# The Assassinator

## THE TRIAL AND HANGING OF JOHN WILKES BOOTH

William L. Richter

*The Assassinator: The Trial and Hanging of John Wilkes Booth*

Copyright © 2015 William L. Richter. All rights reserved. No part of this book may be reproduced or retransmitted in any form or by any means without the written permission of the publisher.

Published by Wheatmark®
1760 East River Road, Suite 145
Tucson, Arizona 85718 USA
www.wheatmark.com

ISBN: 978-1-62787-270-6
LCCN: 2015904434

*In memory of Rick Stelnick, friend, businessman, scholar, outspoken to a fault, whose idea this book originally was. Deo vindice, Rick.*

This is an unapologetic might-have-been story full of actual history—remember, even if it did not happen this way, perhaps it should have....

# Contents

Acknowledgements .................................................................. ix

Introduction by J.E. "Rick" Smith, III ................................................. xi

Preface  "Now, by God, I'll Put Him Through!" ........................... xv

## PART I
"Kill Me Quick!" ..................................................................... 1

1  From Ford's Theater to Locust Hill Farm ............................ 3

2  Last Day of Freedom ........................................................ 14

3  The Yankees Arrive .......................................................... 24

4  The Shooting of John Wilkes Booth ................................. 37

## PART II
"The Most Atrocious Assassination Ever Committed" ......... 47

1  Not Guilty ........................................................................ 49

2  Six of One, Half Dozen of Another ................................. 56

3  Conviction by Hook or by Crook ..................................... 62

4  Weichmann Spins a Tale .................................................. 66

5  Major Rathbone Tells of a Frightful Night ....................... 72

**6** The Prosecution's Closing Argument..................78

**7** Verdict..................84

## PART III
"The Good Do Not Always Win"..................89

**1** Skirting the Regulations..................91

**2** Lincoln and the American System..................99

**3** The Constitution and the Fugitive Slave Act 1850........104

**4** The Constitution and Slavery in the Territories..........110

**5** Cordon Against Slavery..................117

**6** The Dissatisfied Whig..................125

**7** Unconstitutional Presidential Dictator..................135

**8** Military Emancipation..................147

**9** Guilty at Last..................153

**10** What Profit Hath a Man from All His Labor?............160

## PART IV
"I Care Not to Outlive My Country"..................165

**1** Between Heaven and Hell..................167

**2** Lincoln Shall Be King..................173

**3** A New Birth of Freedom..................182

**4** Congress Emerges Supreme..................187

# Acknowledgements

Librarian Sandra Walia, of the Surratt Museum in Clinton, Maryland, for her never-ending, good-natured assistance and encouragement.

Nicholas Scheetz, Head of the Georgetown University Library Special Collections Division; Scott S. Taylor, Manuscripts Processor; Kristina Bobe, Librarian, Government Documents and Microforms Department; and Chris Ulrich, Library Assistant; at Georgetown University Libraries, Lauinger Library.

The over-worked staff at the Inter-Library Loan desk of the University of Arizona, which kept us supplied with numerous, obscure sources from obscure collections.

A special thanks to Betty Ownsby for designing the cover.

An extra special thanks to Lynne C. Richter for making the manuscript ready for the printer.

# Introduction

After shooting President Abraham Lincoln in the back of the head at Ford's Theatre on the night of Good Friday, April 14, 1865, the actor John Wilkes Booth was consumed by three concerns; first, to elude capture by federal authorities and make good his escape; second, how his actions against the federal government and Mr. Lincoln in particular, would be viewed by the world; third, the possibility that he might be taken alive by his pursuers.

Of all these concerns, perhaps the one which most troubled Booth was that of being taken by those who pursued him; to be harried and hunted down like a criminal, to be at bay, encompassed by his enemies, forced to yield and have rough hands laid on his person, dragged in chains back to the City and be placed on display; disgraced, degraded and humiliated to be held up as a spectacle before the masses. This he would never submit to.

Indeed, he had spoken of this very contingency on more than one occasion; once when in hiding and under the care of Thomas Jones and again, to Confederate agent Thomas Harbin after crossing the Potomac River into Virginia.

Jones wrote this of Booth's resolve not to be taken by federal authorities, "He said he knew the United States Government would use every means in its power to secure his capture. 'But,' he added, with a flash of determination lighting up his dark eye,

'John Wilkes Booth will never be taken alive.' And as I looked at him, I believed him."

Later, while in hiding near the Queensberry place and waiting to be moved further down the Secret Line, Booth had this to say to Thomas Harbin, "I will never be taken to be paraded through Washington like some hapless victim of Rome, to be hanged in some ignominious public spectacle, like John Brown, or in mean isolation, like John Yates Beall. I will kill myself first!"

After being shot through the neck and dragged by the heels in a paralytic state from the burning tobacco barn, the 'last Confederate hero' would linger in a dreadfully painful condition until sunrise on Wednesday, April 26, 1865, when the light was finally extinguished from those dark, flashing eyes. And so, in the end, Booth would hold fast to his vow and his words would ring true to a certain extent; that although he was alive when taken at the Garrett's Locust Hill Farm, he would not remain so for long, dying slowly by inches over the course of three hours or so while lying on the porch of the farm house; never to be displayed by his enemies as a public spectacle, "some hapless victim of Rome" as he termed it ... at least not in reality.

Using the interminable three hour period during which it took Booth to die, as he lay grievously wounded, fading in and out of semi-consciousness, author William Richter constructs a compelling "what if" scenario; a drama played out in the hazy and wandering mind of the assassin as his life slowly ebbs, wherein Booth's fears of being captured and "paraded through Washington" take hideous form as he survives his wounding at the Garrett farm and is placed on trial for the killing of Mr. Lincoln.

While the Garrett family, along with troopers of the 16th New York Cavalry and detectives Baker and Conger wait impatiently for the assassin to return to their reality and die, Booth is transported to the City, arraigned, tried, found guilty and sentenced to be hanged by the neck until dead.

Richter's narrative invites us to consider Booth's final imaginings, as his mind gradually dims, all the while realizing, most likely with anxiety and regret, that all he had so carefully planned, all of his endeavors, had come to naught.

Vanity of vanities, all is vanity; all that we see or seem is but a dream within a dream.

Rick Smith
Surrattsville, MD
2014

# Preface

## "Now, by God, I'll Put Him Through!

One hundred and fifty years ago on April 26, 1865, shortly after dawn, John Wilkes Booth died on the porch of the main house at Richard Garrett's Locust Hill Farm just below the Rappahannock River in Virginia. Twelve days earlier he had shot President of the United States Abraham Lincoln dead. Many, then and now, condemn this act as the "Crime of the Century." Lincoln was the third U.S. president to die in office, William Henry Harrison and Zachary Taylor preceded him, but he was the first to be assassinated.[1] Some believed that this re-occurrence every decade since 1840 was an American Indian curse placed on Harrison and his successors by the Shawnee shaman the Prophet for the death of his brother Tecumseh in the War of 1812.[2]

---

1   Richard Lawrence had attempted to assassinate Andrew Jackson in 1835 in the Rotunda of the Congress but both of his pistols had miss-fired. Lawrence was judged insane and committed to an asylum, see Robert V. Remini, *Andrew Jackson and the Course of American Democracy, 1833-1845* (New York: Harper & Row, 1984), 229. Jackson was also the first President to be assaulted when Robert Beverly Randolph grabbed him by the nose in 1833 as the President sat at a table aboard a docked ship. Randolph escaped and when taken, Jackson refused to charge him, *ibid.*, 60-62. See also, John M. Behohlavek, "Assault on the President: The Jackson-Randolph Affair of 1833, *Presidential Studies Quarterly*, XII (Summer 1982), 361-68.
2   The two presidents who died in office before Lincoln, Harrison and Taylor, probably died from septic shock produced by typhoid or paratyphoid, rather than the curse. The south lawn of the White House was a veritable swamp of sewer "night soil" from which disease-laden insects emerged in the warm Washington climate, and the water supply was drawn down-hill from this morass. Both James K. Polk and James Buchanan seemed to have suffered the same symptoms but recovered. See Jane McHugh and Philip A Mackowiak, "What Really Killed the President?" *The New York Times*, April 1, 2014, D-4.

xv

*Preface*

But to call this execution a crime or a curse is to misunderstand its import.[3] The United States was fighting a war with the Confederate States of America. Lincoln was not merely the head of state—he was also the commander-in-chief of his nation's armies. His earlier failed capture and then successful execution were acts of war. His removal from office would cause consummate confusion in the Union war effort. During this disorientation in the Yankee high command, the Confederates hoped to evacuate Richmond and join their several armies in the East and defeat the separate Federal forces in North Carolina and Virginia in quick succession.[4]

In reality, the Confederates were not breaking new ground here. They were simply following the earlier precedents of large cavalry raids into the enemy's capital city set by the Lincoln administration. One was the Stoneman's Raid during the 1863 Chancellorsville Campaign. Two more attempts, the Wistar Raid and the Kilpatrick-Dahlgren Raid prior to the 1864 Overland (Wilderness, Spotsylvania) Campaign. The Kilpatrick-Dahlgren effort actually involved freeing of Union prisoners of war at Belle Isle in the middle of the James River and the capture of Richmond, and the kidnapping or execution of Confederate President Jefferson Davis and his cabinet. The war was getting more vicious and less gentlemanly on both sides day by day.[5]

---

3   David W. Gaddy, "Under a Southern Rose: Of A Time When C.I.A. Meant 'Confederate Intelligence Activities,'" Annual Lecture of the Alexandria Library Company, February 17, 1989 (copy in hands of the author, courtesy of David W. Gaddy), [8] and *passim*. See also William A. Tidwell, James O. Hall, and David Winfred Gaddy, *Come Retribution: The Confederate Secret Service and the Assassination of Lincoln* (Jackson: University Press of Mississippi, 1988), 3-29.

4   In general, see Tidwell, Hall, and Gaddy, *Come Retribution*, 241-52.

5   For the 1863 Stoneman's raid, see Stephen Z. Starr, *The Union Cavalry in the Civil War* (3 vols., Baton Rouge: Louisiana State University Press, 1985), particularly volume 2, *passim*.
The Wistar Raid is treated in David George, Jr., "'Black Flag Warfare': Lincoln and the Raid Against Richmond and Jefferson Davis," *The Pennsylvania Magazine of History and Biography*, 115 (July 1991), 291-318.

The classic work on the Kilpatrick-Dahlgren Raid is Virgil Carrington Jones, *Eight Hours*

*Preface*

Although the Confederates tried to launch massive cavalry raids into Lincoln's summer home north of Washington and Point Lookout prisoner of war compound in Maryland, they lacked the manpower. So they relied on more subtle approaches, such as using their civilian Secret Service operations and Lieutenant Colonel John S. Mosby's guerilla command to infiltrate individual agents into Washington, D.C., from Virginia to blow up the White House and the entire Lincoln cabinet. They also attempted various other harassing operations (freeing prisoners of war in the Old Northwest, burning New York City, and robbing banks in St. Albans, Vermont) in northern cities from secret service headquarters in Canada.[6]

None of these projects, except for the St. Albans bank robberies, succeeded. Although Booth and his gang were to receive Confederate Torpedo Bureau powder man Sgt. Frank Harney and smuggle him into the White House basement to blow the Lincoln government sky-high, Harney never showed up. Booth checked around in the more likely places of information—various whorehouses in the District frequented by Union cavalrymen—and found that Harney had been captured at Burke's Station outside the capital, his fifty pounds of powder trod underfoot

---

*Before Richmond* (New York: Holt, 1957). A more modern approach is Duane Schultz, *The Dahlgren Affair: Terror and Conspiracy in the Civil War* (New York: W. W. Norton & Company, 1998). Other accounts of varying length include, Emory Thomas, "The Kilpatrick-Dahlgren Raid, Part I," *Civil War Times Illustrated*, 16 (February 1978), 4-9, 46-48, and "Part II," *ibid*., (April 1978), 26-33; Bruce Catton, "A Boy Named Martin," in *The Army of the Potomac: A Stillness at Appomattox* (Garden City, N.Y.: Doubleday, 1953), 1-18; Edward G. Longacre, "To Burn the Hateful City: The Kilpatrick-Dahlgren Raid on Richmond, (February 28-March 4, 1864)," in *Mounted Raids of the Civil War* (South Brunswick, N.J.: A. S. Barnes, 1975), 225-57; and Stephen W. Sears, "Raid on Richmond," *MHQ: The Quarterly Journal of Military History*, 11 (Autumn 1998), 88-96. See also, Sears, *Controversies & Commanders: Dispatches from the Army of the Potomac* (Boston: Houghton Mifflin, 1999), 225-51.

6  Tidwell, Hall, and Gaddy, *Come Retribution*, 146-47 (Point Lookout), 235-36, 264, 273 (Old Soldier's Home), 418-21 (Mosby & Harney at Burke's). The efforts against other Northern targets primarily from Canada are in Jane Singer, *The Confederate Dirty War: Arson, Bombings, Assassination and Plots for Chemical and Germ Attacks on the Union* (Jefferson, N.C.: McFarland & Company, 2005). See also, Edward Steers Jr., "Terror—1860s Style," *North & South*, 5 (May 2002): 12–18.

in the fight, and his Confederate escort from John S. Mosby's command scattered.⁷

This left Booth in a quandary as to what was to be done. But this puzzlement did not last long. On April 11, one day after Harney failed to show up in Washington City, Booth and two of his compatriots were outside the White House along with a large crowd listening to Abraham Lincoln give what proved to be his last speech. Speaking from a second floor balcony, with son Tad catching his pages as the President cast them aside after reading them aloud ("Gimme another one," he encouraged his father onward), Lincoln spoke of Reconstruction, specifically of Louisiana.

Lincoln believed that even though the new Louisiana state constitution had been silent as to blacks voting, Congress should be accepted the new document. He reasoned that Reconstruction would be advanced regardless of Louisiana's shortcomings on race. But Lincoln held out hope that some blacks would be allowed to vote in the future, primarily the well educated (Louisiana had numerous mulattoes who were the scions of the finest white families in the state, many with university educations from France), as well as those who wore the blue uniform during the war.

Booth was furious at Lincoln's reasoning. As the crowd politely applauded, the actor turned to Lewis Thornton Powell, his most reliable companion, and snarled, "By God! That means n——r citizenship! Have you your pistol?" Powell nodded. "Well, shoot him! Here and now! Shoot him where he stands!" Powell saw that many in the crowd were now turning to see what

---

7   For Harney's "Gunpowder Plot," see Tidwell, Hall, and Gaddy, *Come Retribution*, 27; Tidwell, *April '65*, 160-96, *passim*.

*Preface*

the disruption was. He freed himself from Booth's grabbing his collar and turned away.

The actor followed Powell fuming and cursing way too loudly and too much. As his other pal, Davy Herold, caught up with the duo, Booth turned on him. "That is the last speech he will every make!" Booth vowed to Herold as he caught up. "Now, by God, I'll put him through!"[8]

Booth had suddenly determined to do individually what Harney was supposed to do in one blast and take out the Lincoln administration, one by one at the same time. Meeting with his whole gang at the Herndon House Hotel on April 13, Booth assigned Powell to kill Secretary of State William H. Seward, and Herold to take Johnson down, and George A. Atzerodt to scout on ahead to see that the bridges across the Eastern Branch of the Potomac were open. He immodestly reserved action against the President for himself. But as happened so many times in the past during several abduction attempts against Lincoln, the President did not show up.[9]

---

8   The speech is in Basler (ed.), *Collected Works*, VIII, 399-405. See also, David Miller DeWitt, *Assassination of Abraham Lincoln* (New York: Macmillan, 1909), 39-40; "Booth's Movements, April 9-13, 1865," box 4, folder 211, David Rankin Barbee papers (DRB papers), Georgetown University (GU); Noah Brooks, *Washington in Lincoln's Time* (Ed. by Herbert Mitgang, New York: Rinehart & Company, Inc., 1958), 225-28. Lerone Bennett, Jr., *Forced into Glory: Abraham Lincoln's White Dream* (Chicago: Johnson, 2000), 588-89, 606-609, 619, sees Lincoln's references, to permitting ("let in," was Lincoln's condescending phrase) some blacks (the educated and soldiers) to vote, as more foot-dragging on the equal rights issue—exactly what Radical Republicans in Congress believed, but the complete opposite of what Booth thought. For a critique of Bennett, see John McKee Barr, *Loathing Lincoln: An American Tradition from the Civil War to the Present* (Baton Rouge: Louisiana State University Press, 2014), 198, 248-51, 262-63, 277-82, 286-87, 288.

Most studies are more complementary to Lincoln. See Peyton McCrary, *Abraham Lincoln and Reconstruction: The Louisiana Experiment* (Princeton: Princeton University Press, 1978); William C. Harris, *With Charity for All: Lincoln and the Restoration of the Union* (Lexington: University of Kentucky Press, 1997); William B. Hesseltine, *Lincoln's Plan of Reconstruction* Tuscaloosa: Confederate Publishing Co., 1960); C. Peter Ripley, *Slaves and Freedmen in Civil War Louisiana* (Baton Rouge: Louisiana State University Press, 1978); T. Harry Williams, "Abraham Lincoln: Principle and Pragmatism in Politics," *Mississippi Valley Historical Review*, 40 (June 1953), 89-108.

9   Tidwell, Hall, and Gaddy, *Come Retribution*, 27-29, discuss Booth altering his abduction

*Preface*

Furious, Booth called his men together the next day, April 14, at the Canterbury Dance Hall and Saloon. This time, Powell still was to take care of Seward but realizing that Davy Herold was not going shoot Vice President Johnson, Booth switched the roles of Herold and Atzerodt. The latter would shoot Johnson at the door to his hotel room. Herold, meanwhile, would act as a coordinator of the movements of the others, seeing to it Powell got to Seward's around the 10:30 p.m. time that Booth would assassinate Lincoln. A new arrival, Michael O'Laughlin would kill Secretary of War Stanton at the same moment. Other supporters would signal the correct time by shouts, whistles, and signal lamps from Ford's Theater, where Lincoln and his party would be facing Booth's derringer. Unfortunately, for various reasons, only Booth would accomplish the job. [10]

---

operation to include Harney's assassination objective. See DeWitt, *Assassination of Abraham Lincoln*, 40-41, 44-45; Wilson, *John Wilkes Booth*, 93-97; E. A. Emerson, "How Wilkes Booth's Friend Described His Crime," *Literary Digest*, (Mar. 6, 1926), 58, 60. See also, "Booth's Movements, April 9-13, 1865," box 4, folder 211, DRB papers, GU.

The idea of Booth attempting to shoot Lincoln on April 13, was first pointed out to us by Booth expert Michael W. Kauffman, who posits that Booth's entry in his diary of "the Ides" on that date with nothing following is key to the notion. See Richter to Kauffman, December 14, 2001, and Kauffman to Richter, December 17, 2001, e-mails in the author's possession. This notion of two assassination attempts seems born out at least circumstantially in other places, especially in Atzerodt's confession

10   Lincoln's final day is detailed in Oldroyd, *The Assassination of Abraham Lincoln*, 7-29; Jim Bishop, *The Day Lincoln Was Shot* (New York: Harper & Bros., 1955); W. Emerson Reck, *A. Lincoln: His Last 24 Hours* (Jefferson, N.C.: McFarland & Co., Inc., 1987); and Bak, *The Day Lincon Was Shot*, 71-104. The wound Lincoln suffered is analyzed in John K. Lattimer, *Kennedy and Lincoln: Medical and Ballistic Comparisons of Their Assassinations* (New York: Harcourt, Brace, Jovanovich, 1980). The possibility of Lincoln surviving his wound with better contemporary or modern medical care is the subject between Dr. Lattimer (no) and Dr. Richard A. R. Fraser, who found Lincoln's medical care close to incompetent. See Art Candenquist, "The Lattimer-Fraser Debate," David C. Dillon (ed.), *The Lincoln Assassination: From the Pages of the* Surratt Courier, (2 vols., Clinton, Md.: The Surratt Society, 2000), II 25-26. Dr. Blaine V. Houmes, "The Wound of Abraham Lincoln," *ibid.*, II, 27-30, believes that Lincoln's wound would have been fatal, regardless of the medical technology available at any time in history.

For an excellent, up-to-date, magazine-length description of Booth's final day, see Michael W. Kauffman, "John Wilkes Booth and the Murder of Abraham Lincoln," *Blue and Gray Magazine*, 7 (April 1990), 8-25, 46-62. More dated, but still with some validity, is Robert H. Fowler, "Album of the Lincoln Murder: Illustrating how It Was Planned, Committed and Avenged, "*Civil War Times Illustrated*, 4 (July 1965), 1-4, 7, 10-11, 15-16, 21-22, 25-26. See also, "Booth's Movements, April 14, 1865," DRB papers, GU.

*Preface*

---

For a brief, point-by-point chapter-length discussion of Booth's last hours, see Kimmel, *Mad Booths of Maryland*, 215-23; a more detailed account with some on Lincoln, is in Gene Smith, *American Gothic: The Story of America's Legendary Theatrical Family—Junius, Edwin, and John Wilkes Booth* (New York: Simon & Schuster, 1992), 133-59; and Dorothy Meserve Kunhardt and Philip B. Kunhardt, Jr., "Assassination!" *American Heritage*, 16 (April 1965), 5-35, and by the same authors, *Twenty Days: A Narrative in Text and Pictures of the Assassination of Abraham Lincoln and the Twenty Days that Followed—the Nation in Mourning, the Long Trip Home to Springfield* (New York: Harper & Row, Publishers, 1965). Dated, but interesting, is George Alfred Townsend, *The Life, Crime, and Capture of John Wilkes Booth* (New York: Dick & Fitzgerald, 1865), 5-10.

See also, DeWitt, *Assassination of Abraham Lincoln*, 7-28, 46-50; Francis Wilson, *John Wilkes Booth: Fact and Fiction of Lincoln's Assassination* (Boston: Houghton-Mifflin, 1929), 106-17, 128-29; J.E. Buckingham, *Reminiscences and Souvenirs of the Assassination of Abraham Lincoln* (Washington: Rufus H. Darby, 1894), 7-17, 73-76; James McKinley, "Death to Tyrants!" in his *Assassination in America* (New York: Harper & Row, 1977), 18; Clara E. Laughlin, *The Death of Lincoln: The Story of Booth's Plot, His Deed and the Penalty* New York: Doubleday, Osage & Co., 1909), 68-99, which is shortened for popular consumption in Clara E. Laughlin, "The Last Twenty-four Hours of Lincoln's Life." *Ladies Home Journal*, 20 (February 1909), 12ff.; Edward Steers, Jr., *Blood on the Moon: The Assassination of Abraham Lincoln* (Lexington: University of Kentucky Press, 2001), 117-130

# PART I

## "KILL ME QUICK!"

"Yonder is the assassinator, none other than J. Wilkes Booth, the man who killed Lincoln!"

—David E. Harold to Pvt. Willie Jett, 9th Virginia Cavalry, serving with Mosby's Rangers, April 24, 1865, Port Conway, Virginia

# 1

## From Ford's Theater to Locust Hill Farm

It was the afternoon of April 24. Ten days had passed since John Wilkes Booth had locked himself into the hallway behind the second story box above the right side of the stage of Ford's theater. Not much had gone right since then for the beleaguered actor. He had waited for the correct time, spying on the presidential party through a bored hole in the door until fellow actor Harry Hawke had given his big laugh line, "you sockdologizing old man trap!"—unknowingly, the signal for Booth to strike.[11]

As the audience roared with laughter. Booth had stepped into the box behind Abraham Lincoln and yelled, "Sic semper tyrannis!" He then fired his single shot .44-caliber derringer pistol. ThSe ball smashed into Lincoln's head and came to rest behind his right eye. Lincoln's guest for the evening, Major Henry Rathbone, jumped from his seat and lunged at Booth. A ripping slash from Booth's double-bladed knife split his arm open from shoulder to elbow.[12]

---

[11] The word "sockdolagizing" means rendering a final, finishing blow. One can wonder along with Laurie Verge, "A Random Thought," *Surratt Courier*, 22 (April 1997), 6, if this line not only brought forth a good laugh, but also had a symbolic significance related to Booth's act of shooting Lincoln. Booth's entry into the foyer and the route he used to access the Lincoln box is detailed in Michael W. Kauffman, "Door Number 7 or Door Number 8?" *Surratt Courier*, 33 (February 2008), 3-4.

[12] On the couple that accompanied the Lincoln's to the theater, see R. Gerald McMurtry, "Major Rathbone and Miss Harris: Guests of the Lincolns in the Ford's Theater Box," *Lincoln Lore* (August 1971), 1-3; Frank Rathbun, "The Rathbone Connection," Michael W. Kauffman (ed.), *In Pursuit of . . .* (Clinton, Md.: The Surratt Society, 1990), 213-20.

Booth then stepped to the edge of the box, facing the audience, many of whom assumed that this commotion was part of the play. He forked over the balustrade leaping twelve feet to the stage below. It was an easy ploy. He had done it dozens of times before in the opening scene to Shakespeare's Macbeth. But this time he caught his spur in one of the flags decorating the outside of the box and landed off-balance.

Something snapped in his back. Booth winced. But this was no time to pause. "The South is avenged!" he bellowed as he raced off the stage, disappearing past the scenery flats and out the back door, sweeping aside all attempts to stop him. After several attempts, he mounted his panicked horse and galloped off into obscurity, avoiding the thousands of soldiers and detectives sent after him.[13]

It was not that Booth could not be traced. It was that after he crossed the bridge over the Eastern Branch of the Potomac the pursuit stayed days behind him.[14] As he rode out of Washington up a slope known locally as Soper's Hill, his horse fell with him and broke the small bone in Booth's left leg.[15]

---

13   Numerous persons saw the murder and wrote about it, in later years. Their stories are collected in Timothy Good (ed.), *We Saw Lincoln Shot: One Hundred Eyewitness Accounts* (Jackson: University Press of Mississippi, 1995). See also, Joan L. Chaconas, "Witnesses to the Assassination," in Dillon (ed.), *The Lincoln Assassination: From the Pages of the* Surratt Courier, II, 3-8.

14   Kauffman, "Booth's Escape Route: Lincoln's Assassin on the Run," 12-13; and Robert H. Fowler, "Album of the Lincoln Murder: Illustrating How It Was Planned, Committed, and Avenged," *Civil War Times Illustrated*, 4 (July 1965), [Special Issue], 29, 32-33, 35-38, 42, 46, 48-49; Roscoe, *Web of Conspiracy*, 137-39, 149-53; Laughlin, *Death of Lincoln*, 119-20. See also, Joan L. Chaconas and James O. Hall, "Crossing the Navy Yard Bridge," *Surratt Courier*, 21 (September 1996), 5-7; Benn Pitman (comp.), *The Assassination of President Lincoln and the Trial of the Conspirators* (Cincinnati: Moore, Wilstach & Baldwin, 1865), 84.

15   Kauffman, "Booth's Escape Route: Lincoln's Assassin on the Run," 13, 17 (sidebar). There is much confusion on where Booth's leg was broken and what bone was broken. The standard version is that he broke it jumping from Lincoln's box to the stage. But if he had, he never could have mounted his flighty horse. In all likelihood, Booth wrenched his back jumping to the stage, hence his fall to the floor and constant complaints to Dr. and Mrs. Mudd about his back bothering him. Where did he break his left leg? Kauffman is probably correct, it happened on the road to Surrattsville, noted for its deep mud, numerous pot holes, and ever-constant, wretched ruts worn by the wheels of passing wagons. Kauffman's theory is expanded upon by Joseph E. "Rick," Smith III, "Break a Leg," Surratt Courier, 28 (June 2003), 4-6.

Stopping briefly at the Surratt Tavern for guns and liquor,[16] Booth's injury forced him and his recently arrived companion, David E. Herold, to seek medical attention from the one doctor they knew was a reliable Confederate agent, Samuel A. Mudd. The physician administered to Booth's leg as his stable hands doctored Booth's battered horse.[17]

Anxious to get moving, in spite of his injury,[18] Booth and Herold followed Mudd's instructions as to how to travel from safe house to safe house in Southern Maryland. The travelers almost bumped into a roving Yankee cavalry patrol, but guided by a local free man of color, Oswell Swann, they arrived at the plantation of Samuel Cox.[19]

Known locally as "Captain," for his Confederate recruiting

---

For the sake of argument, we assume that Booth sprained some muscles or slipped a disk in his back when he hit the stage in Ford's, broke his left leg when his horse fell with him at Soper's Hill, and the injury was to the fibula or small leg bone. The reader may agree or disagree at his or her own pleasure.

16  Clara E. Laughlin *Death of Lincoln: The Story of Booth's Plot, His Deed and the Penalty* (New York: Doubleday, Page & Co., 1909), 212-22; Pitman (comp.), *The Assassination of President Lincoln and the Trial of the Conspirators*, 85, 129. See also, David Rankin Barbee, "Lincoln and Booth," (Unpublished ms. in the David Rankin Barbee papers, Georgetown University), 823-52, *passim*, DRB papers, GU. Locating Soper's Hill on the road to Upper Marlboro, Barbee believes that Booth and Herold never went by Surrattsville, making his interpretation unique among historians.

17  Kauffman, "Booth's Escape Route: Lincoln's Assassin on the Run," 13-14, 17; Nettie Mudd, . *Life of Samuel A. Mudd* . . . (New York: Neale Publishing, 1908, reprinted 1962), 30; Samuel Carter III, *Riddle of Dr. Mudd* (New York: G. P. Putnam's Sons, 1974), 212-33; Edward Steers, Jr., "Deceptive Doctor," *Columbiad: A Quarterly Review of the War Between the States*, 2 (Summer 1998), 114-28; Hal Higdon, *The Union vs. Dr.* Mudd (Chicago: Follett Publishing Company, 1964), 9-11; Theodore Roscoe, *Web of* Conspiracy (Englewood Cliffs, N.J.: Prentice-Hall, 1959), 170-79; Laughlin, *Death of Lincoln*, 123-24. See also, Pitman (comp.), *The Assassination of President Lincoln and the Trial of the Conspirators*, 87-90; Barbee, "Lincoln and Booth," 823-52, *passim*, DRB papers, GU.

18  Mudd, *Life of Mudd*, 30-31; Laughlin, *Death of Lincoln*, 124-25. Some of Herold's conversation is from his later confession in *Verge (ed.), From War Department Files*, 1-19. See also, Kauffman, "Booth's Escape Route: Lincoln's Assassin on the Run," 17.

19  Kauffman, "Booth's Escape Route: Lincoln's Assassin on the Run," 18-19; James O. Hall, "Oswell Swann and the Fugitive Assassins," Kauffman (ed.), *In Pursuit of* . . . , 171-73; Laurie Verge and James O. Hall "Crossing the Zekiah," Dillon (ed.), *The Lincoln Assassination: From the Pages of the* Surratt Courier, IV, 7-8; Laughlin, *Death of Lincoln*, 128-30; Edward Steers, Jr., *Blood on the Moon: The Assassination of Abraham Lincoln* (Lexington: University of Kentucky Press, 2001), 150-51, 156-58, 160, footnotes on 316-316. See also, William A. Tidwell, "April 15, 1865," *Surratt Courier*, 22 (April-May-June 1997), 6-10, 5-10, 4-9; and Otto Eisenschiml,

abilities, Cox was an ardent secessionist and slaveholder who had beaten a runaway bondsman to death early in the war.[20] He sent the fugitives into the nearby woods, where they were cared for by his wily foster brother, another Confederate agent, Thomas A. Jones.[21]

Just how long and how much Booth and Herold had to endure for the next half dozen days is open to debate. Tradition says that they shivered in the wild, fed by Jones, who kept an eye on the desperately searching Federals. But more recent research suggests that they spent some of their time indoors at the Austin Adams Tavern at Newport comforted with shelter and hot food. They slept in the woods at night to avoid surprise from their roaming pursuers.[22]

While at Newport, Booth and Herold saw their horses disguised with dyes, shoe polish, and new hairstyles courtesy of a stableman's rapidly snipping scissors. They were not shot

---

"The Conspirators Who Went Free," *Why Was Lincoln Murdered?* (New York: Grossett & Dunlap, 1937), 296-307; Barbee, "Lincoln and Booth," 823-52, *passim*, DRB papers, GU.

20  Tidwell, Hall, and Gaddy, *Come Retribution*, 446-48; Eisenschiml, "The Conspirators Who Went Free," *Why Was Lincoln Murdered?* 296-307. Mary Swann's statement to the Federals is in box 5, folder 238, DRB papers, GU. See also, Barbee, "Lincoln and Booth," 823-52, *passim*, DRB papers, *ibid*.

21  Kauffman, "Booth's Escape Route: Lincoln's Assassin on the Run," 19; Roy Z. Chamlee, *Lincoln's Assassins: A Complete Account of their Capture, Trail, and Punishment* (Jefferson N.C.: McFarland & Company Inc., Publishers, 1990), 139-42; Thomas A. Jones, *J. Wilkes Booth: An Account of His Sojourn in Southern Maryland . . . and His Death in Virginia* (Chicago: Laird & Lee, 1893), 1-82. For a good account of Jones' activities in the Confederate underground, plus the text of his book, see John M. Wearmouth and Roberta J. Wearmouth, *Thomas A. Jones: Chief Agent of the Confederate Secret Service in Maryland* (Port Tobacco, Md.: Stone's Throw Publishing, 2000).

22  See J. E. "Rick" Smith, III, "The Owens Statement," *Surratt Courier*, 32 (No. 10, October 2007), 3-6; Smith, "The Adams Tavern, Newport, Maryland," *ibid.*, 38 (No. 10, October 2013), 11-13. See also, Osborn H. Oldroyd, *Assassination of Abraham Lincoln: Flight, Pursuit, Capture, and Punishment of the Conspirators* (Washington: O. H. Oldroyd, 1901), 67; Jones, *J. Wilkes Booth*, 83-89, 96-97; Kauffman, "Booth's Escape Route: Lincoln's Assassin on the Run," 19-20; John Rhodehamel and Louise Taper (eds.), *"Right or Wrong, God Judge Me": The Writings of John Wilkes Booth* (Urbana: University of Illinois Press, 1997), 154 and footnotes; William Hanchett, "Booth's Diary," *Journal of the Illinois Historical Society*, 72 (Feb. 1979), 40. For various newspaper columns on the baseness of Booth's assassination, see box 3, DRB papers, GU.

as commonly believed. It was an old Civil War trick, used by cavalry on both sides to conceal their thievery of farmers' stock.[23]

After several days wait, the federals were fooled by false reports that Booth and his companion were seen in a neighboring county. Jones immediately rounded up Booth, Herold and their horses and, helped by Cox's adopted son, took the fugitives down to the Potomac, where they crossed into Virginia. Federal patrol boats came close to their quarry, but failed to make contact with the wanted men.[24]

Traveling up Gambo Creek until the old Confederate Navy raiders' camp, Booth and Herold made contact with Thomas Harbin another Confederate agent, who turned them over to William Bryant, a regional guide. [25] Then it was the usual traveling with local agents between safe houses, with the charming names like "the Cottage," and "Cleydael," until Booth and Harold wound up on the banks of the Rappahannock.[26] Joined

---

23  J. E. "Rick" Smith, III, "What Is Horse-Faking?" *ibid*.., 33 (No. 4, April 2008), 4-6; "More on the Fate of the Horses," *ibid.*, 33 (No. 5, May 2008), 4-5. See also, See also Bruce Catton, *Army of the Potomac: Glory Road*, 246, quoting Crowninshield, *History of the First Massachusetts Cavalry*, 294-95, on how people of the time altered horse appearance to prevent original owners from detecting a stolen animal.
24  Kauffman, "Booth's Escape Route: Lincoln's Assassin on the Run," 21, 38; John F. Stanton, "Mrs. Quesenberry and John Wilkes Booth," *King George Journal*, week of March 31, 2008; Barbee, "Lincoln and Booth," 823-52, *passim*, DRB PAPERS papers, GU. See also, William A. Tidwell, "Booth Crosses the Potomac: An Exercise in Historical Research," *Civil War History*, 36 (No. 4, 1990), 325-33; Rhodehamel and Taper (eds.), *Writings of John Wilkes Booth*, 154-55 and footnotes; Hanchett, "Booth's Diary," 41-42.
25  Kauffman, "Booth's Escape Route: Lincoln's Assassin on the Run," 40; Barbee, "Lincoln and Booth," 853-83, *passim*, DRB papers, GU. Many of the pertinent original sources of Booth's sojourn in Virginia can be found in James O. Hall (comp.), *On the Way to Garrett's Barn: John Wilkes Booth and David Herold in the Northern Neck of Virginia, April 22-26, 1865* . . . . Ed. by David C. Dillon (Clinton, Md.: Surratt Society, 2001). See also, J. E. "Rick" Smith III and William L. Richter, "'I Told Him He Must Go Away'," Elizabeth Rouse Quesenberry and the Escape of Lincoln's Assassin," *Surratt Courier*, 33 (September 2008), 4-7, and Smith with Richter. *In the Shadows of the Lincoln Assassination: The Life of Confederate Spy Thomas H. Harbin*, 123-32. There is some dispute as to the actual identities of one of these guides. See with J. E. "Rick" Smith III) "Behold! I Tell You a Mystery': Who was Mr. Chrisman?" *Surratt Courier*, 38 (March 2013), 11-14, and John F. Stanton, "Another Look at Crismond," *ibid.* (April 2013), 3-5.
26  Kauffman, "Booth's Escape Route: Lincoln's Assassin on the Run," 40, 42. Dr. Stuart's statement to Federal authorities is in Roscoe, *Web of Conspiracy*, 542-43, 361-64. See also

by three Confederate cavalrymen, Private Willie Jett, Private Absalom Ruggles Bainbridge, and Lieutenant Mortimer Bainbridge Ruggles, currently from John Singleton Mosby's guerrilla command to whom Herold confessed that Booth was Lincoln's "Assassinator," as he put it. Soon another Mosby man, Enoch Welford Mason, joined them and all of the five men crossed together on the ferry to Port Royal on the south bank.[27]

As the ferry docked, Mason thundered off on his mount, scouting the pathway south and looking for assistance from more Mosby men, while Jett, being a local boy, tried in vain to get housing for Booth and Herold. No one in Port Royal wanted to risk getting involved. But then Jett remembered a nearby farm that might be amenable to putting up Confederate soldiers coming home from the war, as Booth and Harold claimed to be. And so, ten days after the slaying of Lincoln, Booth, Herold and the three cavalrymen rode off south, down the Bowling Green Road towards Richard Garrett's farm and a rendezvous with destiny: Booth alone on Ruggles' horse, Ruggles up behind Bainbridge, and Jett sharing his steed with Herold.

"You boys certainly have made good your escape. The Yankees have not been seen in the area since the war's end," said Ruggles, referring to Lee's surrender. "We will leave you two at

---

Eisenschiml, " The Conspirators Who Went Free," 296-307; Barbee, "Lincoln and Booth," 853-83, *passim*, DRB PAPERS papers, GU. See also, James O. Hall, "Two Pages From Booth's Diary: Dr. Richard Stuart Meets John Wilkes Booth," Dillon (ed.), *The Lincoln Assassination: From the Pages of the* Surratt Courier, IV 11-12.

27  M. B. Ruggles, "Pursuit and Death of John Wilkes Booth: Major Ruggles's Narrative," *Century Magazine*, 39 (January 1890), 443-46, reprinted in Prentiss Ingraham, "The Pursuit and Death of John Wilkes Booth," Dillon (ed.), *The Lincoln Assassination: From the Pages of the* Surratt Courier, IV, 23-31, which also includes an account by Lt. Bainbridge, 26-27; Kauffman, "Booth's Escape Route: Lincoln's Assassin on the Run," 43-44; Barbee, "Lincoln and Booth," 853-83, *passim*, DRB papers, GU; Pitman (comp.), *The Assassination of President Lincoln and the Trial of the Conspirators*, 90-91; Kate H. Mason, "A True Story of the Capture and Death of John Wilkes Booth," *Northern Neck Historical Magazine*, 13 (December 1963), 1237-39.

Garrett's and go ahead to Bowling Green. It is the junction of many roads."

"Do not worry, Booth, we will find a safe haven for you," Jett promised.

"I am in your hands, gentlemen, do with me as you think best."

Herold mentioned that his shoes were a bit over-worn and that he would like to accompany the Rebel soldiers to Bowling Green to get reshod. Everyone thought that was good idea. It would make for one less stranger at the Garrett's. When asked where he was going after Virginia, Booth professed to be unsure. Ruggles recommended west over the Appalachian Mountains. He said that his father, an unassigned brigadier, believed that the Confederacy could endure in Texas. Herold remarked that he was proud that Booth had stopped Yankee tyranny east of the mountains already, in spite of his injuries and failure of his fellow conspirators.

"That's nothing to brag about." Booth fairly snapped the words out, indicating that he wanted nothing more said about the failures or anything remotely connected with the assassination. The little cavalcade rode on in silence, covering the three miles to the gate of Garrett's farm in good time. Here it stopped. It was mid-afternoon.

"Well, Davy, I reckon this is where we part company," Booth said.

"I will be with you soon, John, Depend on it. Good-bye. Keep in good spirits."

"Have no fear about me," Booth said. He concluded confidently, "I am among friends now." Davy switched horses, riding behind Bainbridge. Jett and Ruggles would take Booth in to the Garretts.

As Bainbridge and Herold left, Ruggles led his mount with its precious cargo, the man who killed Lincoln, into the farmyard. Jett rode along to do the talking, being at least somewhat acquainted with the Garretts. As they entered the farmyard, Booth took a look at his new surroundings. The farm was located on the west side of the Bowling Green road, surrounded by pine and locust thickets. It was close to the road, yet the trees and undergrowth were so prevalent that the buildings were very hard to see as one rode by.

The farm road went through two gates. One was right on the highway, while the other marked the edge of the farmyard about a hundred feet farther in. The farm yard itself was surrounded by a split-rail worm fence, inside of which were a tobacco barn, a cow shed, and a couple of corn cribs. The farm road ran straight west to the tobacco barn at the side of the yard. About midway in, a second smaller road branched off to the left. It passed through a picket fence, with its own gate, and led directly to the house.[28]

The farmhouse was a two-story, balloon frame affair, covered with clapboards and painted white. At the top was a fine attic space, which ran the length of the house. It had a tall, narrow brick chimney at each gable end, and a one story high veranda along the entire front side. The dwelling was surrounded by apple and locust trees, which gave much needed shade from the summer's heat.

In the midst of this domesticated arboreal splendor, Willie Jett dismounted. An older man approached the three strangers with a quizzical look on his face.

"This is Mr. Garrett, I presume?" Jett inquired.

---

28 There is some dispute as to the exact arrangement of the fences and gates at Garrett's Farm, see David C. Dillon, "Where Were the Garrett Farm Gates?" *Surratt Courier*, 28 (August 2003), 3-6.

"Indeed, I am Richard Garrett, sir."

"I suppose you hardly remember me."

"No, sir, you have the advantage of me." Garrett was amiable enough in his reply.

"My name is Willie Jett. I am the son of your old friend Jett of Westmoreland County. My companion is Lieutenant Mortimer B. Ruggles [Lieutenant? Now Booth got a quizzical look on his face, but let it pass], son and aide to the general of that name. And the gentleman on the horse is Mr. John W. Boyd, a Confederate soldier, who was wounded in the battles around Richmond, near Petersburg. He is trying to get to his home in Maryland. Can you take care of him for a day or two until his wound will permit him to travel?"

"Certainly. Nothing is too good for the boys in gray who defended the Cause of the Right. Get down, sir, and welcome!"

"Lieutenant Ruggles and I are on our way to Bowling Green and cannot stay. But we will help Mr. Boyd down so that he may partake of your hospitality, sir."

Ruggles and Jett lifted Booth carefully from the saddle. He winced noticeably, gritted his teeth and audibly sucked in air. Ruggles handed Booth his crutches.

"Welcome to Locust Hill Farm, Mr. Boyd. You seem quite wearied, sir," Garrett said to Booth, "I'll get you some sweet water from the well. Go and take a seat upon the veranda. I'll fetch you a pillow for more comfort."

As Garrett left on his errand, the two Confederate soldiers bade Booth good-bye. "We will return when it is safe to move you. Rest and get well," Ruggles said. All three shook hands.

Garrett met Booth as he hobbled to the porch. "Your wound must pain you very much, Mr. Boyd."

"Yes, thank you, sir, for your consideration," Booth responded.

"It has not been properly cared for and riding has jarred it so. It gives me great pain...."

Garrett went inside and brought out a pillow. Booth placed it in the chair, sat down, and closed his eyes. Garrett could see that he needed rest and not a lot of bothersome questions, so he excused himself and left Booth to doze in the warm afternoon air.

About a half hour later, Mr. Garrett nudged Booth gently and said, "Excuse me, Mr. Boyd. I wish to present my eldest son, Jack, to you. He is just home from the war. He served with General Lee as an artilleryman. No, no. It is not necessary to rise, sir. Hopefully you will get better with time."

"Fredericksburg Light Artillery since 1861," Jack said, "transferred to Lightfoot's Artillery Battalion, Second Corps, and surrendered with them at Appomattox. I was severely wounded in the thigh at Drewry's Bluff last May, so I know how you feel."

Booth looked up and stated, "2nd Maryland, Heth's Division, A. P. Hill's Third Corps. And thank you for your kind consolation." Booth gave an inward sigh of relief. At least Jack was from a different part of Lee's army than the portion indicated by his own pre-planned cover story. But then, maybe Harbin knew few Third Corps troops came from this part of Virginia when he made up Booyth's cover story. Booth said with feeling, "It is indeed a pleasure, sir."

"The pleasure is mine, sir," Jack said. "Always an honor to meet others who have worn the gray. Well, I am on my way over to a neighbor's. I shall see you all later at supper."

Booth sat there a while and pondered all that he endured. He reached into his pocket and took out the little memorandum book. He removed the pencil from the safety of its loop and began to scribble an entry, undated, and yet eerily prophetic:

I have too great a soul to die like a criminal. Oh, may He, may He spare me and let me die bravely.

I bless the entire world. Never hated or wronged anyone. This last was not a wrong, unless God deems it so. And it's with Him, to damn or bless me. And for this brave boy with me who often prays (yes before and since) with a true and sincere heart, was it a crime in him? If so, why can he pray the same? I do not wish to shed a drop of blood, but I must 'fight the course.' 'Tis all that's left me.

With this reference to Shakespeare's cornered king of Scotland (Macbeth, Act 5, Scene 7), Booth returned his pencil to its place and closed his little book. The porch empty, he returned to his thoughts to rest and was soon sleeping soundly.[29]

---

[29] An excellent account is Janine Clarke Dodels, "The Last Days of John Wilkes Booth," (Unpublished ms. in hands of author), 1-4. See also Betsy Fleet (ed.), "A Chapter of Unwritten History: Richard Baynham Garrett's Account of the Flight and Death of John Wilkes Booth," *Virginia Magazine of History and Biography*, 71 (October 1963), 388-407; "Statement of John M. Garrett," *Surratt Courier*, 20 (March 1995), 4-9; "Deposition of William H. Garrett," *ibid.*, 24 (May 1999), 5-7, both reprinted in "Mr. Booth Visits the Garrett Family," Dillon (ed.), *The Lincoln Assassination: From the Pages of the* Surratt Courier, IV, 33-39; Kauffman, "Booth's Escape Route: Lincoln's Assassin on the Run," 44-45; Barbee, "Lincoln and Booth," 884-910, *passim*, DRB papers, GU. The diary entry is in Rhodehamel and Taper (eds.), *Writings of John Wilkes Booth*, 155 and footnotes; and Hanchett, "Booth's Diary," 42.

# 2

## Last Day of Freedom

The next morning, April 25, Jack rose early and went downstairs. Willie arose shortly after and, as he quietly left the room, he collared young Richard on the stair landing and told him to return to the bedroom and assist Booth, whom he knew as Mr. Boyd, when he awoke. Shortly Booth stirred and Richard helped him get into his clothes and handed him his crutches. At that moment Jack came up the stairs.

"Breakfast is ready Mr. Boyd."

"Y'all go ahead without me. No need to wait and let it get cold on my account."

"No hurry, Mr. Boyd," Jack said kindly. "We find soldiers to be a privileged class and you may rest assured that breakfast will be available for you at any time you are ready to come down. We are waiting for Willie to come back from taking the cattle out to graze, anyway."

"Thank you, sir. Go on down with your brother, now, Richard. Thank you for your help. I reckon I will go out back before I eat, if you do not mind."

Later, after a huge country breakfast topped off with steaming mugs of ersatz coffee ("do not ask what it is made of or you may not wish to drink it," apologized Mrs. Garrett), Booth went outside on the veranda. He packed his pipe and had a smoke. Then he wandered around the yard, until his throbbing leg indicated he should go back to the porch and rest. Booth lay down on a long wooden bench and took a nap.

After he had awakened and was sitting up, Willie came out on the veranda. Like his brothers, he had noticed the paleness of Booth's complexion and it troubled him. He was no field soldier. He asked Booth about his wound and got the same story that he had told the night before. He was wounded at Petersburg and had met his cousin on the north side of the Potomac where they got into a scrape with Yankee soldiers. They fled south and recrossed the Potomac, and here they were at Locust Hill.

"Well, sir," Willie said as he stretched his arms, "I got chores to do." Mr. Boyd had held to essentially the same story he had told the night before, with some embellishments, thought Willie. No one was going to trip him up with a few questions. Mr. Boyd would have to do that all by himself.

"And I need to exercise by walking a bit," Booth said. He got up from the bench and hobbled out into the yard. He went down the lane from the house to the tobacco barn, took a turn around the barn and stared at the woods. They would make a good hideaway if it ever became necessary, Booth thought. By the time he got back to the house his leg was crying for more rest.[30]

Back at the Garretts', the star attraction at noon dinner was not Booth, but brother Jack, who had returned from his visit to a nearby shoemaker.

"You know, Father, about that rumor that Lincoln has been assassinated?"

---

30 Dodels, "Last Days of John Wilkes Booth," 4-7; Kauffman, "Booth's Escape Route: Lincoln's Assassin on the Run," 45. The field glasses Booth demonstrated to the Garrett children are described in detail in John C. Brennan, "John Wilkes Booth's Field Glasses," 5-6. See also, Fleet (ed.), "A Chapter of Unwritten History: Richard Baynham Garrett's Account," 388-407; "Statement of John M. Garrett," 4-9; "Deposition of William H. Garrett," 5-7; Barbee, "Lincoln and Booth," 884-910, *passim*, DRB papers, GU.

"It has been around a couple of days," Mr. Garrett remarked, "but I do not believe a word of it. No one has killed a president before. True, there was an attempt on Andy Jackson over thirty years ago. But no one has ever tried such since then. It is some idle report started by stragglers, I reckon."

"Well," Jack said, "hear what I learned over at Mr. Acres' while he was repairing my boots. There was another feller named Geavitt there. While we waited, he told me that he had seen a Richmond newspaper and, among the other news, was a story of how $140,000 was being offered up in Washington City for the arrest of the man who had killed the President of the United States."

Everyone looked at Jack. Mr. Boyd seemed especially interested, although he said nothing.

"Well," Willie said, "he had better not come thisaway or he will be gobbled up!"

"How much did you say had been offered?" Booth asked calmly.

"The man from Richmond said $140,000 for sure," Jack replied. "Why?"

"I would sooner suppose $500,000, or more like $500,000," Booth mused.

Willie did not care how much the actual amount was. "I could use $100,000 dollars just now," he concluded. Everyone laughed, except Booth.

"Would you betray him? For that?" Booth quietly interjected.

"He had not better tempt me," Willie concluded, "for I haven't a dollar in the world."

"I suppose the assassin has been paid," said one of the daughters.

"Do you think so, Miss?" Booth queried with a wan smile. "By whom do you suppose he was paid?"

"Oh," she said off-handedly with a shrug, "I suppose by both the North and the South. There are a great many, North and South, who are anxious to be rid of Mr. Lincoln."

"It is my opinion," Booth said with some authority, "that he was not paid a cent, but did it for notoriety's sake and for the good of his country."

As dinner was completed and everyone arose from the table, Mrs. Garrett noted Booth wince as he stood on his crutches. "Mr. Boyd," she said, "would you like me to change the dressing on your wound?"

"Oh, no, ma'am, thank you. It does not give me the slightest pain," Booth lied.

"You really ought to see a doctor," Mr. Garrett said, looking very concerned. Willie had already told his father that he believed the limb was in need of amputation. He had seen many such wounds in the war.

"Really, I am doing fine, sir," Booth said amiably. "But thank you both for your concern."

A while later, Booth was back at his chair on the veranda, making notes in his diary. Jack Garrett was sitting on the steps. Hearing a noise, Jack looked toward the road and saw some men pass by on horseback.

"There go some of your party from yesterday, now. Headed for Port Royal, looks like."

Booth snapped out of his seeming lethargy of pain. He threw down the diary and got up out of his chair with amazing rapidity. "Go up and get my pistols!" he shouted.

"What do you want with your pistols?" Jack inquired, puzzled at the change that had overcome his porch companion.

Booth turned on Jack and spoke in a voice that Garrett had never heard before. It possessed all of the commanding qualities of a general officer on the battlefield. "Go now and get my pistols!" Each word was distinct, projected from the depths of his soul, precise in its delivery. It was his old stage voice that resounded across the veranda.

Garrett ran into the house and up the stairs. He grabbed the belt with its weapons. Then he looked out the second story window and saw that the riders had passed without coming in. He put the belt back on the bedpost and came down empty handed.

"They have gone past the gate," Jack said.

Booth listened for a minute, grunted in agreement, turned and reseated himself in his old place.

Within five minutes, a lone figure strode down the farm lane. He carried a cavalry carbine slung over his shoulder with a bit of soft cotton rope. "Who is that?" Jack wanted to know.

Booth jumped up again and said, "Oh . . . that is one of our men."

"What do you mean?" Jack retorted, never having seen Davy Herold before.

"Why, one of those who crossed over with me." Booth then asked young Richard to fetch his pistols and knife. Thrilled to be able to handle such fearsome weapons Richard quickly ran up the stairs and returned with them in hand. He gave them to Booth proudly, his heart beating wildly, more from the excitement of touching the weapons than the exertion of climbing the stairs two at a time. Booth strapped them on and tousled the boy's hair by way of a thank you.[31]

---

31 Dodels, "Last Days of John Wilkes Booth," 7-8; Kauffman, "Booth's Escape Route: Lincoln's Assassin on the Run," 46, 48; statement of Miss Halloway, in Wilson, *John Wilkes Booth*, 208-22; Fleet (ed.), "A Chapter of Unwritten History: Richard Baynham Garrett's Account," 388-407; "Statement of John M. Garrett," 4-9.

Booth stepped off the porch and met Herold in the yard. Herold told him about his trip to Bowling Green and the fact that if they could get there, they might receive help to go farther south or west. He was also bubbling over about their stop at a place variously called the Trappe or the Half-way House with a Madam and her very accommodating daughters. Booth told him that Jack Garrett was getting suspicious of who they actually were. Garrett suspected some sort of criminal activity that would bring vengeful Yankess down on the whole family.

Jack Garrett was still sitting on the porch. As Booth and Herold approached, he stood up.

"This is my cousin, David Boyd," Booth lied to him. "Davy, meet Jack Garrett."

"Hey," Herold said shaking hands. "Do you suppose that you all can entertain me for the night?"

"Well, I am not the proprietor of the house. My father is out and I do not know when he will return. I cannot take you in on my own account." By now, Garrett actually wished to get both men off the premises. He was very suspicious of Booth's conduct earlier that evening. This guest was way too edgy to suit Jack.

Garrett assented to Herold awaiting the return of the head of the Garrett family on the front steps. Herold had hardly been comfortably settled in when the pounding of hooves coming up the drive caused everyone to stand up. Garrett recognized Lieutenant Ruggles. He had seen him from the second story bedroom window when Booth arrived the day before. The other was Bainbridge, as Booth and Herold knew. The two fugitives walked out to meet the riders.

"Well, boys," Booth exclaimed, "what is in the wind now?"

"Great Scott, fellers!" Ruggles yelled, loudly enough that Jack Garrett overheard every word. "We hear tell that they are about forty Federal cavalry crossing the Rappahannock down at the ferry. Y'all had better get out of the way! We are cutting out before they take us, too."

Bainbridge advised Booth and Herold to take to the woods. "I'll do as you say, boys," Booth pledged. "Ride on! Good-bye! It will never do for you to be found in my company!"

Then he grabbed Ruggles' leg and said in a low voice so that Garrett could not overhear, "Rest assured of one thing, good friend, John Wilkes Booth will never be taken alive!" With that the two Confederate soldiers turned and spurred their mounts back to the road. They turned south for Bowling Green.

Immediately, Booth and Herold started for the woods west of the house. "I'm damned if I will take their oath," Booth shouted over his shoulder at Jack for effect. But he knew that Jack Garrett, and through him the whole family, would be harder to deal with than ever. And how could the Yankees have found them so fast? Booth questioned himself silently. They were all confused up in Maryland, the last we heard. Booth and Herold could not move very fast, as Booth was loaded down with the pistols, his knife, and the laborious impediment of his crutches. They disappeared into the woods, Herold having to wait for Booth to get there.

Within five minutes, however, Herold was back, wondering aloud if the Federal troopers were really crossing at Port Royal. Garrett saw a black youth coming down the farm road. He knew him as Jim Pendleton, son of a man who did odd chores on the Locust Hill farm. Pendleton confirmed that Union cavalry was crossing on the old ferry, and lining up to head south on the Bowling Green road past the Garrett's. Then he headed for the woods that had swallowed up Booth.

"All is not right with you Boyds," Jack said. "It would please me no end if y'all would leave here. We are peaceable citizens and don't want to get into any difficulty with the Federal authorities." Garret's brief litany was interrupted by the pounding of hooves on the highway. Before Herold or Garrett could properly react, a cavalry detachment thundered by in a cloud of dust, accompanied by the creaking of leather and the clanging of sabers. The soldiers did not even pause as they passed the main gate. Indeed, it would turn out later that they had not even seen it. Jack Garrett made them out to be more like thirty men rather than forty. But they were Yankees, nonetheless, and going Hell-bent for leather toward Bowling Green.

Garrett begged Herold to fetch up Booth and leave the Garrett farm. Two horsemen, trying to catch up with those who had passed a few minutes earlier, punctuated his plea. When Herold inquired about buying a horse, Garrett demurred. Herold then asked about renting a wagon and driver. Garrett referred him to a balck neighbor.

"Ol' Ned Freeman is mighty fond of specie," Garrett informed Herold. "He might do it for five or six dollars. But he probably will not go beyond Guinea Station."

Herold handed Garrett a ten-dollar greenback. Herold took a small stick lying on the ground and stepped into a dusty part of the yard. He made a few calculations, stood there a moment rechecking his figures, and turned back to Garrett.

"I make that as about seven dollars and thirty cents in specie."

"I will go over and do what I can to get Freeman to take you," Garrett promised. With that he started down the lane to Freeman's.[32]

---

32 Dodels, "The Last Days of John Wilkes Booth," 8-11; Kauffman, "Booth's Escape Route: Lincoln's Assassin on the Run," 48; Statement of Miss Halloway, in Wilson, *John Wilkes Booth*, 208-22; Fleet (ed.), "A Chapter of Unwritten History: Richard Baynham Garrett's Account," 388-407; "Statement of John M. Garrett," 4-9; "Deposition of William H. Garrett," 5-7.

When Jack Garrett came back from visiting Freeman's, he had three men with him. They found that Booth had rejoined Herold and that both were awaiting Jack on the veranda. Informed that Freeman was not home, Garrett confirmed that the Yankees were hunting for someone because they had asked Freeman's wife if she had seen any strange white men. But Garrett thought that everything could be handled tomorrow morning.

Three whites had followed him. "They are from Mosby," Jack to Booth and Herold. "Without paroles. I told them they could come over and eat supper with us. They will be moving on later." Before the usual handshaking amenities could be observed, the whole crowd was called in to supper. It was consumed with a minimum of conversation, the atmosphere strained by the presence of the newcomers. Booth and the three Mosby men eyed each other cautiously. Somehow, Booth seemed to divine their true purpose, to kill him to prevent his capture by Union soldiers, if it came to that.

Then Jack Garrett informed Booth that he and Herold could not sleep in the house that night. After some haggling, which angered Booth, always the compromiser, Herold suggested that they sleep in the Tobacco barn and the end of the lot.

As he and Booth set off to the tobacco barn, Jack turned to Willie Garrett and muttered quietly, "We had better lock them in for the night. I am very suspicious of those two. They might try and steal our horses and escape. Pa thinks they might be guerillas, who have done something to cause them to fear arrest. He wants us to keep a sharp eye on them tonight."

"Well, be that as it may, Colonel Mosby wants them to come down to Hanover Junction or Ashland tomorrow. We cannot allow them to leave independently," one of Mosby's men warned. "They might stumble onto that Federal cavalry column that passed through here. Can you lock them in? Without creating a ruckus? And we really need to get that wagon from Old Freeman—and him, too, as driver, if we can. Booth cain't ride a mile."

The Garretts produced a large padlock with which to lock the tobacco barn door. Pleased with the arrangements, the Mosby men bade their farewells and left. They would hide out at their own homes until tomorrow, when they would return to help move Booth and Herold to the Hanover Junction area.

The two Garrett boys went quietly down to the barn. The barn walls were built with wide separations between the vertical boards, which allowed air to circulate and cure the tobacco as it hung from poles laid over multiple cross beams. Jack now laid his ear to one of these crevices to see if he could hear anything of the fugitives' possible plans. Meanwhile, Willie carefully clicked a large padlock on the door hasps.

Jack and Willie returned to the house for the nightly family worship. After prayers, Jack came over to Willie, as he crawled into bed upstairs. "I still do not trust those men. We had better take blankets and sleep out in one of the corn cribs, where we can guard the horses, personal like."

"Good idea," Willie agreed. They took their blankets, a Confederate-issued Enfield rifled musket, and quietly went back down stairs. They left the house silently, not telling anyone what they were doing or where they were going.[33]

---

[33] Roscoe, *Web of Conspiracy*, 375-80; Dodels, "The Last Days of John Wilkes Booth," 11-12. On the Confederate attempt to control Booth's escape, see Smith with Richter, *In the Shadows of the Lincoln Assassination: The Life of Confederate Spy Thomas H. Harbin*, 132-40.

# 3

## THE YANKEES ARRIVE

"This is Garrett's," Willie Jett said. He was outside the Garrett's main gate on the Bowling Green road, along with over two-dozen Union horse soldiers from the Sixteenth New York Cavalry commanded by Lt. Edward Doherty, escorting two civilian detectives. It was the middle of the night.

"Are you sure?" one detective whispered, the implicit tone of warning in his voice. "I am not fooling. I will hang the man who misleads me."

"He is right, Colonel," William Rollins said. Rollins was a Port Conway man impressed into service as a local guide yesterday evening. "This is Garrett's main gate. I swear it."

After ascertaining the layout of Garrett's farmyard from Jett, Lt. Col. Everton Conger boldly rode into the farmyard, taking Lieutenant L. Byron Baker with him. The two men had been in the First District of Columbia Cavalry, but now operated as civilian detectives with the National Detective Police, a sort of private governmental law enforcement group headed by Baker's cousin, Col. Lafayette C. Baker. He had organized the First D.C. Cavalry, but now operated under Secretary of War Edwin McM. Stanton, as a civilian in charge of any dirty business that needed solving off the books.[34]

---

34 See Lafayette C. Baker, *History of the United States Secret Service* (Philadelphia: L. C. Baker, 1867; Jacob Mogelever, *Death to Traitors: The Story of General Lafayette C. Baker, Lincoln's Forgotten Secret Service Chief* (New York: Doubleday & Company, 1960).

Pursuing Booth was one such job. Lafe Baker had received information that two men had crossed the Potomac some days before. The men were actually Thomas Harbin and his assistant and telegrapher, Joseph Baden, but Baker mistakenly thought them to be Booth and Herold. No difference; the Yankees had cornered Booth at last.

The two men had hardly entered when the hounds started baying and yelping at this undesired invasion of their territory. The two detectives soon returned, having confirmed the truth of Jett's description of the farm's layout.

"Hold on a little longer, men. Booth's in there, for sure! Lieutenant Doherty, have your men follow me and surround the house. Move quietly, no noise, no talking!"

Doherty gave the signal to move forward, leaving several men to watch Jett and Rollins. Byron Baker spryly leaped up on the porch and banged on the door with his revolver butt. Out in the yard, one of the more aggressive dogs yipped off in pain as a well-placed kick from a cavalry boot found its mark. The remainder of the pack still raised a ruckus, but from a safe distance.

"Open up in there! Be quick about it!" Baker shouted.

There was a rustling noise and the sound of wood scraping against wood. A window next to the door was raised. Old Richard Garrett stuck his head out to see what the matter was. Baker grabbed his arm and put his pistol to the man's head.

"We are Federal officers," Baker snarled.

"Open the door! Get a light and be right quick about it!" The new voice belonged to Conger, who had just arrived on the porch.

Garrett did as he was ordered. He opened the door, a lighted candle in his hand.

"Where are they? What do you mean by sheltering the murderers of the President?" Conger shot his questions so quickly that none could have been answered.

Garrett was bewildered and frightened. He had a tendency to stutter, and the affliction seized upon him in all its magnitude now. His response was a tongue-tied, "wha'... wha'... I ... I ..."

"Where are the two men who have been staying here the past two days?" Conger yelled.

"Th-th-they are no, no ... not he-here," Garrett stammered.

"Do not tell me that," Conger warned, cocking his pistol. "They are here!"

Garrett, his body convulsed with tremblings, could do nothing but attempt to stutter out more gibberish.

Conger turned to a trooper, "Soldier go get a rope! I aim to put this old miscreant to the top of one of these trees, and right now!"

In the midst of this exchange, Mrs. Garrett called out from behind a door down the hall, "Father, here are your clothes, dress yourself!" Nineteenth century propriety could be asserted at the oddest times.

"Search this place, Lieutenant!" Conger raged.

"But there are unclad women about, sir!" Doherty objected. More of that Victorian propriety intervened, once again.

"Do not hang him, sir, please," the voice of Mrs. Garrett begged. Lucinda Holloway, her sister, also pleaded for mercy. The youngest Garrett girl began to sob and moan, "Papa, oh, Papa!" in the midst of her tears.

Conger dragged Garrett out of the house and made him stand on a chopping block. A rope was thrown over a tree limb above his head and fastened to his neck. Half a dozen men stood ready to hoist him up so that he would slowly strangle.

"Colonel!" The voice was from a trooper, who had been detailed to guard the back of the house. "Hold on, sir! I have someone here from behind the house that can help out."

Into the midst of federals came a man, dressed in Rebel gray, escorted by a trooper in Union blue.

"I heard the uproar and came up to help out," said the Confederate soldier. "This man nearly shot me. I am Jack Garrett. This is my father. Do not hurt him. Give him time. He is tongue-tied and cannot talk hurriedly. What do you gentlemen want with the two men the corporal says you are looking for?"

"That is none of your business, Reb," Conger said icily. "We know they are here. We have Jett out at the road and he says he left them here. We mean to have them. If you do not tell us instantly, we will hang you and the old man and burn this house to the ground. Now make haste, my patience is wearing mighty thin."

"Please, don't hurt my father. Father, it is best to tell them. Gentlemen, if you want to know where those men are, I will take you to the place. They did not sleep in the house tonight, but are in an outhouse."

In those days, an outhouse could be any building away from the main home, not specifically a privy, as is commonly thought today. So, Jack Garrett pointed to the darkened barn-like structure off to the west.

"My brother and I locked them in last night—they cannot get out."

"What brother?"

"Willie. He and I have been sleeping in the corncrib to guard our horses. We were afraid the men might try to steal them. Some of your men have him out back there. He has the key."

"Baker, take that boy," he pointed to young Richard, who

had come down to watch the proceedings, "and go get the key from brother Willie. Jack Garrett and I will meet you at the barn. Bring everyone along, including Willie. Doherty, leave a half dozen men under Sergeant Wendell to guard the house. And keep the old man on the block, ready to swing. The rest of you surround the tobacco barn. Doherty, you and Sergeant Corbett, get them moving. Now!"35

Meanwhile, the commotion from the farmyard had already rousted the half-asleep Booth. "Dave, they are here."

"Huh? Humph. What is the matter? Is it time to go?"

"A cavalryman has just ridden around the barn. I could hear his saber clanking. There! He stopped and looked in at the back corner! There he goes, back up towards the house!"

"What? Oh, no. Oh my God! Aw-w-w, mother! . . . We had better give up."

"I will suffer death first," Booth swore. "Come on. They are still up at the house. The door is still locked. Let us see if we cannot break through the wall and take to the woods."

Both men went to the back wall of the barn away from the house.

"Look for a weak or loose board," Booth said.

---

35 Dodels, "The Last days of John Wilkes Booth," 12-15; Jacob Mogelever, *Death to Traitors: The Story of General Lafayette C. Baker, Lincoln's Forgotten Secret Service Chief* (New York: Doubleday & Company, 1960), 353-55; William L. Reuter, *The King Can Do No Wrong* (New York: Pageant Press, Inc., 1958), 41-43; Chamlee, *Lincoln's Assassins*, 154; Roscoe, *Web of Conspiracy*, 381-83; Laughlin, *Death of Lincoln*, 147; Townsend, *Life, Crime, and Death of John Wilkes Booth*, 30-31; Kauffman, "Booth's Escape Route: Lincoln's Assassin on the Run," 48; Barbee, "Lincoln and Booth," 959-84, *passim*, DRB papers, GU.

See also, Statement of Miss Halloway, in Francis Wilson, *John Wilkes Booth: Fact and Fiction of Lincoln's Assassination* (Boston: Houghton Mifflin, 1929), 208-22; Baker, "An Eyewitness Account of the Death and Burial of J. Wilkes Booth," 425-46; Doherty's "Official Report on the Capture of John Wilkes Booth," *Surratt Courier*, 25 (May 2000), 3-7; Fleet (ed.), "A Chapter of Unwritten History: Richard Baynham Garrett's Account," 388-407; Miller (ed.), "A Trooper's Account of the Death of Booth," 5-9; "Statement of John M. Garrett," 4-9; and Steven G. Miller (ed.), "Boston Corbett's Long-Forgotten Story of Wilkes Booth's Death," *Surratt Courier*, 26 (May 2001), 5-7; *ibid.*, 26 (June 2001), 4-6.

"I cain't find any," Herold whined.

Booth sat down and began to kick at one wood panel with his good leg. "Here, Davy, help me! Let us kick together!"

The board moved but a few inches, not yielding enough to let either man through.

"John, I cannot kick hard enough left footed. Cain't we switch sides?"

"Be careful of my broken leg. Now, kick!"

But left-footed or right-footed, the panel yielded only a few inches more to Herold's desperate battering. Still not enough to pass either man through.

Herold began to thrash about angrily in the straw, kicking at the blankets that had once covered him.

"Sh-h-h," Booth cautioned him quietly. "Someone is coming down. Do not make any noise. Maybe they will go off, thinking we are not here."

This hope filled fragment of naïveté was quickly blown away, when Lieutenant Baker yelled out, "You men had better come out of there. We know who you are. I want you to surrender. If you do not, I will burn the barn down in fifteen minutes."

Herold looked at Booth. Even through the darkness, Booth knew his companion's eyes were wide with fear. Booth wondered if these were Confederates who had come to rescue them or Yankees who had come to arrest them. The actor thought a moment, lining out his part, as it were. Then he spoke, putting on a bold front, "Who are you?"

Conger whispered quietly in Baker's ear. "Do not, by any remark made to him, allow him to know who we are. You need not tell him who we are. If he thinks we are Rebels, or thinks we are his friends, we will take advantage of it. We will not lie to him about it, but we need not answer any questions that have any reference to that subject. Simply insist on his coming out . . . if he will."

Lieutenant Baker nodded. "Never mind who we are. We know who you are and you had better come out and deliver yourselves up."

The outside of the barn grew bright, as the weary troopers of the Sixteenth New York gathered brush and loose boards and began to build numerous small fires. Some of the men gathered around the flames to warm themselves. Others actually fell asleep. Conger was furious. He turned to Lieutenant Doherty, who was petulantly standing aside, as usual, letting Conger and his minion, Baker, run things.

"Lieutenant Doherty," he shouted, "you damned cowardly scoundrel"—this unfairly to a man who had served with distinction in four crack combat units since 1861—"can you not control your men? Damn it! If you do not keep those cowards in their places here, those fellows in the barn will get away. Get their asses back in position now!"

The two officers went down opposite sides of the barn, rousting out the tired soldiers from their fires and blankets and placing them back in line. "You, Sergeant Corbett," Conger said, placing a stick on the ground near the rear of one wall and standing him next to it, "do not leave your post Sergeant, on any condition."

"Yessir," Corbett intoned.

Returning to the front door, Lieutenant Doherty said, "I think we ought to wait for daylight. They are trapped and cannot go anywhere."

"Hell, no! We are going to flush them out, here and now." Although Conger did not say it, he was not about to share the reward money with any possible reinforcements the dawn might bring. It was bad enough to split with twenty-eight others of all ranks.

Colonel Conger grabbed hold of Jack Garrett. There was a rustling and creaking about the main door. Booth heard the lock snap open. "Now listen carefully, Reb," Conger whispered threateningly in his ear, resting his revolver along Garrett's shoulder with the barrel pointed at his neck. "You are going to go in there to your friends and demand their arms and bring them out. If you fail, we will burn this barn down on top of them."

Baker opened the door and Conger gave Garrett a rude shove. He stumbled into the dark maw of the building, momentarily blind from the blackness of the interior. Baker shouted after him, "We are going to send in this man, on whose premises you are, to get your arms, and you must come out and deliver yourselves up."

"Gentlemen," Garrett almost whispered as he talked. "The cavalry are after you. You are the ones. You had better give yourselves up."

"You have implicated me," Booth snarled. "You damn Judas! Get out of here! You have betrayed me!"

Lieutenant Baker, hearing the oaths Booth threw at Garrett, spoke up once again. "We sent this young man, in whose custody we find you. Give him your arms and surrender or we shall burn the barn and have a bonfire and a shooting match."

"There are nearly fifty armed men out there," said Garrett, amazed at Booth's hesitation in the face of such odds. "Escape is impossible. Be reasonable and surrender yourself."

Booth glowered at Garrett, who could just make out the hatred in those piercing, hazel eyes, glowing like those of a wild, enraged cat.

"The word surrender is not in my vocabulary," Booth

snapped. "I have never learned the meaning of that. You vile traitor! I have half a mind to kill you right here!" He reached to his belt. Garrett thought he was going for one of his revolvers and beat a hasty retreat.

"Captain, let me out. I will do anything I can for you, but I cain't risk my life in here. Lemme out!"

"Sir," Garrett said to Colonel Conger, once safely outside, "he will not give up. I will not go back in there again. He has threatened to kill me."

"How do you know he was going to harm you?" Conger said with incredulity in his voice.

"He reached for his pistol in the hay behind him, and I came out. My life is very dear to me. I would not like to risk it in that barn again."

Then Garrett looked at the lit candle that Lieutenant Baker had been holding in his hand during the negotiations. "You had better put that out or he will shoot you by its light," Garrett said.

Baker placed the candle down in the dirt near the door, so that its glow would illuminate the front of the barn. He wanted no one to slip out in the dark. But in the romantic fashion of thousands of men who had died on both sides during that bloodiest of all American wars, he refused to stand in the darkness. Honor demanded that he stand within the arc of light, to be seen by all, friend and foe alike. He placed Jack and Willie nearby, but separated, each with a guard, ordered to shoot them down at the first shot fired from the barn.

"Come, come, gentlemen," Baker called out. "Time's awastin'. Surrender now. I will give you no more than ten minutes. Then, we torch the barn."

"Gentlemen," Booth yelled back; or, rather, his voice boomed back, so resonant and full of timbre that it could be heard clear to the highway, as it reverberated out on the night zephyrs. There was no fear in it. Rather, it rang with the note of command. "Give me time for reflection! You have spoiled my plans; I was going to Mexico to make my fortune."

"Your fortune has already been assured. Come out!"

"Now, now, gentlemen, if I have done anything, I did it for the good of my country; at least I pray that I did so."

After some pause, Booth spoke again. "I am alone; there is no one in here with me."

"No, sir. We know that two men went in there and two must come out," Baker asserted firmly.

"Oh, God, Johnny!" pleaded Herold, in quiet desperation. "I do not want to die. Le's give it up. Please!"

"I am not going to surrender only to be mocked and hanged later. Come on, Davy! Let us give them one last, good fight, just like Richard III."

"What the Hell has some English king from hundreds of years ago got to do with this? I want to go out and save me—in the here and now!"

"Surrender, boy, if you must. But as for me, I will die like a man!"

"Please, Johnny," Herold pleaded. The term "boy" had cut through his soul like a knife, but fear and self-preservation overrode all other emotions in Herold's panic-stricken mind.

"Alright Davy. I will do what I can to save you." Booth raised his voice aloud again. Again Baker was impressed with its force and clarity. "There is a man here who wishes very much to surrender."

Then Booth turned on Herold and snapped loud enough for Baker to hear, "Leave me, will you? You little rat! Go! I would not have you to stay with me. Get out before I shoot you and blow my own brains out!"

Herold did not catch on to the ruse Booth had created for him. "I am going! I do not intend to be burnt alive!" Herold ran up and shook the door, which had the lock slipped through the hasp again. "Let me out! I know nothing of this man in here."

"Let him out, Captain," Booth said resignedly. "This young man is innocent." He thought for a moment, and then spoke again, "I want you to take careful notice of one thing. The gentleman whose place this is, Mr. Garrett, nor any of his family, knows who I am, or what I have done."

Lieutenant Doherty, attempting to assume a larger role for himself after Conger's previous rebuke, yelled back to Herold, "Bring out the arms and you can come out."

"I have no arms," Herold cried out, then beginning to sob.

"But you have," Lieutenant Baker insisted, jockeying for a more commanding position, as befitted a cousin of the head of the National Detective Police. "You brought a carbine across the river. You must hand it out!"

Booth interjected loudly here. "He has no arms. They are mine and I have them."

Baker yelled back, angrily, "This man carried a carbine, and he must hand it out!"

"Upon the word and honor of a gentleman, he has no arms. The arms are mine, and I shall keep them."

"Please, God!" Herold prayed again. "He will shoot me! Merciful Jesus! Please let me come out!"

"We had better let him out," Doherty said to Baker.

"No," Baker replied. "Wait until Colonel Conger comes—here he is!"

"I got one of the Garrett boys piling up pine boards and

twigs at the rear corner next to the straw inside. Never mind the arms," Conger ordered, gasping in pain from his exertions, which had caused his old unhealed wounds to be aggravated. "If we can get one of the men out, let us do it, and wait no longer. I am going back to supervise preparations for the fire."

Richard Garrett ran up to Conger as he went to the back of the barn. "I cain't pile up no more wood and sticks, Mister. He said he would shoot me if'n I did."

"That's all right, sonny," Conger reassured him. "We have got enough to do the job up right."

Back at the front door, the competition between Doherty and Baker intensified. "I will take that man out myself!" Lieutenant Doherty said, as Conger disappeared around the corner once again. He motioned to a trooper by the door who then took the lock out of the hasp and opened the door slightly.

"Whoever you are, put out your hands! Let me see your hands!" Doherty ordered. Herold did as he was told, and Doherty grabbed him and pulled the badly frightened, tear-stained boy out into the night.

"I am not Booth!" he whined. Nobody paid any attention to his blubbering. Herold was relieved of his gloves, pocketknife, and a piece of a page out of an atlas. It was part of a map of Virginia from a schoolbook. Manacles were then placed on his wrists.

Doherty grabbed him by the collar. "Come and stand up by the house," he said, pulling Herold along. Herold continued whimpering, sometimes crying like a child.

"Let me go away," Herold pleaded.

"Not on your tintype, sonny boy," Doherty said, gruffly.

"Let me go around here, then. I will not leave. I will not go away."

"No, sir," Doherty said, again.

"Who is that man in the barn?" Herold asked, feigning a wide-eyed innocence.

Doherty could not believe his ears. "Why, you know very well who it is."

"No, I do not," Herold insisted. "He told me his name was Boyd."

"It is Booth and you know it," Doherty retorted.

"No, I did not know it. I did not know that it was Booth."

Lieutenant Doherty called out to a trooper at the Garrett house, "Trooper! Tie this fool to a tree with your picket rope. If he keeps on whimpering, gag him."

"No, don't. Let me stay loose, I will not run."

"Who was in the barn with you? Was it Booth?" Doherty tried one more time.

"Yes," Herold owned up. "Booth is in the barn."

"Tie him up!" Doherty ordered.

"That is not fair, sir! I told you what you wanted.... Ahh! Not so tight!" Herold complained as the trooper lashed him to a tree beside the Garrett's front porch.

"Shut up, Reb," came the trooper's insensitive reply.

Herold kept trying. "You know, I always liked Mr. Lincoln's jokes...." The rest Doherty could not hear as he rushed back toward the tobacco barn, still shaking his head in amazement.[36]

---

36 In general, see Dodels, "The Last Days of John Wilkes Booth," 15-22; Mogelever, *Death to Traitors*, 355-57; Reuter, *The King Can Do No Wrong*, 43-46; Chamlee, *Lincoln's Assassins*, 153-54; Roscoe, *Web of Conspiracy*, 383-87; Laughlin, *Death of Lincoln*, 150; Townsend, *Life, Crime, and Death of John Wilkes Booth*, 35; Kauffman, "Booth's Escape Route: Lincoln's Assassin on the Run," 49; Barbee, "Lincoln and Booth," 959-84, *passim*, DRB papers, GU.

See also, Statement of Miss Halloway, in Wilson, *John Wilkes Booth*, 208-22; L. B. Baker, "An Eyewitness Account of the Death and Burial of J. Wilkes Booth," *Journal of the Illinois State Historical Society*, 39 (Dec. 1946), 425-46; Edward P. Doherty's "Official Report on the Capture of John Wilkes Booth," *Surratt Courier*, 25 (May 2000), 3-7; Fleet (ed.), "A Chapter of Unwritten History: Richard Baynham Garrett's Account," 388-407; Miller (ed.), "A Trooper's Account of the Death of Booth," 5-9; "Statement of John M. Garrett," 4-9; Miller (ed.), "Boston Corbett's Long-Forgotten Story of Wilkes Booth's Death," *Surratt Courier*, 26 (June 2001), 4-6.

# 4

# The Shooting of John Wilkes Booth

Back at the barn, Doherty's temporary absence left the field to Baker. He called out to Booth, "You had better come out, too, and surrender. You have five minutes or we fire the barn!"

Evidently, Booth still was not sure if he faced Yankees or possibly a Confederate unit come to rescue him. "Tell me who you are and what you want of me," he demanded. "It may be I am being taken by friends."

"It makes no difference who we are," Baker said. "We want you. We have fifty well-armed men around this barn. You cannot escape and we do not wish to kill you."

Booth paused to ponder a bit. "Captain, this is a hard case, I swear. I am a cripple; I have got but one leg. Give me a chance. Draw up your men in line of battle twenty yards from the door and I will fight your whole command."

"We are not here to fight you," an exasperated Baker retorted. "We are here to take you. You are now free to come out and surrender."

"Give me a little time to consider," Booth stalled.

"Very well," Baker said with a sigh. "You can have two more minutes."

Booth took most of the allotted time before he answered. "Captain, I believe you to be a brave and honorable man. I have had half a dozen chances to shoot you. I have a bead drawn on you now, and could pull the trigger, but I do not wish to do it. Withdraw your men from the door, any distance, and I will come out. Give me this chance for my life, Captain, for I will not be taken alive."

"Your time is up!" snapped Lieutenant Baker. "We shall wait no longer. We shall fire the barn."

"Well then, my brave boys, you may prepare a stretcher for me.... One more stain on the glorious old banner!" Booth said, referring to his love of the pre-war Old Glory and Lincoln's defiling of it, as stated in his "To Whom It May Concern" letter,[37] which he had locked up some time ago in his brother-in-law's safe.

Colonel Conger came around the corner of the barn. "Are you ready?" he asked.

"Yes," Baker said.

Conger limped back around the corner to the rear of the barn, where he picked up a six inch twisted straw fuse and lit it with a match. The acrid smell of sulfur drifted in the night air. Conger waited a moment for the fuse to flare up and get going. Then he threw it through the crack into the hay and straw on the other side. The dry straw flashed so quickly, it was as if it exploded. The flames raced along the length of the barn where the straw and fodder were piled. The open walls of the tobacco barn let in massive amounts of air, which fueled the blaze and sucked the flames all the way to the rafters. It followed the trail of straw under the dry, wooden furniture piled in the back of the barn. The loosely stacked, prized pieces, so meticulously rescued from the war, now fell victim to its Götterdämmerung. The very

---

37  Rhodehammel and Taper, *The Writings of John Wilkes Booth*, 124-27.

cobwebs seemed to breathe fire, as they disappeared in a waft of super-heated air.[38]

Before the blaze was set, the soldiers had all been easily visible around their lights and bonfires to Booth in the darkened barn. Now the situation was reversed. Booth was in the spotlight he cherished so much while on stage. He spun around as agilely as his crutches would allow, carbine in hand, working the lever. He moved along the wall, peering through the ventilation cracks between the boards, looking for the man who set the fire. But the pace and ferocity of the flames seemed to blind him, temporarily.

He leaned back from the fierce heat and bumped a small table in the middle of the floor. Throwing the carbine down, he grabbed the table by one leg, as if he would flip it over and extinguish the blaze with its top. But the fire was too far-gone to submit to half measures. Already the roof was catching. Smoke rolled along the ridgepole and out through the openings in the walls. Booth consigned the table to the flames.

Now fully aware of the fire's intensity, Booth turned back toward the front door. Conger raced around the barn to meet him in front. Booth threw down one crutch and drew a revolver. The other was holstered on his belt next to the sheathed Bowie knife. It was his moment in the sun, the thing he had treasured all his life. He drew himself up to full height. His hair blew in the wind created by the miniature firestorm behind him. The light flickered all around, crowning him with a ghostly aura, outlining his tousled hair like the halo highlighting a holy figure in some medieval painting. His alabaster forehead glowed red from

---

[38] Rob Wick, "Why Did Everton Conger Burn Down Richard Garrett's Tobacco Barn?" *Surratt Courier*, 33 (May 2008), 6-7, theorizes that Conger was suffering from the extended ride to find Booth and wanted to get the ordeal over with posthaste. While not in disagreement with this analysis, we think that Conger's fear of the arrival of more federal troops and the subsequent dilution of the reward money also had great influence on his decision to speed up events by setting the barn on fire.

the reflected fire, his pupils glistened like lumps of coal, his lips drawn tightly in a grim, determined frown.

Outside, the soldiers temporarily scattered from the flames. Their officers stood transfixed by the drama unfolding before them. Booth threw down his second crutch. He was standing free on his own legs for the last time. The Booth of old. The premier actor of his day. The greatest scene-stealer of the era. This was in his finest hour, his final role, standing bravely without a sign of fear at the tremendous odds arraigned against him. He was the last Confederate hero, the embodiment of Richard III at Bosworth Field, fighting gamely to the end. He sprang forward, oblivious to the sudden pain that shot up his leg, his revolver ready for action.

He remembered something he had said to his sister, Asia, when she asked him why he had to have the east-facing bedroom in the garret. No setting sun for me. It is too melancholy—let me see him rise.

But he would not see his beloved rising sun. His father had pronounced his fate years before. The good do not always win, he had said. So, too, had his sister, Asia. I am not to drown, hang, or burn, although my sister has believed I am a predestined martyr of some sort, Johnny remembered. And it was his own stated desire as a youth that he should die with the satisfaction of knowing he had done something never before accomplished by any other man; something no other man would do. But he was damned if he would die strangling at the end of a Yankee noose in a dank prison courtyard, as had his friend John Yates Beall before him, or swing in front of a sensation-seeking public, like old Osawatomie John Brown.

A shot rang out. Booth pitched forward on his face. Baker fumbled with the lock, tearing it out of the hasp and desperately throwing it aside. He sprang into the barn, closely followed by Doherty, who had just returned from securing Herold. Conger and Jack Garrett piled in after them. Baker grabbed Booth's gun hand and wrenched the revolver away. Jack Garrett leaped toward the fire.

"Save my property! Help put out the fire," he shouted.

"You men," Conger shouted at the soldiers congregating at the door. "Get in here and put out the flames!"

Conger then looked at the dying Booth, held up in Baker's arms. The wound at the back of his neck was visible. "He has shot himself," Conger asserted, more than a little astonished.

"No, he did not either," Baker retorted firmly.

"It is Booth, all right," Doherty interjected. "I know him, personally, from a theater party."

Conger produced a photograph and the reward poster, with its written description of Lincoln's assailant. They confirmed Doherty's statement.

"It is John Wilkes Booth, the famous actor," said Baker, as if he could not trust Doherty. Standing nearby, Richard Garrett realized for the first time who the wounded, alleged Confederate soldier, Boyd, really was. He ran to spread the news to his family.

"Whereabouts is he shot?" Conger asked. "In the neck or the head?" Baker indicated the location of the wound, just below Booth's right ear. It was as if he had placed the revolver behind his ear and it slipped as he jerked on the trigger. A perfect suicide. Oddly, the bullet had entered Booth's head at about the same spot as the one he had put in Lincoln. Their trajectories, of course were ninety degrees apart—Lincoln's traveling through the brain, Booth's severing his own spinal cord. But the entry wounds were remarkably similar.

"Yes, sir," Conger said with finality, "he shot himself!"

"No, he did not!" Baker refused to yield the point. "Someone shot him, and whoever did it goes back to the City under arrest."

A shot whizzed by, followed by a series of popping noises. Davy Herold's abandoned box of Spencer cartridges was burning up.

"Well," Conger said, "let us carry him out of here. This whole place will soon be burning."

The three officers grabbed Booth like a sack of potatoes and hauled him out of the path of the advancing fire. They were followed by Garrett and the soldiers who had vainly tried to control the flames.

But Baker was not yet willing to stop the argument. "What on earth did you shoot him for?" he said to Conger accusingly.

"Damn it! I did not shoot him!"[39]

Baker looked at the Colonel a moment. Maybe it would be better, if Conger did do the shooting, not to spread it about. Baker knelt and placed Booth's head and shoulders in his lap. He motioned for a bucket of water that had been drawn for putting out the fire, before it was decided to let the holocaust burn itself out.

Baker splashed water in Booth's still pale, handsome face. His eyes blinked. They opened up with a shocked look, as if he

---

39  The question of whether Booth committed suicide or Sgt. Thomas "Boston" Corbett shot him is discussed in William L. Richter with J. E. "Rick" Smith III) "Could John Wilkes Booth Have Committed Suicide?" in *Surratt Courier*, 38 (May 2013), 3-8.

See also, Otto Eisenschiml, "Who Shot Booth?" in *O. E.: Historian Without an Armchair* (Indianapolis: Bobbs-Merrill, 1963), 159-66, concludes that Conger shot Booth to stop him from incriminating Stanton or other unnamed persons of note, in or out of the Federal government. We doubt that. Booth shot himself in the back of the head to save his pretty face (Lattimer, *Kennedy and Lincoln*, 75). His weapon slipped and the shot cut his spinal cord instead of blowing his brains out—the final piece of the bad luck that had attended all of his efforts since January 1865. The standard version is Blaine V. Houmes and Steven G. Miller, "The Death of John Wilkes Booth: Suicide by Cop?" *American Journal of Forensic Psychiatry*, 25 (No. 2, 2004), 25-36.

wondered how these soldiers could have followed him into the very depths of Hell. If Yankees were here, it surely could not be Heaven!

He was still alive! Baker took a military-issue, collapsible, metal cup from his pocket and filled it with water. He poured it into Booth's open mouth. The actor coughed and spewed it back, nearly hitting Baker in the face.

"Tell mother," Booth began. He paused, thought a moment, and repeated it. "Tell mother...." Booth's head slumped to one side as he passed out, again. Baker took his kerchief from around his neck, dampened it in the bucket, and gently bathed Booth's forehead.

His eyelids began to flicker again, batting furiously at first and then locking wide open. Booth was staring intently, although it seemed as if he could not focus on any one object or idea. Conger got down on one knee. He did not want to miss a word of possible confession. His boss, Colonel Lafayette C. Baker, and Baker's boss, Secretary of War Stanton, would want to hear it all.

Booth concentrated on him. "Tell mother... I die... for my country," Booth whispered. Conger had put his ear close as Booth's lips moved.

Conger thought a moment and repeated the sentence. "Tell mother I died for my country. Is that what you say?"

"Yes," came the hoarse reply. "I did... what... I thought... best."

Baker repeated the phrase again and asked, Booth, "Do I get it correctly?" Booth half-nodded his head affirmatively.

"Captain," Booth cried out painfully, as loudly as he could. Conger bent down to hear Booth's hoarse whisper. "It is hard... that this... man's property should... be destroyed.... He does ... not ... know who ... I am." The Garretts had been saved from being hanged by the Federal juggernaut, although there would be plenty of tough days of jail and interrogation to follow for Jack and Willie.

Conger and Baker looked at each other, and then at the remnants of the still blazing barn. The heat was intense. Baker motioned to some nearby soldiers watching the little scene before them. The soldiers picked up Booth and moved him to the safety of the long porch of the Garrett house. In response to a request from Baker, and with the help of the children, Lucinda Holloway and Mrs. Garrett brought a mattress out.

Booth was placed on it, protesting all the while, "No, no! Let ... me die ... here! Let me ... die here!"

"The damned Rebel is still living!" Doherty exclaimed. "Sergeant! Send a man into Port Royal and bring out a doctor! Miss," he said to Lucinda Holloway, "do you perchance have a pillow for his head?"

Miss Holloway put the pillow under Booth's head. "Would you like some wine? Some water?" Booth refused everything. Presently, however he changed his mind and stuck out his tongue. Miss Holloway took her handkerchief, wetted it in water and a bit of wine, and placed it on his extended tongue. She then moistened his lips.

Booth then saw Willie Jett, standing among the soldiers. "Did that ... man ... betray me?" he inquired haltingly. Booth's eyes seemed briefly to flash as of old. Then they grew dull again. No answer followed.

"Turn me," Booth begged.

Conger and Baker rolled him to his left. Booth cried out

in agony. "No! . . . Other way!" The two officers obliged and revolved him to his right.

Booth again groaned in pain. "On my . . . face!"

"You cannot lie on your face," Conger protested. They rolled Booth again on to his back.

"Press . . . your hand . . . down on . . . throat."

Conger did as he was instructed.

"Hard . . . er!"

Conger pressed again with more force. Booth tried to cough. He wanted to clear his throat. To make it function again—the most melodious and famous throat on the American stage. He had much to say. But he could not. He was losing muscular control.

"Open your mouth and put out your tongue," Conger said. "I'll see if it bleeds." Booth complied. Conger looked down his throat then used his finger to clear any obstruction. Nothing. No blood.

"The bullet has not gone through any part of it there," Conger told him.

Lieutenant Doherty reached down where Booth had been rolled and picked up an object that had fallen out of his coat pocket. "What is this? Great Scott, gentlemen! It is a diary! Look!" Doherty thumbed through it rapidly. "It covers events for the last year or so."

Conger and Baker gathered around to see the prize Doherty had found. Conger rudely snatched the little volume from the lieutenant's hand.

"It names names, it reveals the whole conspiracy! This is fabulous!"

"My God!" Baker breathed out in a whisper.

Booth's physical suffering was intense, but when he realized that his diary was in the hands of the enemy, his agony was beyond bearing. "Oh . . . kill me . . . kill me . . . quick!" he pleaded.[40]

---

[40] Dodels, "The Last Days of John Wilkes Booth," 22-28; Mogelever, *Death to Traitors*, 357-60; Reuter, *The King Can Do No Wrong*, 46-51; Chamlee, *Lincoln's Assassins*, 155-57; Roscoe, *Web of Conspiracy*, 387-98; Oldroyd, *Assassination of Abraham Lincoln*, 70-78; Laughlin, *Death of Lincoln*, 147-53; Townsend, *Life, Crime, and Death of John Wilkes Booth*, 32-39; Kauffman, "Booth's Escape Route: Lincoln's Assassin on the Run," 49-50; Barbee, "Lincoln and Booth," 959-84, *passim*, DRB Papers, GU.

See also, Conger's and Baker's testimony, R. Sutton, *et al. (comps.)*, *The Reporter: Containing . . . Trial of John H. Surratt, on an Indictment for Murder of President Lincoln* (Washington: Sutton, 1867), III, 260-73; Doherty's "Official Report on the Capture of John Wilkes Booth," *Surratt Courier*, 25 (May 2000), 3-7; Baker, "An Eyewitness Account of the Death and Burial of J. Wilkes Booth," 425-46; Statement of Miss Halloway, in Wilson, *John Wilkes Booth*, 208-22; Otto Eisenschiml, "Death Visits Garrett's Farm," *Why Was Lincoln Murdered?*, 153-61. See also, Wilson, *John Wilkes Booth*, 171-93; Miller (ed.), "A Trooper's Account of the Death of Booth,"5-9; Fleet (ed.), "A Chapter of Unwritten History: Richard Baynham Garrett's Account," 388-407, more easily accessed in Richard Baynham Garrett, "End of a Manhunt," *American Heritage*, 17 (June 1966), 40-43, 105.

# PART II

## "The Most Atrocious Assassination Ever Committed"

John Wilkes Booth is "[o]ne whose name and reputation will go down to the latest times in this country associated with the most atrocious assassination ever committed."

—Joseph Bradley, Sr. to the Court in the John H. Surratt, Jr., trial, quoted in Francis Wilson, John Wilkes Booth: Fact and Fiction of Lincoln's Assassination (Boston: Houghton Mifflin, 1929), vii

# 1

## Not Guilty

Booth drifted in and out of consciousness. The whole world seemed cloudy. In the distance he heard a rhythmic banging noise.

"Order! The Court will be in order.... The Clerk will read the Charges and Specifications," a voice intoned.

Another voice began to read rapidly from a legal document in front of him:

> CHARGE I. Treason against the Government of the United States in that he, the said John Wilkes Booth, did combine, confederate, and conspire with Mary E. Surratt, John H. Surratt, Lewis Thornton Powell, Samuel A. Mudd, David E. Herold, George Andrew Atzerodt, Samuel Arnold, Michael O'Laughlen, Edman Spangler, and others unknown, maliciously, willfully, and traitorously, to aid the then existing armed rebellion against the United States of America, on or before the 26th day of April, 1865, said rebellion being conducted by an illegal combination of former states styled as the so-called Confederate States of America, in violation of the laws and customs of war.
>
> SPECIFICATION. That he, the said John Wilkes Booth, did combine, confederate, and conspire with

John H. Surratt, Lewis Thornton Powell, David E. Herold, George Andrew Atzerodt, Samuel Arnold, Michael O'Laughlen others to abduct and ultimately assassinate Abraham Lincoln, President of the Unites States and Commander-in-Chief of the Union Armies and Navy, and important members of his administration as part of a well-financed secret service campaign in 1864and 1865. That effort included spying and conveying communications between the Rebel government and its agents in US and Canada; plans for forcibly freeing enemy soldiers held in Northern prison camps; sabotage, and military assaults on Union territory from the relatively safe haven of British Canada; the instigation of disturbances against the Northern military draft; the introduction of infectious diseases into selected Union cities; the destruction of New York City by arson; and the blowing up of the White House and its occupants during a cabinet meeting.

CHARGE II. Attempted kidnapping of Abraham Lincoln, President of the United States and Commander-in-Chief of the Union Armies and Navy of the United States, in violation of the laws and customs of war.

SPECIFICATION 1. That he, the said John Wilkes Booth, did combine, confederate, and conspire with Mary E. Surratt, John H. Surratt, Samuel A. Mudd, David E. Herold, George Andrew Atzerodt, Samuel Arnold, Michael O'Laughlen, Edman Spangler, and others unknown, on the 18th day of January, 1865, to abduct Abraham Lincoln, President of the United

States and Commander-in-Chief of the Union Armies and Navy, at Ford's Theater 511 Tenth Street, Washington City.

SPECIFICATION 2. That he, the said John Wilkes Booth, did combine, confederate, and conspire with Mary E. Surratt, John H. Surratt, Samuel A. Mudd, David E. Herold, George Andrew Atzerodt, Samuel Arnold, Michael O'Laughlen, Edman Spangler, and others unknown, 17th day of March, 1865, attempt to abduct Abraham Lincoln, President of the Unites state and Commander-in-Chief of the Union armies and Navy, on Seventh Street near the entrance to Campbell Military Hospital, in Washington City.

CHARGE III. Assault and Attempted Murdering of members of the Government of the United States, in violation of the laws and customs of war.

SPECIFICATION 1. That he, the said John Wilkes Booth, did combine, confederate, and conspire with Mary E. Surratt, John H. Surratt, Samuel A. Mudd, David E. Herold, George Andrew Atzerodt, Samuel Arnold, Michael O'Laughlen, Edman Spangler, and others unknown, on the 14th day of April, 1865, at or around 10:30 p.m., to attempt to murder Andrew Johnson, Vice President of the United States, at his room in the Kirkwood Hotel, on the northeast corner of 12th Street and Pennsylvania Avenue, in Washington City.

SPECIFICATION 2. That he, the said John Wilkes Booth, did combine, confederate, and conspire with Mary E. Surratt, John H. Surratt, Samuel A.

Mudd, David E. Herold, George Andrew Atzerodt, Samuel Arnold, Michael O'Laughlen, Edman Spangler, and others unknown, on the 14th day of April, 1865, at or around 10:30 p.m., to attempt to murder William Henry Seward, Secretary of State of the United States, at his home at 17 Madison Place, or 15 ½ Street between Pennsylvania Avenue and H Street North, in Washington City.

SPECIFICATION 3. That he, the said John Wilkes Booth, did combine, confederate, and conspire with Mary E. Surratt, John H. Surratt, Samuel A. Mudd, David E. Herold, George Andrew Atzerodt, Samuel Arnold, Michael O'Laughlen, Edman Spangler, and others unknown, on the 14th day of April, 1865, at or around 10:30 p.m., to attempt to murder Edwin McM. Stanton, Secretary of War of the United States at his home near Franklin Square, in Washington City.

SPECIFICATION 4. That he, the said John Wilkes Booth, did combine, confederate, and conspire with Mary E. Surratt, John H. Surratt, Samuel A. Mudd, David E. Herold, George Andrew Atzerodt, Samuel Arnold, Michael O'Laughlen, Edman Spangler, and others unknown, on the 14th day of April, 1865, at or around 10:30 p.m., to attempt to murder Lt. Gen. U. S. Grant, Commander of the armies of the United States, at Ford's theater at 511Tenth Street, Washington City.

CHARGE IV. Murdering a member of the Government of the United States, in violation of the laws and customs of war.

SPECIFICATION. That he, the said John Wilkes

Booth, did combine, confederate, and conspire with Mary E. Surratt, John H. Surratt, Samuel A. Mudd, David E. Herold, George Andrew Atzerodt, Samuel Arnold, Michael O'Laughlen, Edman Spangler, and others unknown, on the 14th day of April, 1865, at or around 10:30 p.m., to murder Abraham Lincoln, President of the United States and Commander-in-Chief of the Union Armies and Navy, at Ford's theater at 511 Tenth Street, Washington City.[41]

As the clerk droned on, Booth suddenly realized that he was sitting at a table in front of a board of military officers. He shook the cobwebs out of his head. In front of him lay another legal paper. He perused it quickly, as he would a part of a play, when he had to "wing it," that is read a part he was unfamiliar with just before he went on a theatrical stage. The relevant parts read:

Executive Chamber
Washington City, May 1, 1865
    Whereas, The Attorney General of the United States hath given his opinion:
    That the persons implicated in the murder of the late President, Abraham Lincoln ... are subject to the jurisdiction of, and lawfully triable before a Military Commission. . . .

---

41   The form of the indictment is from "The Court Martial of Henry Wirz," www.civilwarhome.com/wirzcourtmartial.htm, and Benn Pitman (comp.), *The Assassination of President Lincoln and the Trial of the Conspirators* (Cincinnati: Moore, Wilstach & Baldwin, 1865), 18-21. Wirz's "court martial was actually a military commission, as were the trials of Booth and his co-conspirators. For an excellent study of the operations of military commissions, see Detlev Vagts, "Military Commissions: The Forgotten Reconstruction Chapter," *American International Law Review*, 23 (No. 2, 2007), 231-74.

Special Orders, No. 211, Adjutant General's Office, series 1865.

A Military Commission is hereby appointed to meet at Washington, District of Columbia, On Monday, the 8th day of May, 1865, at 9 o'clock A.M. . . . for the trial of John Wilkes Booth, and such other prisoners as may be brought before it. . . . [42]

Booth looked to the side as a hand was laid on his shoulder. The seemingly incessant vocalizations of the court clerk continued unabated before him.

"I am Charles O'Connor, Mr. Booth," the man whispered. "Your volunteer attorney from yesterday—remember? This is the third day of the hearing."

Booth did not. He looked puzzled. He had missed two days already? "I cannot afford you," he murmured back.

"That is ok, sir, I am working for free, pro bono publico as we lawyers say."

"Are you any good at your trade?" Booth asked.

"I am, Mr. Booth, I am. Although I am from New York State, I have a long record in representing Southerners and defending the slave system before the war. I was on the side of the plantation owners in the case of Lemmon v. The People back in the 1850s. . . . You know, when the state of New York tried to seize a Virginian's slaves as they awaited a Texas-bound boat on the dock?"

---

[42] See Pitman (comp.), *The Assassination of President Lincoln and the Trial of the Conspirators*, 17-18. For the preferred use Pitman version of the military commission testimony, see John C. Brennan, "The Three Versions of the Testimony in the 1865 Conspiracy Trial [Benn Pittman, Ben: Perley Poore, and T. B. Peterson]," and "More on the Three Versions of the 1865 Trial Testimony," in Kauffman (ed.), *In Pursuit of . . .* , 175-84, 185-88. Another viewpoint, defending the Poore version as best, can be found in Steers, *Blood on the Moon*, xii-xiii. Peterson, the first published, is error-ridden.

"How did you do?"

"Well we lost...."

"Oh, great!" Booth muttered, sarcastically. He rolled his eyes.

"... But the case was up on appeal and I assure you we would have won in the U.S. Supreme Court, after the manner of the Dred Scott Case—you have heard of that one, surely? The outbreak of the war has since made the issue moot."

"Yeah, I know Dred Scott, everyone knows Dred Scott."[43]

"Soon, the Court will ask you to enter a plea."

"I will plead guilty and make my case to the people—honor demands it."

"Like hell it does!" O'Connor exploded. "You plead 'guilty' and you will hang tomorrow. They will not even wait to build the scaffold. Any tree will do. You will not be allowed to make a speech of any kind. Anything you say will be dismissed as a conflict of interest. You will plead 'not guilty' to all charges and specifications. Believe it or not you have a good chance to beat everything, except the murder of the President. But I think we can give them a run for their money on that one, too. You hear me?"

"All right, Counselor, all right," Booth said wearily.

"We are going to make them work for a conviction, harder than they ever supposed," O'Connor promised.

---

43  Arthur T. Downey, *Civil War Lawyers: Constitutional Questions, Courtroom Dramas, and the Men Behind them* (Chicago: ABA Publishing, 2010), 15-37, 43-44, 331.

# 2

## Six of One, Half Dozen of Another

The following day, O'Connor took the oath of loyalty to the Union to please the Court. It was the ironclad oath, an affirmation that he had not aided the Confederacy in word or deed during the Rebellion, as the North had named the Civil War.

Later, he met Booth in his cell at the Old Arsenal. Both men were locked in, each sitting on a three-legged stool.

"Did you hear about the kerfuffle over in the trial of your co-conspirators? No? Well," O'Connor said, "it was a beaut, as the young folks say nowadays. Old Reverdy Johnson, a well-respected attorney from your home state of Maryland, refused to take the oath of loyalty. Said he had already taken it as a U.S. Senator some years before. General Thomas Harris begged to differ. He said that Johnson had hinted last year that the oath need not be obeyed. Harris said that Johnson lacked the integrity to take the oath and be believed. It took a secret session to get Harris to drop his opposition. But Johnson was so insulted that he withdrew, leaving the defense of his client, Mrs. Mary E. Surratt, in the hands of junior subordinates."

"That does not bode well for Mrs. Surratt."

"Perhaps not. But Johnson will aid us outside the courtroom, so his able mind is not lost to any of us, be we counsel or defendant. I have consulted with him and we shall use his arguments in your case."

"What has Johnson for us?"

"Essentially he argues that President Andrew Johnson has no authority under the U.S. Constitution to order the convening of a military commission to try civilians, rather than soldiers or sailors. The war power is a legislative grant in Art. 1, section 8, clause 11, and regulate the same, in clause 14. All of this is reinforced through legislation, and persons not belonging to the Army or Navy are not subject to its jurisdiction.

"Further, Johnson continues, that all of you are essentially charged with treason, a civilian crime, not a military one. He finds it bizarre that President Jefferson Davis has been indicted by a civilian grand jury, while your lesser persons are charged in a military commission. As private citizens, you and your fellow conspirators all have that same right of indictment, plus a right to due process under the Fifth Amendment and a right to a public trial by an impartial jury under the Sixth Amendment.

"That really destroys the whole case against us, does it not?"

"Not according to the Attorney General of the Unites States. He say that you can be tried by a military commission—indeed, you ought to be tried by the military court. You can bet that President Johnson will go by that decision.[44]

"So I am in trouble again."

"Well, your consolation is that you can sue the military board for personal liability of the Attorney General is wrong."

"Yeah, if I live that long!" Booth chuckled bitterly.[45]

---

[44] Attorney General James Speed's argument is in Pitman (comp.), *The Assassination of President Lincoln and the Trial of the Conspirators*, 403-409.
[45] See Downey, *Civil War Lawyers*, 263-67.

"Well. Let us take a look at your military board. The senior officer and chief judge seems to be General William F. Barry. He is an artilleryman, served under General Irwin McDowell at Bull Run, at the Washington garrison, and then under General Sherman in the Atlanta Campaign and the March to the Sea.

"Then in no particular order, we have General George J. Stannard, a Vermont man, once a prisoner of war, hero of Gettysburg helping defeat Pickett's charge, generally served in the eastern theater of War, wounded four time, losing an arm at Petersburg.

"General Charles Francis Adams, grandson of the President of the United States is next served in the Fifth Massachusetts Cavalry, a colored regiment. There is General Charles C. Doolittle, a Michigander out of Vermont. Let us hope he lives up to his name, huh? He served mostly west of the Appalachians. Real fighter, saved Sherman's butt at Jonesboro outside of Atlanta.

"Ah! Ranald Slidell Mackenzie, a young buck, General U.S. Grant has called him the most promising young officer in the Army. Fought under General Phil Sheridan in the Shenandoah Valley and Grant at Petersburg. Oh-ho! His uncle was the Confederate commissioner to France. John Slidell of Mason and Slidell fame? Let us hope a little of uncle's Louisiana corruption rubs off on him!

"Then, we have the lawyers with connections. First there is General Francis Preston Blair, Jr., of the old Jacksonian Democratic Party. Brother was President Lincoln's Postmaster General. Good! Fired from cabinet because of alleged pro-slavery views. Oops! You Rebs burned the family mansion out in Sliver Spring to the ground in 1864.

"Bringing up the rear of this distinguished board is General

Hugh Boyle Ewing. Big political family, the Ewings. His brother is representing a couple of your pals, Edman Spangler and Dr. Sam Mudd. He is presenting Reverdy Johnson's argument against using military commissions to try civilians to the other court.[46] But the Ewings also have a couple of flaws as far as you are concerned. His brother issued General Orders No 11, which tried to combat Missouri's Confederate guerrillas by moving their supporters out of their farms. And then there is their brother-in-law, General William Tecumseh Sherman. Ouch!

"The last member of your trial board is General James Oaks, an expert on serving on military boards of all kinds. As junior member, he will be the clerk."[47]

Booth looked glum. "Still think I have a chance?"

"Actually, yes. Six of one, half-dozen of another. But better than you will ever think."

"Of course, all of this is challenged by the fact that the chief prosecutor in all the Lincoln and related assassination cases will be the Judge Advocate of the Army, Brigadier General Joseph Holt. He is a devout, uncompromising Union man out of Kentucky. He and Stanton were instrumental in transforming the Federal war effort into the hard emancipationist, anti-Southern policies that ultimately defeated the Confederacy. He sees this trial not as a final shot of the War of the Rebellion, but as an opening salvo for the Reconstruction of the Union that is to come, as do most so-called Radical Republicans in Congress—you know, men like Thad Stevens, Charles Sumner,

---

46  See Pitman (comp.), *The Assassination of President Lincoln and the Trial of the Conspirators*, 264-67 (illegal trial argument), 276-87 (Spangler), 318-32 (Mudd).

47  For brief biographies, in alphabetical order, of the select board, see Mark Mayo Boatner III, *The Civil War Dictionary* (New York: David McKay Co., Inc., 1959), 3, 38-39, 47, 67, 243-44, 269-70, 499-500, 603, 791-92.

and your own Maryland representative Henry Winter Davis. Their notion of peace is not that General Grant extended to General Lee at Appomattox."[48]

"So my goose is cooked . . . again!"

"Holt will not conduct the prosecution in person, however. He will use Colonel Henry B. Carrington, his favorite attack dog. He looks formidable, but his sweeping Indiana clean of treason late in the war centered on prosecuting the head of the Knights of the Golden Circle in the state. (I believe you are a suspected member if the Maryland Castle, as local units are called).[49] A man with the intriguing name of Lambdin P. Milligan. This man's hanging conviction is headed to the U.S. Supreme Court, appealed on the same basis as Reverdy Johnson's objections to

---

48  The best Holt biography from a political point of view is Elizabeth D. Leonard, *Lincoln's Forgotten Ally: Judge Advocate General Joseph Holt of Kentucky* (Chapel Hill: University of North Carolina Press, 2011), *passim*. For identification of Radical Republicans, see David Donald, *The Politics of Reconstruction, 1863-1867* (Baton Rouge: Louisiana State University Press, 1965), *passim*.

What exactly Lincoln had in mind for reconstructing the Union after the shooting stopped is open to much interpretation. See, e.g., Lloyd Lewis, "If Lincoln Had Lived," in Edward Wagenknecht (ed.), *Abraham Lincoln: His Life, Work, and Character* (New York: Creative Press, 1947), 533-40; William Hesseltine, *Lincoln's Plan of Reconstruction* (Tuscaloosa: Confederate Publishing Co., 1960); Harold Hyman, *Lincoln's Reconstruction: Neither Failure of Vision Nor Vision of Failure* (Ft. Wayne, Ind: Louis A. Warren Lincoln Library and Museum, 1980); and John C. Rodrigue, *Lincoln and Reconstruction* (Carbondale: Southern Illinois University Press, 2013).

49  The Knights of the Golden Circle was a pre-war organization dedicated to create a massive slave empire, centered on Cuba, and stretching from the American South through Mexico and Central America, over to Colombia, Venezuela and into all of the Caribbean isles. It had local chapters called Castles, all over the Northwest and the South, see David C. Keehn, *Knights of the Golden Circle: Secret Empire, Southern Secession, Civil War* (Baton Rouge: Louisiana State University Press, 2013).

On the Knights of the Golden Circle, consult Robert E. May, *The Southern Dream of a Caribbean Empire, 1854-61* (Baton Rouge: Louisiana State University Press, 1973), 3, 20, 49, 91-94, 148-55; Olliger Crenshaw, "The Knights of the Golden Circle," *American Historical Review*, 47 (1941), 23-50; C. A. Bridges, "The Knights of the Golden Circle: A Filibustering Fantasy," *Southwestern Historical Quarterly*, 287-302; and Joe A. Stout, Jr., *The Liberators: Filibustering Expeditions into Mexico, 1848-1862, and the Last Gasp of Manifest Destiny* (Los Angeles: Westernlore Press, 1973). Both Booth and neighbor T. William O'Laughlen (if not his brother Mike, too, later a co-conspirator against Lincoln) were rumored to be members of the Golden Circle. See Keehn, *Knights of the Golden Circle*, 9, 17, 110, 144-45.

your trial, which I will soon present to the military tribunal here. So there is still hope. Patience, sir, patience!"[50]

"It is not your neck, sir, not your neck."

"No, I daresay it is not. But oddly enough, Mr. Booth, you have done one thing correctly. You have connected anyone who might testify against you so closely that they appear to be co-conspirators, even if they are not. In common law a man cannot be convicted solely upon the word of a cohort. The same will apply to military commissions when civilians are the object of the trial."

Booth smiled a wry smile. He had known that all along.[51]

---

50   Milligan won his case, see *ex parte* Milligan (1866), 71 U.S. (4 Wall.) at 2. For more, see Frank L. Klement, *Dark Lanterns: Secret Political Societies, Conspiracies, and Treason Trials in the Civil War* (Baton Rouge: Louisiana State University Press, 1984); Lewis J. Wertheim, "The Indianapolis Treason Trials, the Elections of 1864, and the Power of the Partisan Press," *Indiana Magazine of History*, 85 (1989), 236-60; and Mark E. Neely, "Treason in Indiana: A Review Essay," *Lincoln Lore*, (February/March 1974), 1-4, 1-3; Kenneth M. Stampp, "The Milligan Case and the Election of 1864 in Indiana," *Mississippi Valley Historical Review*, 31 (June 1944), 541-58.
51   Booth's cleverness in manipulating the law of conspiracy is a prime thesis of Booth biographer and expert Michael W. Kauffman, *American Brutus: John Wilkes Booth and the Lincoln Conspiracies* (New York: Random House, 2004), xiv, 384-95.

# 3

## Conviction by Hook or by Crook

There was one good outcome to Attorney General Speed's opinion—the Federal authorities, Holt with Stanton's approval, decided to open the trials to the public—attendance by ticket signed by General John Hartranft, a special provost marshal and commander of the prison guard, because of limited seating space in the courtrooms. The court also issued morning press releases to the newspaper reporters, the same as those given attorneys.[52]

The prosecution's first tack was to charge that Booth was in cahoots with the worst elements of the "so-called" Confederate government—that part connected to the secret service and operating more or less surreptitiously out of British Canada. These men sent their minions into the Northern States to wreak havoc by interfering with the draft levies; committing arson, especially burning parts of Manhattan in New York City; freeing captured Confederate soldiers from Yankee prison camps; robbing the banks in St. Albans, Vermont; spreading disease and pestilence into New York City, Washington, D.C., Norfolk, and New Bern; and the blowing up of the Union government during a cabinet meeting at the White House.[53]

---

52   Edward Steers, Jr., *Blood on the Moon: The Assassination of Abraham Lincoln* (Lexington: University Press of Kentucky, 2001), 222.
53   These and other "black flag" operations, as they were called in the Civil War, are brought forth in Pitman (comp.), *The Assassination of President Lincoln and the Trial of the Conspirators*, 46-63. See also, Singer, *The Confederate Dirty War: Arson, Bombings, Assassination and Plots*

Worse than this, was the testimony of three men as to the presence of Booth and several fellow conspirators in Canada, where they allegedly conferred with former Union Secretary of the Interior, the hated and corrupt Jacob Thompson, and a professional revolutionary from Kentucky, George N. Sanders. The three government witnesses were Richard Montgomery, James B. Merritt, and Charles A. Dunham, who testified under his pseudonym, Sandford Conover.[54]

All admitted seeing Booth in Canada talking in confidence with various Confederate commissioners but only Conover admitted to seeing him several times, hunched over drinks and speaking conspiratorially with Sanders and others at the St Lawrence Hotel. O'Connor went to work on Conover during his cross-examination.

"Where are you from—I mean where were you born?"

"Croton, New York," Conover answered smugly.

"Tell me about your education."

"I had the usual schooling as a child. Then I went to law school."

"Did you graduate? Did you pass the bar?"

"Sadly, I failed to pass the bar."

"It has come to my attention that you made a career of finding heirs to alleged fortunes."

"Yes, I would seek out lost relatives, as it were, for a percentage of the inheritance."

"No, no. My reading of your record indicates that you took a payment ahead of time, and then absconded with the funds without finding the inheritable fortune."

---

*for Chemical and Germ Attacks on the Union* (Jefferson, N.C.: McFarland & Company, 2005); Edward Steers Jr., "Terror—1860s Style," *North & South*, 5 (May 2002): 12–18.
54  Steers, *Blood on the Moon*, 223-25. On Conover, see Carman Cumming, *Devil's Game: The Civil War Intrigues of Charles A. Dunham* (Urbana: University of Illinois Press, 2004).

"Well, the payment was to finance my expense—it can be very difficult to find the sought-for relative."

"The war was a windfall for you, was it not?"

"I have done my patriotic duty for the Union, sir, I assure you."

"Oh yeah, les see . . . raised a New York regiment with you as colonel."

"Nothing wrong with that!"

"But the enrollment officer reported you for claiming to have raised five hundred men—but he could only find thirty-six actual recruits."

"That was an merely unfortunate bookkeeping error, sir."

"Ah! You were sort of a spy, I see. You had many endeavors that involved cross enemy line. Hazardous work, I assume? I see that you published several article in magazines of suspect repute about your adventures. The Rebels locked you up in Castle Thunder, their form of the Bastile."

"I had a dreadful time there, sir, dreadful."

"But fortunately you did not stay long. Instead you hung around the enemy government, observing it operations."

"All in the cause of Union."

"I hear that you purloined enough letterhead to function as any branch of the Confederacy out of any desk in the North American continent."

"That is a base falsehood, sir!"

"Be that as it may, I see you became a newspaper reporter next, huh? Well, how convenient! You operated out of Canada. Arrested nosing around the trial of the St. Albans raiders. The Canadian authorities arrested you as a nuisance. Look here! They released you into the care of none other than George N. Sanders!"

"You make it sound so illegal. I did nothing wrong."

"Oh, come on, you are crooked as a snake, are you not? Your newspaper articles are all made up out of whole cloth. You really know nothing about what you write. You started out as a flim-flam man and you have done little else but improve upon your own brand of deceit!"

"That is an outrage, sir!"

"No, sir! The real outrage is that the Federal government would rely on someone as loose with the truth as you to make a case against my client, John Wilkes Booth! Your talents as forger, propagandist and agent provocateur are renown. You have invented a veritable collection of fictional identities, some of which fomented fake military and political plans, while others reported on these imaginary plots in Northern newspapers to arouse public ire and smear alleged Copperhead opponents of the war. Hell, at one point you even offered a reward for your own capture and were duly arrested! At war's end, your machinations grew so murky, as to be unfathomable—indeed unbelievable."

O'Connor turned away and slammed his notes down on the defense table in disgust. "I am through with this lying, piece of trash, your Honor."[55] But no matter what the legal aspects of the Conover testimony, the revealed falsehoods and double talk, the Yankee public believed that the Confederates and their government looked mighty guilty in President Lincoln's death.[56]

---

55   O'Connor's final tirade is a synopsis from a review in *Publisher's Weekly* (Reed Business Information, a division of Reed Elsevier Inc.) currently (May 2014) offered on Amazon.com. On Sanders and the cover-up of Confederate participation in Lincoln's demise, see William A. Tidwell, *April '65: Confederate Covert Action in the American Civil War* (Kent, Ohio: Kent State University Press, 1995), 148-54. For a history of how effective the cover-up was and how it became the standard view of the assassination see, William Hanchett, "Lincoln's Murder: The Simple Conspiracy Theory," *Civil War Times Illustrated*, 30 (November/ December 1991), 28-35, 70.
56   Steers, *Blood on the Moon*, 224-25.

# 4

## WEICHMANN SPINS A TALE

Louis J. Weichmann exuded an air of outward confidence. Inwardly, however, Weichman's whole system shook with nervous anticipation—or, was it dread? His mouth was dry, his clothes, a natty suit of dark black, white starched shirt and collar, neat string necktie, were full of nervous sweat—stinking sweat. His hair was piled on his head in its usually oily glop. He looked studious behind his pince-nez eyeglasses, nearly steamed over with the heated vapors from his damp body, like the effeminate religious student he really was. In reality, he was just a step away from the priesthood. But it would be a long step, marred by his dubious connection to the plot to assassinate President Lincoln.

The real problem facing Weichmann was how close was he to the plotters? Union Secretary of War Edwin McM. Stanton had his doubts that Weichmann was an informer. He feared that the big, pudgy, lisping wimp or Nancy Boy as they said in those days,[57] disrespectfully called "Fatty" behind his back by the Surratt family with whom he roomed, was actually an active participant. But Weichmann claimed he was innocent, a by-stander, a good, honest citizen who wanted to "cooperate," as he put it. "As God is my witness...."

Fine. Stanton needed a good "impartial witness, one who

---

57  Weichmann was evidently bi-sexual, according to a letter from "Clara," possibly Sarah Slater, a well-known Confederate spy with connections to the Surratts. See Kauffman, *American Brutus*, 362, and 469n24.

would spell it out," as it were, but very carefully as instructed by the prosecution and the erstwhile secretary himself. "But one mistake," Stanton warned, "Weichmann would change his guise from informer to defendant." He had had several weeks in the Old Capitol prison, that filthy den of malefactors who had opposed the war effort, to help remind him of his course of action when the time came. And that time was now.

"Louis Weichmann," the bailiff called. He was big beefy sergeant from the Army of the Potomac's II Corps, who had lost an arm at Weldon Station in the summer of 1864. But from the looks of the man, he could still wrestle most troublemakers to the floor with relative ease. Weichman stepped forward and took the oath. He stated his name as asked.

"When did you first meet John Wilkes Booth?" Prosecutor Carrington asked.

"I reckon it was two days before Christmas in Washington City. I was walking with my roommate John H. Surratt up Seventh Street from the Avenue, Pennsylvania Avenue, that is, when we were hailed from the other side of the street by Dr. Samuel Mudd. He and Surratt live in close proximity in Southern Maryland before the war. Mudd was walking with a companion, who turned out to be Booth."

"Continue, please."

"Well, Booth invited all of us to his room at the National Hotel where we shared a pitcher of milk punch. Surratt asked Mudd to step out in the hall, leaving me and Booth behind. What they discussed, I do not know. Shortly, Mudd reentered the room and asked Booth to step out in the hall, too. Booth bade me to finish the last of the milk punch, which I did."

"Then what passed?"

"I got curious as to what was so secret so I edged up to

the door and listened at the jamb. Booth got Surratt to swear his silence and told him that he was going to abduct President Lincoln. I accidentally bumped a chair and had to retreat to my old place to hide my nosiness. I acted like I was reading some papers left behind by a congressman who had the room before Booth. They reentered the room and proceeded to draw a map of Southern Maryland with various roads and pathways on it. I was told they were interested in land sales."

"What did you do?"

"I tried to convey this information to my superior at the War Department where I work, Major D.H.L. Gleason, but he doubted that such a plot to capture Mr. Lincoln could be effected. But he reported the possibility to his superiors. When nothing happened on the March day, the fourth, I believe, when the plan was to take place, I was dismissed as a fraud or jokester."

"Anything else?"

"Yeah, once in mid-March I went up to the attic floor looking for Surratt and bumbled onto him, Booth, and the man known as Wood, more recently identified a co-conspirator Lewis Powell, gathered around pistols, spurs, and Bowie knives. But Mrs. Mary Surratt, John's mother said it was nothing as they all often rode out at night and needed personal protection. But a couple of days later, March 17, I would say, they all came in splattered with mud and very angry about something. When Booth came in and saw me in their midst, everyone had gathered in my room, he motioned all to go out and they went up to the attic. They soon came thundering down the stairs and I never saw them together again."

"How did you find out about Booth's participation in the assassination?"

"I was asked to carry Mrs. Surratt from the Washington

townhouse onto the countryside to her old tavern at Surrattsvillle several times. The last of these was on April 14. She owed or was owed some money from a Mr. Nothey. On our way back, she seemed awfully curious about when he Union cavalry pickets would be called in. I did not think much of it at first, but as we came over the hills at dusk the whole city was lit up before us. She was quite disturbed at the sight. She said something about the whole world being excessively licentious and she feared that everything would turn into sadness. She also seemed to pay special care as how I used the password and the countersign."

"What were they?"

"Tee Bee and Tee Bee Road."

"When did you suspect Booth had killed the President?"

"That night when the police came and searched the house, looking for John Surratt. When I figured it out I accompanied he police out to Surrattsville and later to Canada looking for John Surratt. A fellow boarder Mr. John Holohan went with us. I had confessed everything to Chief of Metropolitan Police, A. C. Richards. He kept me under house arrest at his office, until I was transferred to the Old Capitol Prison under orders of Secretary of War Stanton."

Carrington indicated that he was finished with Weichmann and O'Connor arose and walked over to Weichmann's chair.

"Mr. Wickman," he began.

"That's Weichman, with a long i," Weichmann retorted, obviously a little peeved. Both was right, O'Connor smiled to himself. Mispronouncing his name was a good subtle way to needle him.[58]

---

58  It is this author's opinion that Booth always got Weichmann's name wrong unless he was

"I see you are a candidate for the priesthood, sir. Saints should always be judged guilty until they are proved innocent, do you not agree?"[59]

"The Church is very meticulous about conferring sainthood, yes."

"As a fellow Roman Catholic, so am I. Let us look into your sainthood, as it were. Did you not ask Booth to let you in on the plots to kidnap and even kill Mr. Lincoln?"

"That is a base canard, sir. The rankest falsehood! I can neither shoot nor ride."

"You supplied information from the War Department, where you worked in the Bureau of Prisons under Col. Hoffman, I believe to Booth and others. Things like passwords across bridges for travel after dark and such, did you not? Things that require no shooting or riding?"

"I only used such a password when Mrs Surratt and I were out late on April 14, and only as an emergency. A woman of refinement as Mrs. Surratt could not be expected to be turned away at the gates to her own home in the city."

"That is it, huh?"

"Yessir," Weichmann insisted. O'Connor looked amazed and shook his head in disbelief.

"There never was a kidnapping of Mr. Lincoln was there, Mr. Weichmann? Answer yes or no, do not go further."

"No, sir."

"You never heard Booth say in your presence that he was going to assassinate the President, or kill the President or anyone else, did you? Answer only yes or no."

---

trying to schmooze him. See telegram in Rhodehammel and Taper (eds), *The Writings of John Wilkes Booth*, 142-43. See also, Tidwell, Hall, and Gaddy, *Come Retribution*, 415.

59  A line unabashedly borrowed from George Orwell, "Reflections on Ghandi," *Partisan Review*, 16 (No. 1, January 1949), 85.

"No, sir."
"No further questions, your Honor." O'Connor turned and sat down.[60]

---

60   Weichmann's story is from Louis J. Weichmann, *A True Story of Abraham Lincoln and of the Conspiracy of 1865* (Edited by Floyd E. Risvold. New York: Alfred A. Knopf, 1975), 11-17 (before the war), 29-36 (Booth meeting Surratt), 66-78 Surratt joins plot), 109-10 (tells Gleason), 96-114 (guns, spurs, failed kidnapping), 133-34, 171, 163-74 (visits Surrattsville). 174-79, 217-33 (cooperates with police), 263-64. For an early essay on Weichmann and the part he played in the Lincoln conspiracies, which has become a fairly standard treatment of the subject, see Osborn H. Oldroyd, *The Assassination of Abraham Lincoln: Flight, Pursuit, Capture, and Punishment of the Conspirators* (Washington: O. H. Oldroyd, 1901), 153-93.

On whether [yes] and how much Weichmann lied [a lot], see Thomas R. Turner, "Did Weichmann Turn State's Evidence to Save Himself? A Critique of *A True History of the Assassination of Abraham Lincoln*," *Lincoln Herald*, 81 (Winter 1979), 265-67; and Joseph George, Jr., "Nature's First Law: Louis J. Weichmann and Mrs. Surratt," *Civil War History*, 28 (No. 2, 1982), 101-127. One assumes that most of what Weichmann left out was his active role in the abduction plot, securing passwords for the bridges, and the giving of information on Confederate prisoners held in the North.

Technically, Weichmann's family spelled the name Wiechmann, but its spelling and pronunciation have been butchered for so long that even he changed it to Weichmann. For a modern author who refuses to follow this convention, see Steers, *Blood on the Moon*, 80, *et seq.*

# 5

## Major Rathbone Tells of a Frightful Night

Major Henry Reed Rathbone was the only man to witness the death of President Abraham Lincoln from close-up. He was approximately five feet away when John Wilkes pulled the trigger on the squat, little Derringer pistol and change American history forever. As a military man, he had received a captain's commission in the Twelfth United States Infantry as soon as it was organized in 1861. It was a "Lincoln Regiment." That meant that instead if the standard ten companies of fighting men, the Twelfth had three battalions of eight companies each. This allowed Lincoln to enlarge the U.S. Army by three times the amount that it seemed. It was of dubious executive power, but Congress approved of all such actions when it came into session in the summer of 1861.

Rathbone owed his appointment to the influence of his stepfather, U.S. Senator Ira Harris, a solid Republican. Rathbone's birth parents had died before he reached his majority, and the Harris family had taken him in. Well, his mother had married the Senator and the boy came along as part of the package. Senator Harris had a pretty daughter the same age as Henry and the two soon became engaged when he marched off to war. Although the Twelfth was chewed up in some of the biggest battles around Washington, Henry saw little combat, usually being detailed as a staff officer.

In Washington, Henry's fiancée Clara Harris became friend with Mrs. Mary Lincoln, a relationship the last to the end of the war. She would spend much of the night as the President lay dying consoling Mrs. Lincoln at the Peterson house across the street from Ford's Theater. In any case, when the Lincolns could not find anyone else to go to the theater with them on April 14, she turned to Clara Harris and her handsome officer, now sporting a major's shoulder boards.

So, Major Henry Rathbone and his fiancée wound up in the box at Ford's theater with the Lincoln's on that fateful Good Friday eve. The president was seated in his favorite rocker with Mrs. Lincoln to his right. They cuddled occasionally. Mary Lincoln thought the young couple seated off to their right on a sofa facing them might be embarrassed, but Lincoln told her to ignore them. None of the box inhabitant could see much of the stage. Rather they listened to the dialogue, until Booth entered the box and fired the bullet into Lincoln's head.

Rathbone rose to grapple with Booth and received a gashing knife wound to his left arm. Booth then jumped to the stage as Rathbone spewed blood from his artery all over the box. But, now several weeks later, he was ready to appear as the chief eyewitness to Lincoln's last moments on earth. He walked slowly up to the bar and was sworn in.

"Good morning Major," Col. Carrington said amiably, "how are you doing today?"

"Well, considering that my arm is still weak and pains me a little."

"Would you relate to the Court your experiences on he night of the 14th ultimo?"

"Beginning when?

"When your party arrived in the reserved presidential box at Ford's theater, if you please."

Well, we, that is the President, Mrs. Lincoln, and my fiancée Clara Harris came into the box. The play was interrupted by Miss Laura Keene from the stage and the orchestra struck up the piece called 'Hail to the Chief.' Then we all sat down, the president in the rocker, Mrs. Lincoln next to him and Miss Harris on a chair sort of in front of me and I on a couch facing toward the President. None of us could rightly see the stage or the actors. We essentially listed to the dialogue."

"I see, please continue."

"I do not really know how long we sat there. Finally, the play came to the point, second scene, third act, when the American Cousin, I believe that was Harry Hawke, was along on stage and he called the English mother a "sockdologizing old mantrap.' Everyone broke out into a boisterous laughter. Out of the corner of my eye, I saw Booth enter the box and yell, 'Freedom!' and 'Sic Semper Tyrannis!'[61] He fired his pistol. Everyone just sat there stunned. Smoke filled the box and drifted out toward the stage. The President seemed to stand up and half-turn before Mrs. Lincoln spun him back into his chair. Oh, my God, it was positively horrible!" Rathbone sobbed into his hands as he drew them up to his anguished face.

"Easy, Major, we know the outrageous frightfulness of that moment. No one blames you, sir. It takes steel nerve, real sand, to go after an armed opponent with your bare hands, We salute

---

61 "Thus ever to tyrants," is the motto of the Commonwealth of Virginia.

you, sir. Please, pull yourself together. Major?" Rathbone seemed to be briefly in another world. Then he gathered his emotions and resumed his testimony as if nothing had gone awry.

"At first I thought it must be an addition to the play. Then I realized it was real. I immediately arose from the sofa and grappled with Booth. He threw his pistol down and slashed at my breast with a knife, but missed as I parried the blow. Suddenly a great pain shot down my arm. He had sliced me to the bone with some sort of dagger."

"It was a double-bladed knife popularly called an Arkansas Toothpick, sir. Is this the weapon?"

"I cannot say for sure. Is that my blood still on the blade? My God, blood was everywhere!" Rathbone broke down again. "I lost hold on Booth and he jumped out of the box onto the stage. As he jumped, I reached deep into my soul and grabbed at his coattails. I caught him but could not hold on—I was too weakened from my wound.

"I ran to the edge of the box and shouted, 'Stop that man! Catch him!' Mrs. Lincoln's screams punctuated my plea. Booth stood on the stage holding his knife covered with my dripping blood, faced the audience and yelled, 'the South is avenged!' He ran off the stage and out the rear of the theater."

"I quickly ran to the back of the box, through the door into the hallway and found the door to the Dress Circle blocked with a bar, wedged between the door and the wall. It took considerable force on my part to release it as the more the crowd tried to push in the more the door became locked in place. I finally removed the wooden bar and the door opened with a bang and let in several persons representing themselves as surgeons.

"Then Miss Harris and I escorted Mrs. Lincoln over to

the Peterson House across Tenth Street, where her husband lay, mortally wound. I know nothing after that; I passed out from loss of blood."

All at once, Rathbone's whole countenance changed and he cried out in agony, "What could I have done differently? I was the only man in the world who could have stopped Booth and save President Lincoln. I should have see Booth sooner! I waited too long!" He began to sob and breath in great gulps. Then it seemed that he could not breathe at all.

"Is there a doctor in the court?" Col. Carrington called out. "Please come forward!"

A young woman of some personal beauty stood and passed over the legs of those seated outside of her. "Excuse me," she implored. "Please excuse me."

Rathbone continued his ranting, wrapped in a make-believe world of his own, "Could I have restrained John Wilkes Booth in spite if my arm wound? Why did I not grab him harder? Surely I could have saved the President of the United States?"

The major then grabbed Col. Carrington by his uniform. "Why did he die and I survive? Can you tell me why, sir? Why? Why?"

The young lady hurried to the front of the room. A sergeant acting as bailiff sought to restrain her. "Let me go!" she insisted.

"Who are you, Miss?" General Barry called from the bench.

"I an Clara Harris, his fiancée. Please let me calm him!"

"Release her, Sergeant. Allow her to proceed."

"Henry," she cooed, "Henry, come to me, come with me. It is all right—everything is all right." Slowly she propelled the distraught Major down the aisle and out of the courtroom.

"That shot rings in my ears every day," Rathbone yelled in

agony. Then more quietly, he turned to Miss Harris and said, "Clara, every day—that shot rings in my ears every day."

"I know, Henry, I know."

Suddenly, Rathbone straighten his uniform and walked out as if nothing had happened.

O'Connor stood and spoke quietly to the bench, "No questions, your Honor."

After the war the couple would marry and have three children. Rathbone would work abroad in the diplomatic service. He still had "episodes," as the family came to call them. Then one day, while serving in the newly created Germany, he would pull a knife and attack the children. Clara stepped in to save them and was stabbed to death. Rathbone turned the knife on himself, stabbing himself in the chest numerous times. But he would recover in time and spend the rest of his life in a German insane asylum, refusing to talk of that horrible April night when his whole world seemed to collapse forever.[62]

---

62  On the couple that accompanied the Lincoln's to the theater, see R. Gerald McMurtry, "Major Rathbone and Miss Harris: Guests of the Lincolns in the Ford's Theater Box," *Lincoln Lore* (August 1971), 1-3; Frank Rathbun, "The Rathbone Connection," Kauffman (ed.), *In Pursuit of. . .* , 213-20. See also, Michael E. Ruane, "A Tragedy's Second Act," *Washington Post*, (Sunday, April 5, 2009), and Pitman (comp.), *The Assassination of President Lincoln and the Trial of the Conspirators*, 78-79. For a recent volume that looks into post-traumatic stress disorder (PTSD) and the part it might have played in Rathbone's tragic life, see Caleb Jenner Stephens, *Worst Seat in the House: Henry Rathbone's Front row View of the Lincoln Assassination* (Fredericksburg, Va: Willow Manor Publishing, 2014).

# 6

# The Prosecution's Closing Argument

The next day, at the usual 10 A.M. starting time, Colonel Henry B. Carrington, the Special Prosecutor in the case of John Wilkes Booth, the successful federal official who had cleaned out the so-called disloyal element in Indiana the preceding Spring, stood and addressed the court.

"May it please the Court: The conspiracy here charged and specified, and the acts alleged to have been committed in pursuance thereof, and with the intent laid, constitute a crime the atrocity of which has sent a shudder through the civilized world. This crime constitutes a combination of atrocities with scarcely a parallel in the annals of the human race.

"Indeed, the issue joined involves the highest interests of the accused and, in my judgment, the highest interests of the whole people of the United States. It is also a matter of great moment to all the people of this country that the prisoner at your bar be lawfully tried and lawfully convicted or acquitted.

"This case is not simply a crime of murder. It is the crime of killing and murdering, on the 14th day of April, A.D., 1865, within the military department of Washington and the entrenched lines thereof, Abraham Lincoln, then President of the United States and commander-in-chief of the army and navy thereof, conspiring in the assaulting with intent to murder William H. Seward,

Secretary of State of the United States, Andrew Johnson, currently President of the United States, and Ulysses S. Grant, Lieutenant General and commander of the armies of the United States, a treasonable conspiracy entered into by the accuse and others, with intent to aid in the existing rebellion and subvert the Constitution and laws of the United States.

"This so-called rebellion was prosecuted for no vindication of right, no redress of wrong, but was itself a criminal conspiracy and a gigantic assassination of the whole nation. What wrong had this Government of any of its duly constituted agents done to any of the guilty actors in this atrocious rebellion? None whatsoever. This rebellion is nothing but an armed insurrection to resist the lawful authority of the United States Government.

"The Government does not indict the whole people of any state or section, but only the an alleged party to this unnatural and atrocious conspiracy and crime. The President of the United States has constituted you a military commission to hear and determine the issue joined against the accused. The defendant has pleaded, first, that this court has no jurisdiction, and second not guilty to all charges and specifications.

"The Court had already overruled the plea as to its jurisdiction. We would pass over this assertion in silence, but for the grave and elaborate argument made. They deserve to be answered in full. It has been declared that for the president of the United States to cause a military court to be formed to answer this conspiracy is usurp the normal processes of law. The Civil Courts are adequate say the defendant's attorneys.

"This is utter nonsense. The civil courts operate here only by force of 50,000 bayonets. There are still uncounted Union armies in the field daily losing casualties to the Rebel forces. Does anyone think that any of these conspirators, especially this defendant, John Wilkes Booth would have been taken without the force of arms? This was a military operation from start to finish."

"Yeah, and a civil court, with typical Washingtonians on it would find me not guilty," Booth whispered to O'Connor.

Col. Carrington went on, ignoring Booth's editorial comment, if he heard it at all. "Another misconception is that military courts exist solely to try crimes committed in or by the army or naval forces, or State militia forces called into Federal duty. This board is called by the orders of the President of the United States as commander of the military forces and is authorized to exercise it judicial power in this case, no matter what the half-baked arguments of any former United States senator with pronounced Rebel leanings. Besides this court has no authority to rule against the lawful orders of the President.

"Most relevant here is the law passed through both houses of Congress on March 3, 1863. Said law not only suspended the writ of habeas corpus as provided by the Constitution, it also declared that the order of the President of the United States carried out by any governmental authority shall be a defense against prosecution, civil or criminal, in either State or Federal courts, including court cases already in action or in the past or the future. Hence a military commission ordered into being by the President under this law is fully legal, and within the president's right to employ any action necessary to defeat the rebellion or any conspiracy to aid and abet same.

"May it please the Court: It is only necessary to sum up the evidence and present the rule of law as to the actual crimes of the defendant, John Wilkes Booth. Two questions arise: Did John Wilkes Booth conspire with any other party as charges? Did John Wilkes Booth as alleged in the indictment of charges and specifications, commit any or all of the several acts of which he is accused?

"What is the evidence, direct and circumstantial, that the accused together with John H. Surratt, Jr., Jefferson Davis, George N. Sanders, Beverley Tucker, Jacob Thompson, William C. Cleary, George Harper, and George Young, did combine, confederate, and conspire in the aid of the existing rebellion, as charged to kill and murder, within the military district of Washington, and within the fortified and entrenched likes thereof, of Abraham Lincoln, late President of the United States of America and Commander-in-Chief of the Army and the Navy thereof; Andrew Johnson, Vice President of the United States; William H. Seward, Secretary of State of the United States; and Ulysses S. Grant, Lieutenant General of the Armies thereof, and then in command, under the direction of the President?

"There is the sworn testimony of Messers. Conover, Montgomery, and Merritt of the conspiracy operating out of Canada and the presence of the defendant in consultation with known Confederate agents. The Court must be satisfied, by the manner of these and other witnesses to the transactions in Canada, as well by the fact that they are wholly uncontradicted in any material matter that they state, that they speak the truth revealing that defendant Booth entered into conspiracy with the agents of Jefferson Davis, President of the so-called Confederate States of America, there to promote the rebellion. The same is true of the testimony of Louis Weichmann."

"Humpf! That goddamned Weichman wanted to be in on the plot, but I would not let him. He could neither ride nor shoot," Booth kibitzed.

"Admittedly, Carrington continued, "there is circumstantial evidence, but the Court will remember the rule before recited, that circumstances cannot lie; that they are held sufficient in every court where justice is judicially administered to establish the fact of a conspiracy. But we must recognize that every substantive averment against John Wilkes Booth has been established by more than one witness.

"By all the testimony in the case, it is, in my judgment, made clear as any transaction can be shown by human testimony, that John Wilkes Booth and others did with intent to aid the existing rebellion, and to subvert the Constitution and laws of the United States, in the month of October last, and thereafter, combine, confederate, and conspire with Jefferson Davis, et al., to kill and murder, within the military district of Washington and the entrenched lines thereof, Abraham Lincoln per the indictment.

"If this treasonable conspiracy has not been wholly executed, thereby leaving the people of the United States without a President or Vice President, without a Secretary of State, who alone is clothed by the law to call an election to fill the vacancy, should any arise, in the offices of President and Vice President; and, without a lawful commander of the armies of the republic, it is only because the conspirators were defeated by the vigilance and fidelity of the executive officers, whose lives were mercifully protected on that night of murder, by the Infinite Being, who has, thus far, saved the Republic, and crowned its arms with victory.

"If this conspiracy was thus entered into by the accused; if John Wilkes Booth did kill and murder Abraham Lincoln in pursuance thereof, then it is the law that all the parties to that conspiracy, whether present at the time of its execution or not, whether on trial before this Court or not, are alike guilty of the several acts done by each in the execution of the common design. I leave the decision of this dread issue with the Court, to which it alone belongs. It is for you to say, upon your oath, whether the accused, John Wilkes Booth, is guilty.

"Whatever else may befall, I trust in God that in this, as in every other American court, the rights of the whole people will be respected, and that the republic in this, its supreme hour of trial, will be true to itself and just to all, ready to protect the rights of the humblest, to redress every wrong, to avenge every crime; to vindicate in Constitution, whether assailed secretly or openly, by hosts armed with gold, or armed with steel."[63]

"Well, Counselor," Booth whispered, "Looks like you lost another one!"

---

63  This argument borrows from the final statement by Special Prosecutor and former Ohio Congressman John A. Bingham, in Pitman (comp.), *The Assassination of President Lincoln and the Trial of the Conspirators*, 351-402, *passim*.

# 7

## Verdict

"Well, Booth, this is it," O'Connor said.

"The defendant will rise," ordered General Barry, the board president. Booth and O'Connor stood up.

In rising, Booth was assisted by two beefy soldiers, who lifted him into a standing position and put crutches under his arms. The "Assassinator" was standing in front of the bar on only one leg—his left pant leg was empty below the knee and pinned up to keep everything neat and proper.

As he stood, Booth vaguely remembered the trip up the Potomac in the steamer John S. Ide. When he arrived at the Washington Navy Yard, he was thrown onto a medical stretcher and carried aboard one of the ironclads riding at anchor in the middle of the Eastern Branch of the Potomac, or the Anacostia as it is called nowadays. The ironclads were ready to receive the co-conspirators into the stuffy, humid bowels of the ship. Marine guards with Spencer breech-loading, seven-shot rifles stood by, to keep the murderous crowd along the riverbank from swimming out to do vengeance against the man who killed Lincoln.

Unlike the others, Booth, still lying on the stretcher, was set down outside on two sawhorses under the huge canopy that covered the deck of the USS Montauk against the glaring heat of the mid-day sun. A Navy medical assistant cut his left trouser leg off near the hip and scanned his leg, broken during his flight to avoid arrest and prosecution.

"Probably at the knee Doctors?"

The two surgeons looked at the leg and then each other. "That's right, Corpsman. At the knee. The infection is too far advanced and his leg reeks of the beginnings of gangrene. Knock him out and apply the clamps."

Within a couple or three minutes, Booth was anesthetized and his lower leg below the knee joint was removed and unceremoniously thrown overboard. John Wilkes Booth would never again tread the boards, as thespians called stage acting in those days. He had been saved from blood poisoning and gangrene for the skills of the hangman. He, sure as shooting, was not going to cheat the Union authorities with a mere medical death![64]

"The clerk will please read the verdict," Barry commanded.

"Pursuant to Special Orders, No. 211, Adjutant General's Office, series 1865," droned the clerk in his all-too familiar voice that reeked of repeated boredom, "which appointed a Military Commission to meet at Washington, District of Columbia, on Monday, the 8th day of May, 1865, for the arraignment and trial of

---

64 Booth's broken leg and his constant activity while being pursued had caused the military men, Lt. Mortimer B. Ruggles, Pvts. AR Bainbridge, Willie Jett, Enoch W. Mason, and even the Garrett boys just back from the army, who had seen him during his flight to wonder about amputation. See M. B. Ruggles, "Pursuit and Death of John Wilkes Booth: Major Ruggles's Narrative," *Century Magazine*, 39 (January 1890), 443-46, reprinted in Prentiss Ingraham, "The Pursuit and Death of John Wilkes Booth," Dillon (ed.), *The Lincoln Assassination: From the Pages of the* Surratt Courier, IV, 23-31, which also includes an account by Lt. Bainbridge, 26-27; Kate H. Mason, "A True Story of the Capture and Death of John Wilkes Booth," *Northern Neck Historical Magazine*, 13 (December 1963), 1237-39. See also, statement of Surgeon General C. R. Reynolds to David Rankin Barbee, March 30, 1936, "Autopsy and Identification of Body," box 4, folder 812, DRB papers. GU.

The procedure for field amputation common in the Civil War is described in C. Keith Wilbur, M.D., *Civil War Medicine* (Old Saybrook, Conn.: The Globe Pequot Press, 1998), 51-55. See also George A. Otis (ed.), *Medical and Surgical History of the War of the Rebellion* (3 vols. in 6 pts., Washington: Government Printing Office, 1876), *passim*, for beautifully illustrated pictures of any and all procedures in vivid color.

John Wilkes Booth, and of which Brevet Major General William F. Barry, United States Volunteers, is President, to which charges and specifications said John Wilkes Booth pleaded 'not guilty.'

"The court, having considered the evidence adduced, finds the accused, John Wilkes Booth, as follows:

CHARGE I. Treason against the Government of the United States. Of the charge and the specification, not guilty.

The courtroom broke out in a cacophony of disagreement. Booth smiled crookedly under his moustache.

"Order!" Shouted Commission President Barry. His gavel hit the pad in from of him. "Order in the court! Continue," he motioned to the clerk.

The clerk did as he was bade:

CHARGE II. Attempted kidnapping of Abraham Lincoln, President of the United States, etc.,
Of the first specification, not guilty,
Of the second specification, not guilty,
Of the third specification, not guilty,
Of the charge, not guilty.

The courtroom audience growled and snarled in crescendo to each "not guilty" and then cried and shouted, "no, no, no! Impossible! Is there no justice?" Once again, Booth smiled inwardly.

The Commissioner banged his gavel incessantly calling for "order! Order in the court. Sergeant of the guard! Turn out the guard!" A dozen soldiers with fixed bayonets caused the crown to quiet down. "Continue reading the verdict!"

Once again the clerk obeyed, this time reading with renewed interest in his own survival in front of the angered crowd. He stepped behind a big, burly private soldier for cover and raised his voice. It squeaked. He paused, cleared his throat and swallowed the cotton out of his mouth, and tried to speak again, this time with more success.

CHARGE III. Murdering members of the Government of the United States,
    Of the first specification, not guilty,
    Of the second specification, not guilty,
    Of the third specification, not guilty,
    Of the charge, not guilty.

The courtroom went into a frenzy. Men were screaming and women shrieking and crying. The Commission president banged his gavel until it broke and its wooden head flew off into the crowd.

"Charge bayonet!" the sergeant of the guard yelled. The soldiers lowered their rifles and took a step forward with a shout, bayonets fixed, pointed forward at the crowd, ready for action.

The commission president banged his table again. This time it was with an old, heavy Colt's .44 Cal. Dragoon model. "One more outburst like this and I will have the soldiers clear the room, he said turning is revolver around and cocking it before aiming it an the crowd. "By God! I will have order! And that is final!" The commission president barked in a by-now hoarse voice.

"The clerk will continue the reading of the verdict," he commanded once again. The clerk looked at him quizzically. "Go on, read the verdict on the last charge!

# PART III

## "The Good Do Not Always Win"

"It is to be regretted that history should have to tell so many lies as it will tell, when it shall declare Lincoln's intrigues and foolishness models of integrity and wisdom, his weakened and wavering indecision and delay far-sighted statesmanship, and his blundering usurpation of legislative power Jacksonian courage and Roman patriotism, but one cannot help it. History goes with the powers that be."

—Alonzo Taft (future Attorney General and Secretary of War) to Senator pro tem Benjamin Wade, on September 8, 1864, in David Rankin Barbee Papers, Box 3, Archives, Georgetown University.

# 1

## SKIRTING THE REGULATIONS

Meanwhile, as the courtroom was exploding in disappointed anger, Booth's attempt to get around the inability to speak in his own defense before the court and present his views out to the public nonetheless had continued on unabated outside the courtroom. Booth's lawyer, Charles O'Connor, had asked the bench to consider permitting Booth to speak before the Court contrary to defendants not being allowed to speak as their utterances were usually considered biased, possible untruthful and prejudicial to the proper order to the proceedings, but the plea had been rejected out of hand. Besides with Booth's reputation as an actor and a smooth talking one at that, the bench was not about to let his well-known glib tongue influence the verdict.

But Booth was adamant that his views be made public, and several things had already been put in place, without O'Connor's knowledge, indeed even before he had been installed as Booth's attorney, to achieve just that. This effort involved two people, George N. Sanders, a Confederate operator and professional revolutionary in Canada, and his agent, the superb Rebel spy, Sarah Antoinette Slater.

Sanders was born and raised in Kentucky. His grandfather had campaigned for Virginia's approval of the U.S. Constitution in 1787, but ten years later had supported the Kentucky Resolves, which favored the States, not the Supreme Court, declaring Federal laws unconstitutional. His grandson was now imbued with the notion of state rights, slavery, and secession.

George was influenced by a New York newspaper that had his same views, so he wrote the editor, Anna Reid, fell in love with her, moved to New York City, courted, and married her. She stuck with him to the end, ignoring his generally unkempt nature and reluctance to bathe. They returned to Kentucky to live.

An unapologetic believer in Manifest Destiny (God's approval of American growth westward),[65] Sanders supported the "Young America" branch of the Democratic Party, the Independence of Texas and it eventual annexation by the United States, the War with Mexico, a cross-isthmus canal, and expansion to the Pacific coast in the Columbia Quadrilateral, which became Oregon Territory. But Sanders went much further, He supported anti-monarchial constitutional nationalists in Europe and became involved the unsuccessful Revolutions of 1848.

The losers in the Revolutions of 1848 fled their homelands to London, the center of exile communities from all over Europe. Sanders soon joined them as American Consul General in London and communicated and cooperated with other supporters of Young America. These included August Belmont, John Y. Mason, Pierre Soulé, James Buchanan, and Daniel Sickles. These men promoted the assassination of Napoleon III of France and the Ostend Manifesto advocating American seizure of Cuba from Spain.

Recalled from his diplomatic post, Sanders returned to the United States and advanced the Mississippi Valley movement,

---

[65] Frederick Merk, *Manifest Destiny and Mission in American History: A Reinterpretation*. (Cambridge: Harvard University Press, 1963); Julius Pratt, "The Origin Of "Manifest Destiny", *American Historical Review*, 32 (No 4, 1927), 795–98; Paul Finkelman and Donald R. Kennon, *Congress and the Emergence of Sectionalism*. (Athens:Ohio University Press, 2008).

the union of all states along the Mississippi River and its tributaries against the East. He also joined the Knights of the Golden Circle, a pro-slavery, pro-expansionist movement that joined the secessionist movement after Abraham Lincoln's election as president in 1860. With the creation of the Confederacy, Sanders joined the South along with his uncle, Richard Hawes, Confederate governor of "seceded" Kentucky.

Sanders soon returned to Europe to promote Confederate schemes to purchase guns and ammunition and set up diplomatic posts to recognize the Confederacy. He also suggested that Confederate President Jefferson Davis run all Confederate Secret Service spy missions out of Canada, thus avoiding the Yankee blockade of Southern ports.

Then Sanders went north to Canada to become a part of these missions. He met presidential secretary John Hays to discuss the Niagara Peace Movement, met and coordinated John Wilkes Booth's kidnapping and assassination plots, and defended the Confederate bank robbers, by proving them to be Rebel cavalry raiders. It was in this last endeavor, that he met Sarah Slater.[66]

---

66   For Sanders, see William L. Richter, *Historical Dictionary of the Civil War and Reconstruction* (Lanham, Md.: Scarecrow, 2012), 567-69. See also, Merle E. Curti, "George Nicholas Sanders," in Dumas Malone (ed.), *Dictionary of American Biography* (New York: Charles Scribner's Sons, 1935), XIV, 334-35. On his son Reid Sanders, see Meriwether Stuart, "Operation Sanders: Wherein Old Friends and Ardent Pro-Southerners Prove to be Union Secret Agents," *Virginia Magazine of History and Biography*, 81 (April 1973), 157-99. The Hudson's Bay Claims represented by Sanders are treated in John S. Galbraith, "George N. Sanders: 'Influence' Man for the Hudson's Bay Company," *Oregon Historical Quarterly*, 53 (September 1952), 159-76. A newer, sadly as yet unpublished massive study on Sanders, one of the principal characters in the Confederate Canadian operations, is Randall A. Haines, "The Notorious George N. Sanders: His Career and role in the Lincoln Assassination" (unpublished ms. in the James O. Hall Library, Surratt Museum, 1994). Published (and a sort of combination of Leonard F. Gutteridge and Ray A. Neff, *Dark Union: The Secret Web of Profiteers, Politicians, and Booth Conspirators that Led to Lincoln's Death* (Hoboken, NJ: Weilet, 2003), and Haines, "The Notorious George N. Sanders"), is Charles Higham, *Murdering Mr. Lincoln: A New Detection of the Nineteenth's Century's Most Famous Crime* (Beverly Hills: New Millenium Press, 2004), especially 1-51, who puts Sanders at the center of the Lincoln assassination plot as its prime architect.

Born Sarah Antoinette Gilbert (pronounced in the French manner, with a soft, sibilant 'g') in Middletown, Connecticut, in 1843, her parents came from the French West Indies, which allowed Sarah to carry a French passport and all the privileges that went with it. What that meant was she could not be effectively arrested as an American, without the French government intervening in her case. She spoke both French and English with no notable accent in either.

Sarah's father rolled pills of varying efficacy, which earned him the title "Doctor," and her mother ran a boarding house in Middletown. Sarah must have been an obliging chambermaid because she wound up pregnant. The birth split the family, and Sarah followed her father and brothers to New Bern, North Carolina. There she met a dance instructor. Married to Rowan Slater, Sarah moved to Goldsboro, where Slater became a Confederate purchasing agent. Eventually he joined the army and Sarah never saw him again. After the war, Slater returned to North Carolina and searched for his wife, but found nothing but her death notice. That was more than anyone at that time found; indeed it would take until 2010 before her life after the war was pieced together with any certainty.

Searching for her husband, Sarah appeared in the office of Confederate Secretary of War James A. Seddon in January 1865 with a letter of introduction from her congressmen, asking that she, a possible war widow, be allowed to pass through Confederate military lines to go see her mother in New York City.

But Seddon saw possibilities in this sweet, young thing. He offered her a job of carrying dispatches from Richmond to Montreal by way of New York City, Confederate headquarters in Montreal and back again. She was allowed to stop and see her mother each time she passed through the Empire City.

Sarah Slater smiled. Her new career would not last long, she knew, because the Confederacy was on its last pegs. She could see that, even if men like Seddon seemed oblivious to the truth of it. She would make three trips for Seddon and Judah P. Benjamin, traveling variously with Gus S. Howell and John H. Surratt, Jr. Howell was very business-like, but young Surratt was panting the entire way whenever they traveled together, like a rutting, buck elk. Her last trip brought paper that proved the St. Albans bank robbers to be Confederate soldiers on a military mission.

Returning quietly to her mother's residence in New York City, Nettie was dismayed to be arrested in the general sweep of all suspected Confederate agents. Giving her name as Antoinette Gilbert and appealing to the French Embassy, she managed to gain release from the Carrol Annex of the Old Capitol Prison in a matter of days. The April journey with John Surratt was to have been her last trip for the Confederates, anyway.

Back in New York, Sarah was surprised to answer a knock on her mother's front door only to see none other than that Confederate agent—what was his name? Oh, yes, George N. Sanders, scruffy cloths, beard full of orts from his last meal, standing on the stoop. In spite of her protestations that she was done with the Confederacy, Sanders managed to convince her otherwise with a large sum of money. All he wanted her to do was to get into the United States Department of War on Seventeenth Street, the real "lunatic asylum," as it was called, go into Secretary of War Stanton's office, crack the safe, edit John Wilkes Booth's diary by ripping out pages incriminating to high officials, military and civilian, and replace the book otherwise unharmed. There was a big bonus if she brought the pages back to Sanders.

"That is all?"

"Oh" Sanders added as an after thought, "here is the key to

the safe, to help you out. By the way, in exchange, the Confederacy will forgive your prior attempt to pilfer government funds."67

"Anything else?"

"Well, yes. John Wilkes Booth has been captured and returned to Washington City to stand trial for the 'military execution' of President Lincoln. He was grievously injured and lost his leg in the fight down in Virginia. Since an accused man cannot defend himself in his own words in any court in the land, we would like to see his motives revealed to the world. We want you to become his nurse, working for one of the numerous Sanitary Commissions in the District. You can use your time 'nursing' Mr. Booth to take his statement. It may take days, you know. You will provide his confession, as it were, to our designated agent in the City."

"God," She whispered to her own amazement. "How much?" she said aloud.

"Ah, let us say we will double you offer on the diary. You can retire for life somewhere nice."

"You may depend upon it!"68

Before she left New York, Sarah went for an interview with Frederick Law Olmsted, famous for writing several travel books

---

67  James O. Hall, "The Saga of Sarah Slater [orig., "Lady in the Veil," *Maryland Independent* (Waldorf), June 25, July 2, 1975]," Kauffman (ed.), *In Pursuit of* . . . , 69-88; Hall, "Veiled Lady: The Saga of Sara Slater," *North & South*, 3 (August 2000), 34-44; Tonia J. Smith, "[Sara Slater]," (August 17, 1997), at users.nbn.net/tj1. The newest and most intriguing interpretation of Sarah Slater is John F. Stanton, "Some Thoughts on Sarah Slater," *Surratt Courier*, 32 (February 2007), 3-6, which we have used partially. Her appearance at the Kentucky spy reunion is in John F. Stanton to Laurie Verge, February 20, 2008, e-mail in the author's possession, and amplified in Stanton's "Anne Olivia Floyd: 1826-1905," *Surratt Courier*, 33 (June 2008), 5-8, especially 7-8, Sarah Slater's short stay in the Old Capitol prison is in Lomax, *Old Capitol and Its Inmates*, 153-54, as confirmed in Michael W. Kauffman, *American Brutus*, 327, 336. Historian John F. Stanton finally traced Sarah's life until her death in 1920. See Stanton, "A Mystery No Longer: 'The Lady in the Veil,'" *Surratt Courier*, 36 (October 2011), 5-9. Also of interest is the exchange in Lincoln-Assassination.com, General category, All Things Lincoln Assassination, Lady in the Veil (2011), posts 10, 14, 17, 31, 34.

68  These events are written to coordinate with the story presented in Richter, *Last Confederate Heroes*, II, 363-73.

about the Antebellum South, developing landscape architecture, and developing New York City's Central Park. Olmstead had taken leave as director of Central Park to work as Executive Secretary of the U.S. Sanitary Commission, a precursor to the Red Cross in Washington, D.C. He tended to the wounded during the failed 1862 Peninsular Campaign against Richmond.[69]

"I am most impressed with your talent as a medical nurse, Miss Slater," Olmstead said. Like most men he fell for Sarah's charm immediately. She was not flashy but pretty and sincere. She put men at ease with her vivacious smile, nice but not overwhelming figure, and musical voice.

"Thank you, Mr. Executive Secretary. I hoped that you might write me a letter of introduction to the head of your Washington office—ah, I believe he is Col. William Hammond, or should I say, 'doctor?'"

"He answers to either, but I suspect he likes 'doctor' the best. Once a medical man, you know...."

Olmstead escorted Sarah into his front anteroom where he had one of his clerks write up the letter, which he signed with a flourish.

Sarah took the night train to Washington, D.C. She took care of Booth's diary first. Then she turned her attention towards his prison "hospital" cell.

"Dr. Hammond?" she inquired, as she entered the offices of the United States Sanitary Commission.

"I am Sarah Slater. I lost my husband early in the war and I have been volunteering to help others recover from their wounds so that they may travel home to reassure their families as to their recovery. I have a letter of introduction from Secretary Olmstead

---

69    For the United States Sanitary Commission, see William L. Richter, *Historical Dictionary of the Civil War and Reconstruction*, 666-67.

up in New York for your perusal. Hopefully I can be of service here."

Hammond smiled and read Olmstead's letter, which had three years of mythical service on various battlefields on the bloody route to Richmond.

"You know that we are liable to be replaced soon by the new Red Cross, do you not?"

"Why, yes sir, I do. Which is my reason for haste that I might join the true service organization approved by President Lincoln, God rest his soul, so many years ago. I am appalled that this upstart group with so little military discipline should replace one of the President's finest acts for the men of our armies and navy. His murder was such a shock to me and every good American."

"You know, Miss Slater," Hammond said after they had chatted a while about the unprecedented assassination of "our beloved President" by the "traitor Booth," "I have just the job for you."

"Excellent, sir!"

"It is to care for the murderer Booth in his jail cell. It is no hospital birth, but he needs the best of care that he might survive until he can be properly hanged. He has had his left leg removed, a casualty of his attempted flight to avoid justice."

"Thank you, so much Doctor. That is just the job I want—the job I have earnestly prayed for. I assure you that I will have him fit to hang higher than Haman, as God is my witness!"

# 2

# LINCOLN AND THE AMERICAN SYSTEM

The nice-looking nurse stood outside Booth's cell in the arsenal prison patiently waiting for the guard to unlock the door.

"Visitor, Mr. Booth," the guard called as he worked the lock. "A nurse from the Sanitary Commission to check your amputation and write letters or read a book or whatever for you. By orders of Judge Advocate General and Col. Carrington, the prosecutor."

Booth sat up in the straw filled bed and swung his legs around, placing the right foot on the floor. The left leg was crowned at the knee with a bloody bandage. Most of the blood was dried, but his stump was still suppurating in the bandage.

"My name is Nettie Slater, Mr. Booth." Sarah used her middle name, Southern style, when she was being friendly. She looked around for the guard, but he had locked Sarah and Booth in and walked back to the head of the alley. "Mr. Sanders sent me. You know, George N. Sanders of Canada? I believe you spoke with him several months ago—October, I think."

"I believe that we have a formality or two to dispense with first, Miss Nettie. Come Retribution."

"Complete victory," came the reply. "Please, let me see the web of your left thumb and hand."

Booth extended his had, palm down. There, Sarah examined

the junction between thumb and hand for the faded initials, "J.W.B.," made in ink during misspent moments as a youth. Sarah nodded with approval. "OK," she said.

"Are you going to break me out of here?" Booth asked with a grin. "I am not sure I can run fast enough to beat these bluebellies." He laughed and coughed.

"No, sir, I am here to tend your wounds and take down your statement for the American public, now that the nation had been forcibly reunited. I understand they will not let you speak on your own behalf in court? I will get your feelings to the outside another way. I have contacts, you know."

"Well, let us get down to brass tacks," Booth said excitedly. "We can start our look at the Great Emancipator by examining the Lincoln Myth that sprang up after I executed him as Commander-in-chief of the Union armies and Navy. Lincoln was a master politician and an expert rhetorician, which meant he was a near genius of a wirepuller," Booth maintained. Booth pointed out that "Lincoln was the smartest of parliamentarians and a most cunning logroller, a man who admired DeWitt Clinton, the former governor of New York. It was Clinton who introduced the spoils system into American politics," Booth explained, "not Andrew Jackson. One discovers that much of Lincoln's present-say praise is not so much an attempt to explain history as to devise rationalizations or excuses for Lincoln's behavior."[70]

Booth then claimed, "the real purposes usually attributed to the Emancipation Proclamation was to keep European monarchies out of the war and to incite a slave rebellion to assist the floundering Union invasion of the South.[71]

---

70 Thomas DiLorenzo, *The Real Lincoln: A New Look at Abraham Lincoln, His Agenda, and an Unnecessary War* (Roseville, Ca.: Prima Publishing, 2002), 10-11. See also Thomas J. Pressly, "'Emancipating Slaves, Enslaving Free Men'," *Civil War History*, 46 (2000), 254-65.
71 Dilorenzo, *The Real Lincoln*, 4, 33-52, especially 45.

"You know," Booth said to Sarah, "and I am not alone in this notion, I believe that the war and the emancipation that flowed from it had an even more sinister purpose. And that the ultimate goal of Lincoln and the Republicans explains why slavery in the United States had to be ended by violence rather than peacefully as in the rest of the Americas."

"What was their real aim?" Sarah inquired.

"Everywhere else the Industrial Revolution had destroyed slavery, a most inefficient type of labor ill-suited to the new order. Did you know, we Booths hired our black labor and did not use slaves? But in the United States the Whig version of how to achieve industrialism had been voted down by the American people from the time of Jefferson and was seen as corrupt, a replication of the crooked English colonial approach that had led to the American Revolution, and therefore unconstitutional.[72]

"The reason that there had to be a war to end slavery in the United States was to guarantee the institution of Henry Clay's American System," Booth said, "of which Lincoln was the prime proponent in 1860. First put forth in Alexander Hamilton's 1791 'Report on Manufactures,' Lincoln, under the cover of saving the Union by executive fiat, and the new Republican majority in both houses of Congress, could pass their economic system, so long blocked by Democrats, particularly from the South."

"I believe that Lincoln seethed in frustration at the lack of constitutional and popular support for the American system," Booth asserted. "Lincoln's plan was a mercantile ideology, a system that used faulty economic theory to build empires and subsidize individuals or groups or industries favored by the state. It was financed by a protective tariff, which prevented free trade

---

72   Ibid., x, 38, 52-53, 83-84. See also, Walter Williams, "The Civil War Wasn't About Slavery," Jewish World Review, (December 2, 1998); "The Real Lincoln," ibid., March 27, 2002; and Secession or Nullification," at http://www.townhall.com/walterwilliams/ww20020410.shtml.

competition and raised local prices to consumers. It was a fancy cover for corporate welfare for select industries that ultimately led to empire—at first in the American South and then the Great West.[73]

"Because Southern Democrats had been so long the central group around which opponents to the American System had coalesced," Booth stated, "it was imperative to keep the South out of the Union long enough to allow the Republican majority to enact its programs as war measures. By late 1862 or early 1863, Congress had enacted the American System in full with the new National Banking System and its paper money to inflate credit, the Pacific Railroad Act, and the Protective Tariff. Indeed, the tariff with its new rate of 80% was so central to Republican economic aspirations," Booth posited, "that Republicans claimed that secession was merely an extension of the old Nullification argument over the Tariff of Abominations of Andrew Jackson's day. And like in 1832, Lincoln expected that the South would come crawling back to the Union, in time.[74]

"To justify the Republican war, Lincoln also claimed secession to be illegal, following a dubious constitutional theory advanced (1832) and later repudiated (1850) by Daniel Webster, that the Union preceded the states in origin. This was what might be called 'Lincoln's Spectacular Lie.' Lincoln pointed out that there was no clause creating perpetual Union in the Constitution, that the states had not declared independence and signed the Treaty of Paris in 1783 as separate entities, and ignored that three states (Virginia, New York, and Rhode Island) had ratified the Constitution, reserving secession as a right that might be exercised later.[75]

---

73  Dilorenzo, *The Real Lincoln*, 3, 4-5, 54-84, 234.
74  *Ibid.*, 118-19, 121, 126, 128-29.
75  *Ibid.*, 5, 85-129.

"Finally," Booth said, "the Lincoln prosecution of the war had the long-term legacy of destroying the notion that the nation was a voluntary association of states, which had existed from the time of the Founding Fathers. The war destroyed the concept of state rights and secession to check the power of the federal government, which had been advocated by Thomas Jefferson and James Madison to attack the Alien and Sedition Acts in 1798; by the Hartford Convention to protest the War of 1812 in 1814; and by South Carolina to nullify the Tariff in 1832.

"The Republicans prefer the Federalist Party solution advanced by Chief Justice John Marshall, that the U.S. Supreme Court would reserve this state-asserted nullification function to itself in a case by case manner. Lincoln saved the Union by increasing the central political control coming out of Washington and destroying the Ninth Amendment (which guarded against government intrusion upon personal liberty) and Tenth Amendment (which reserved all powers not specifically granted to the federal government to states and the people).

"As John C. Calhoun once wrote, the essential question of American politics was whether ours was a federal or consolidated government; a constitutional or absolute one; a government resting solidly on the basis of the sovereignty of the States, or on the unrestrained will of a majority; a form of government, as in all unlimited ones, in which injustice, violence, and force must ultimately prevail." Booth now put it a little differently: "Lincoln had let the genie of centralism out of the bottle never to be returned. Ending slavery was a by-product designed to cover the real Republican economic domination of the Union program."[76]

---

76   *Ibid.*, ix, xi, xii, 2, 8-9, 122, 257-79. See also, Thomas J. DiLorenzo, " Great Centralizer: Abraham Lincoln and the War Between the States," Independent Review, 3 (No. 2, Fall 1998), 243-71

# 3

# THE CONSTITUTION AND THE FUGITIVE SLAVE ACT 1850

"Well. Let us talk secession. Have you seen my speech I planned to give to a public gathering in late December 1860 in Philadelphia?[77] No? I am not surprised. The Federal officers have seized everything. Or so my sister Asia tells me. So we will start with secession. I learned all of this during my stay in Richmond before the war. I will give no names but several gentlemen were interested in my views as I was a public person and others allegedly listened to me."

"You were a secessionist, were you not?"

"No, quite the contrary. Not until 1864 and my 'To Whom It May Concern' letter.[78] I was what people in 1860 called then a Cooperationist. I believed that the South could maintain it cultural ways best by staying in the Union. It was explained to me that we had all sorts of advantages, not the least was the Constitution of 17887.

"These gentlemen I was talking to in Richmond were lawyers, trained to draw the legal distinctions necessary to understand why secession is an inappropriate response to the Southern position on slavery. They appreciated my interest and support of the South and her customs against the insidious Yankee political

---

77  Rhodehammel and Taper, *The Writings of John Wilkes Booth*, 55-64, especially 64.
78  *Ibid.*, 124-27. See also Richter, *Sic Semper Tyrannis*, ch. 3.

attack that is sweeping much of the North before the war. They wanted me to be correct in my understanding."

"Then secession was not the ultimate position of the South?" Sarah asked in open-eyed wonderment.

"Not at all, Miss Nettie," Booth said. "The South's real position was to stay within the Union at all costs and use the powers granted and withheld under the Federal Constitution to protect our rights to hold slaves. Secession was only a poor alternative, should we fail in our endeavors."

"And how is the South to act to protect herself under the Constitution?" Nettie wanted to know.

"Are you able to keep up with me?"

"Oh, yes, I am able to use a fast form of writing called phonography. It has been taught to secretaries for some twenty years now. I believe it was invented in England before it was brought here. A man named Isaac Pittman invented it and his brothers introduced it over here. They will be taking notes at the trials of you and your co-conspirators, as the Yankees dub them."

"I see," Booth said. "Well, to continue. The Cooperationist program called for the rigorous enforcement of the fugitive-slave law, equal rights for slaveholders in the territories, and ultimately, the clarification of all this in a federally enacted slave code. Before he left the Union and became the President of the Confederacy, the U.S. Senator from Mississippi, Jefferson Davis, was working on the latter point."

"Were these things are possible? The Republicans were opposed to all of this. How were we to win?"

"By a vigorous reading of the Constitution of 1789. Not by relying on political philosophy, but a legal concept. The North's greatest weakness was that they rarely read or followed the Constitution.

"First, the abolition of slavery was not the issue. Any state had the right to abolish slavery within its own borders. No Federal measure to abolish slavery was ever been seriously entertained over the past eighty years of this country's existence. Not even by the Liberty Party in the '40's or the Free Soil Party of a decade ago. Funny thing, it was the Yankees who believed in the so-called state rights doctrine. They wished to interpose themselves between the national government and the citizens to stop the application of Federal law. We wanted the Federal government to rigorously apply and enforce U.S. laws, as regards slavery.

"Slavery could be ended everywhere only by the passage and ratification of a constitutional amendment. That required the agreement of three-fourths of the states. The South had half, so it could not be done."

"I did not know that," Sarah said in awe."

"Yeah, not many understood that, then or now. Actually, the question at issue is not the institution of slavery within the boundaries of any state. Instead, the real issues were the fugitive law and slavery in the territories. This was first expressed by the late Mr. Abel Upshur, when he was Secretary of State under President John Tyler, over a decade ago. Congress could deal slavery a blow only outside the boundaries of the slave states, if the South were not vigilant. The Republicans called this policy the Cordon of Freedom, to isolate slavery in the Southern states.[79] To put it in a word, what we were interested in protecting is the extraterritorial nature of slavery, guaranteed in the Constitution. That is to say, we slaveholders were justified in controlling the internal policies of non-slaveholding states in the matter of slavery and none other."

---

79  James Oaks, *Freedom National: The Destruction of Slavery In the United States, 1861-1865* (New York: Norton, 2013), 256-300.

"How is that so?" Sarah asked, switching pencils. She had many of them already sharpened and ready to go.

"The essence of extraterritorial power comes in two realms. One is the fugitive clause, which guarantees that anyone held to service or labor under the laws of one state cannot be liberated should he escape to another state under whose laws he would be free. Instead, the Constitution guarantees that the fugitive shall be turned over to the original state's jurisdiction, upon proper legal claim being filed with the state to which the fugitive fled."

"I thought that extradition was for criminals."

"It is, but this is different. Extradition of criminals is not guaranteed. A state may refuse it. But the claim on a fugitive slave, a person held to service or labor, cannot be refused. Our slave law functions in any state because of this guarantee. The Northern states claimed that they had concurrent jurisdiction and could refuse to return runaway slaves at will. The U.S. Supreme Court shot that to pieces in the appeal of a Pennsylvania case in 1842. So when a more stringent fugitive law passed Congress as a part of the Compromise of 1850, the Yankees then held that they would nullify the Federal law with their own state ordinances, called 'personal liberty' laws."[80]

"I have heard of them," Sarah said.

"Yes, the North claimed that the new fugitive law was too summary. And it had to be, to get around their unwillingness to enforce the original fugitive act passed back in 1793. The

---

80  On state rights before the secession movement, much of which occurred in the North rather than the South, see Thomas J. DiLorenzo, *The Real Lincoln*, 85-129, and DiLorenzo, "Yankee Confederates: New England Secession Movements Prior to the War between the States," in David Gordon (ed.), *Secession, State and Liberty* (New Brunswick, N. J.: Transaction Publishers, 1998), 135-53; James M. Banner, Jr., *To the Hartford Convention: The Federalists and the Origins of Party Politics in Massachusetts, 1789-1815* (New York: Knopf, 1970); William W. Freehling, *Prelude to Civil War: The Nullification Crisis in South Carolina, 1816-1836* (New York: Harper & Row, 1965); Thomas D. Morris, *Free Men All: The Personal Liberty Laws of the North, 1780-1861* (Baltimore: The Johns Hopkins University Press, 1974).

Yankees maintained that the Federal commissioners created under the new law to hear fugitive cases were unfair, because jury trials were excluded, no Negro testimony could be heard."

"Have you ever heard of such travesty? A colored man testifying against a white man?" Sarah was horrified.

"Typically a Yankee sort of thing to do," Booth opined. "Where was I? Oh, yes. . . . No Negro testimony was compounded by the fact that the commissioner received twice the court fees if he found against the fugitive, and that the decision of the commissioner was full answer to any habeas corpus petition from any other court, state or Federal. The whole thing was settled just before the war in a Wisconsin case before the U.S. Supreme Court. It had an interesting name, Ableman v. Booth."

"Was he a relative of yours?" Sarah asked.

"No, no, of course not. This Booth was an abolitionist newspaper editor who was convicted of stealing slaves out of Missouri and he was set free by State interposition against the decision of the Federal court. Well, anyhow, the Chief Justice ruled that each state is sovereign within its own borders provided that its sovereignty does not cross certain limitations and restrictions set forth in the Federal Constitution, one of course being the extraterritorial nature of the fugitive law."

"So Federal policy was supreme to that of the states?" Sarah asked.

"It was the exact reverse, actually. What the Court did was deny the Federal government or non-slaveholding states any discretionary, policy-making functions in the matter of slavery. They must follow the provisions of the Federal Constitution exactly because only the slavery provisions of the Constitution have extraterritoriality. And the Federal courts will protect those rights. Hence the personal liberty laws were null and void.

"Now the Yankee states would have the same privileges, if they but still owned slaves, as most of them did at the time of the Revolution and writing of the Constitution. It is not our fault that they freed them, but perfectly constitutional and legal that they did, as they are sovereign in taking that action. No one has to own slaves, after all.

"Let's adjourn for this evening, Miss Nettie. Your hand must need a rest. It is getting late. What say we continue this discussion tomorrow?"[81]

---

81  The argument here generally follows the materials presented in Arthur Bestor, "State Sovereignty and Slavery: A Reinterpretation of Proslavery Constitutional Doctrine, 1846-1860," *Journal of the Illinois State Historical Society*, 53 (1960), 117-80. See also, William L. Richter, "Out of the Sahara of the Bozart: The Pre-War Political Thought of John Wilkes Booth," in his *Sic Semper Tyrannis: Why John Wilkes Booth Shot Abraham Lincoln* (Bloomington, Ind.: iUniverse, 2009), 79-133. In 1860, the South would personalize its concern with the fugitive issue, preferring to see Lincoln's oral pledges to return escaped slaves as duplicity rather than separate from Radical Republican promises to end the system. See Bennett, *Forced into Glory*, 288-91.

# 4

# THE CONSTITUTION AND SLAVERY IN THE TERRITORIES

The next evening, Sarah met with Booth again. After changing his bandage on the amputated leg, she sat and listened to more of Booth's beliefs.

"Now," Booth said, "as to slavery in the territories. You may or may not be aware, Miss Nettie, that the foundation-stone of the Bill of Rights, those sacred, first ten amendments that Virginia and other states made a condition of their joining the Union in the 1780s, is the Tenth Amendment, buttressed by its sister proviso, the Ninth. Often we erroneously speak of rights when what we really are taking about is power. Rights are something possessed by individual persons. But no government on any level has rights.

"What governments possess are powers," Booth continued. "The Tenth Amendment says that all powers not specifically granted to the Federal government in the Constitution, or denied to the states by the Constitution, are reserved to the states, or the people. Its sister amendment, the Ninth, says that the enumeration in the Constitution of certain rights guaranteed the people shall not be construed to deny other rights retained by the people.

"Thus, certain powers, but no rights are delegated to the Federal government," Booth said. "Certain other powers, but again no rights, are reserved to the states. Other powers, not granted to either the Federal or the state governments, remain in the hands of the people, thus creating a body of inalienable or indefeasible rights. Now state sovereignty, our theory, is not a defensive concept. States' rights is. It is completely reactive to what the Federal government does. We, rather, hold that the Federal government in the realm of slavery must act, it must command, it must assert its power, the extraterritorial power that is granted to it by the Constitution and its Amendments, regardless of what the states might say.

"You see, Miss Nettie, the right of slaveholders to take their slaves into a territory and hold them there, and exploit their labor, is properly described as an extraterritorial right, just as the recapture of runaways up North is. Unfortunately, unlike the fugitive clause, it is not specifically stated in the Constitution, so it must be interpolated. The problem is that the Founding Fathers left the territories out of the Constitution when they wrote it. The Constitution speaks of the Federal government and the states. But there are three, not two, elements to the nation: the Federal government, the states, and the territories.

"What is important in the territories is what jurisdiction, federal or territorial, will wield the police power, under which slavery is maintained everywhere. Normally, the police power (the inherent power of a state government to exercise reasonable power over persons and property within its jurisdiction in the interest of the general security, health, safety, morals, and welfare, except where constitutionally prohibited), is a function of the individual states. But in the territories, which state's police power should be used? Virginia's, Indiana's, Vermont's? Whatever police power exists in the territories, prejudiced toward slavery or freedom as regards African people, will determine whether a territory will be friendly or hostile to slave owners."

"I thought the Missouri Compromise of 1820 settled that problem?" Sarah inquired.

"It did, until the aftermath of the Mexican War. From the very beginning, when the seaboard states gave up their land claims in the west and turned them over to the Federal government to administer on behalf of all the states, there had grown up a custom. That was that the Congress admitted new states on a fifty-fifty basis. Each new free state was balanced by a new slave state. When Missouri came along, she threatened to upset the balance, until Massachusetts agreed to let her northernmost county, Maine, apply for statehood, too. At the same time, we foolishly compromised and unconstitutionally agreed to permit no further slavery in the territories above the southern boundary of Missouri, the famous $36^0\ 30'$ line. So things rested until the War with Mexico brought much new land into the Union, Texas and the area to its north and west."

"How did the Mexican War change all that? I thought we had another compromise in 1850 to solve that!" Sarah queried, once again.

"We did. The problem was that the Yankees could not abide that Texas was admitted with a provision that she could become five states. That has never been done, o' course, but it could. Also, most of the territory we got from Mexico lay below the $36^0\ 30'$ line. The Yankees got some of the Mexican Cession and Oregon Territory from the British. But along comes this meddler from Pennsylvania, David Wilmot. He was a congressman. That dunderhead introduced a measure, the Wilmot Proviso, that called for making all the Mexican Cession free territory. And the House of Representatives, dominated by the increased Yankee population, mostly immigrants, passed it! We were saved only because we had an equal number of Senators, each state being guaranteed two in the Constitution."

"Was there not a problem with that Compromise of 1850?"

"Yes, ma'am, one could consider it to be flawed. It had five provisions. California was admitted as a free state, upsetting the balance in the Senate. But it has not mattered much. California has elected one pro-slave Senator since, solely by accident, I am sure, but it disgruntles the North. Texas got her Republic debt paid off after she gave up her claims to her western area. That was made the Territory of New Mexico. Then, the area north of that, settled by those polygamy-loving Mormons, the so-called Latter-day Saints—against whom the Republicans have a specific plank in their political platform, by the way—was set up as the Territory of Utah. Congress agreed to admit them as states without looking into stands on slavery, when they got enough population."

"Oh, yes! Popular sovereignty," Sarah exclaimed.

"Squatter sovereignty," Booth corrected her. "Bear with me a while and you will see the essential difference. Where was I? . . . Oh, yes, New Mexico and Utah. Then we agreed to prohibit the trading of Negroes in the District of Columbia. Seems the noble Yankees who objected to slavery could not bear to see a servant sold. But in exchange we got them to pass that fugitive slave act that recognized half of our concept of extraterritoriality. Now here is where popular sovereignty comes in, Miss Nettie."

"I knew it had something to do with slavery out West."

"You are correct in that. But, o' course, like all political and constitutional issues, it is a mite more complicated that the average man cares to think about. It actually embodies, however, the essence of our stand on the extraterritoriality of slavery, so listen up carefully, if you will, Miss."

"Yessir, I am all ears!" Sarah leaned forward eagerly, pencil and paper at the ready.

"Squatter sovereignty was a concept introduced by old Lewis Cass out of Michigan," Booth continued, "who ran for President on the Democratic ticket back in '48. He proposed that the population of a territory vote on whether to have slavery and Congress would accept that decision."

"Sounds great—on the surface," Sarah said.

"On the surface," Booth agreed. "But the problem is that the territories are federally administered on behalf of all the states and admitted into the Union in three phases. In the first, Congress administers the territory through a series of officials appointed by the President with the concurrence of the Senate. All sovereignty or power to rule rests with the Federal government. In the second phase, Congress shares power with the residents of the territory who get to elect a territorial legislature. Obviously, sovereignty is shared between the Federals and the local residents. Finally, in the third phase, the new territory is granted the ability to elect a constitutional convention and draw up a proposed state constitution. If Congress approves, the territory becomes a state on an equal basis with all the other states. You got that?"

"I think so. There is no real sovereignty in the territory until it becomes a state?"

"Well, sovereignty is in the state convention, the most representative body we have in democratic theory, responsible directly to the people for one purpose, drawing up a constitution or fundamental law. Now squatter sovereignty advocates that the people of the territory could decide the slavery issue at any time. But that is not so. So long as the Federal government is ruling or sharing rule, the territory must be ruled under the principle of extraterritoriality. You see, the police power, including the right to slaves, cannot be but the prerogative of a sovereign. A sovereign cannot share power. The Federal government has never been delegated police powers in any way; they are state powers. But the territories are not yet states. So the Federal government is not ruling the territories as a sovereign. It is merely a trustee of the several states. It is there to act not as the government of the United States but as the government of the States United."

Booth emphasized each word with great deliberation, making sure that Sarah caught each vital nuance in meaning. God! Sarah thought to herself. These politicians parse every word to a fault. She nodded her head to indicate she was following Booth's argument fully.

"As a trustee and not as a sovereign, the Federal government can only administer the extraterritorial rights of the states, because the territories are outside of each state's jurisdiction. And the only extraterritorial right in the Federal constitution is. . . ."

"The right to slaves as guaranteed in the fugitive clause!" Sarah cried out triumphantly.

"Correct! Miss Nettie, you have it! Bless me, if you have not got it!"

"Slavery is thus a national institution!"

"Right! And that is the significance of Chief Justice Taney's Dred Scott decision of the U.S. Supreme Court, two years ago. He ruled that Scott, by virtue of being of African descent, was not a citizen of any state and could not sue. No matter where he went with his master, to the free territory of Minnesota, north of the 36°30' line, or the free state of Illinois, covered by the old Northwest ordinance of 1787, he was always covered extraterritorially by the slave law from his home state, Missouri.

"But more important, Taney said that the extraterritoriality of slavery in the territories or the states was guaranteed by the Constitution and that any interference with it, in this case by the Missouri Compromise, was utterly unconstitutional. This means there can be no decision against slavery in the territories until the convention meets to draw up a constitution for statehood. And that is popular sovereignty! It means the non-exclusion of slavery from any western territory, until the time of its statehood."[82]

---

82  Bestor, "State Sovereignty and Slavery: A Reinterpretation of Proslavery Constitutional Doctrine, 1846-1860," 117-80, and Richter, "Out of the Sahara of the Bozart: The Political Thought of John Wilkes Booth." The most comprehensive work on the Dred Scott decision is Don Fehrenbacher, *The Dred Scott Case: Its Significance in American Law and Politics* (New York: Oxford University Press, 1978). See also, F. H. Hodder, "Some Phases of the Dred Scott Case," *Mississippi Valley Historical Review*, 16 (June 1929), 3-22; and Bennett, *Forced into Glory*, 260-63, where he voices the opinion that Lincoln's concern with the constitutional issued raised by Dred Scott was an expression for white migration to the west free of any black competition, slave or free. This is not totally fair, because in his "House Divided" speech, Lincoln revealed that he feared that the U.S. Supreme Court would expand the Dred Scott decision to make slavery legal within all of the states, even the free ones. See Roy Basler (ed.), *The Collected Works of Abraham Lincoln* (9 vols., New Brunswick: Rutgers University Press, 1953), II, 464-65, for Lincoln's expert analysis of Dred Scott. See also, Alexander Gigante, "Slavery and a House Divided," at http://afroamhistory.about.com/library/prm/blhousedivided.htm. Lincoln's fear of legal slavery in all states and territories was threatened in Lemmon v. People of New York, but the case never reached the Supreme Court because of the war and its results." See Downey, *Civil War Lawyers*, 43-44.

# 5

## CORDON AGAINST SLAVERY

"The War Between the States was deliberately and personally conceived and its inauguration made by Abraham Lincoln, and he was personally responsible for forcing the war upon the South," Booth asserted with no hesitation in his next meeting with Sarah. [83] He called Secession "a fire lighted and fanned by Northern fanaticism," and said that Lincoln's nomination as the Republican presidential candidate was but a declaration of "war, war upon Southern institutions. His election proved it.[84] Miss Nettie, we would do well to remember the old adage: 'history is written by those who have hanged the heroes.'"[85]

"Is that not a bit cynical?"

"Not really," Booth retorted. "I am surprised at you. I thought you more a realist."

"I am a realist, but that does not make your statement about hanging the heroes any less cynical, does it?"

"But you do not contradict my assertion that Lincoln started the war on purpose."

"I do not, but you need to explain it further."

"To begin with, one must realize what was at stake in 1860—that abolition of slavery in the existing states was not the issue. In fact, Lincoln and the Republicans said that they were willing

---

83  Merrill D. Peterson, *Lincoln in American Memory* (Oxford University Press, 1994), 251, quoting the *Confederate Veteran*, 30 (1922), 286-86.
84  Rodehamel and Taper (eds.), *The Writings of John Wilkes Booth*, 59, 124.
85  Robert the Bruce in the voice-over introduction to the movie *Braveheart* (1995).

to guarantee slavery where it existed by a new irrevocable constitutional amendment, before the war put an end to it.

"Indeed, the only real way slavery could be destroyed in the states was by a constitutional amendment, which was practically impossible to achieve. This is because it takes three-fourths of the states to amend the Constitution, and the Slave South, being nearly half of the states, thus had a veritable veto. But, in agreeing to maintain slavery in the states where it existed, Lincoln and the Republicans never consented not to constrict slavery where it was or hamper the spread of slavery, elsewhere.[86]

"Before the creation of the Republican Party in 1854, no other political party had really seriously challenged the westward expansion of slavery.[87] By 1860, however, fortified by cobbling together the diverse supporters of what Southern apologist George Fitzugh called the pre-Civil War "infidel Isms of the North," ranging from Madmen, Madwomen, Bloomer-wearers, Men with beards, Dunkards, Muggletonians, Shakers, Spiritual Rappers, Come-outers, Groaners, Agrarians, Grahamites, Seventh-Day Adventists (Millerites), Quakers, Abolitionists Calvinists, Unitarians, Philosophers, Those against slavery in the territories, Anti-Masons, and Anti-Mormon polygamists, Did I miss any?"[88]

"I declare! I certainly hope not! I never heard of most of those."

"Only real Yankees ever have. Anyhow, Republican activists sent cases of "Beecher's Bibles (.52 cal. Breech-loading rifles) to

---

86  Bestor, "State Sovereignty and Slavery, 122-27.
87  David Brion Davis, "American Slavery and the American Revolution," in his *From Homicide to Slavery: Studies in American Culture* (New York: Oxford University Press, 1986), 299.
88  Kevin Phillips, *The Cousins' Wars: Religion, Politics, and the Triumph of Anglo-America* (New York: Basic Books, 1999), 353-62 (especially 357-58 and 362), and 383 (Fitzhugh quote).

'civilize' Kansas. No more 'milk and water' policy against slavery. Everyone now realized what Republican policy, despite all of its duplicitous protect slavery promises, meant for the future of the South and its domestic institutions. The Republicans would attack slavery as soon as Lincoln came into power."[89]

"And that is why you say Lincoln started the war?"

"Certainly! The Republican program against slavery, characterized by Charles Sumner, master orator and U.S. senator from Massachusetts, as making Freedom National and Slavery Sectional,[90] was comprised of two elements: The Cordon of Freedom, and Military Emancipation. The Cordon of Freedom was an old anti-slavery belief that if bondage could be isolated to the existing slave states with no hope for expansion into the West or the Caribbean, it would wither away in time and die out. Military Emancipation was the notion that should the South secede it would lose all the slavery protections guaranteed in the Constitution, and slavery could be abolished out-right by the advancing, all-conquering, Federal armies.

"Lincoln and the Republicans believed that their inability to impose the Cordon of Freedom legally or constitutionally before the war was because of the existence of what they saw as the 'Slave Power Conspiracy,' which they believed infected the Federal government at all levels. Between 1789 and 1861, in a nation where free, white males (potential voters) in the Northern states outnumbered Southern whites at least two to one, the South secured fully half of all major cabinet and diplomatic appointments, and had twenty-two extra representatives in the lower house of Congress from counting three-fifths of its slaves.

---

89   Don Fehrenbacher with Ward M. McAfee, *Slaveholding Republic: An Account of the United States Government's Relations to Slavery* (New York: Oxford University Press, 2001), 295-96.
90   James Oaks, *Freedom National: The Destruction of Slavery in the United States, 1861-1865* (New York: Norton, 2013), 32.

The Old South, more or less, according to this theory, unfairly and disproportionately ran the whole nation.[91]

"Not counting numerous clerkships, secretaries, sergeants at arms, and pages in every executive and congressional department of the federal government, which, in that age of difficult and expensive travel, frequently went to local Washingtonians, Marylanders, and Virginians (who generally backed the institution of slavery if they were not slaveholders themselves), individual presidential administrations were tended to be very lop-sided in their appointment policies. Fifty-one percent of John Adams' appointments were Southern slave owners; and, although Adams was a temporary apologist for the Old South's peculiar institution to get Virginia's support during the American Revolution and South Carolina's backing in his election to the Presidency, he reverted to being an opponent of slavery later in life. But Thomas Jefferson made around fifty-six percent of his appointments from the Old South, while Andrew Jackson found even more of his appointments among slaveholders.

"In the 62 years between 1789 and 1850, slaveholders controlled the presidency for 50 years, and five of these slaveholders (George Washington, Thomas Jefferson, James Madison, James Monroe, and Andrew Jackson) served two consecutive terms.

---

91  In general, see William L. Richter, *Historical Dictionary of the Old South* (Lanham, Md.: Scarecrow Press, 2013), 10-13. More specific studies include Larry Gara, "Slavery and the Slave Power: A Crucial Distinction," *Civil War History*, 15 (1969), 5-18; Alfred W. and Ruth G. Blumenrosen, *Slave Nation: How Slavery United the Colonies & Sparked the American Revolution* ((Napierville, Ills.: Sourcebooks, Inc., 2005); David Waldstreicher, *Slavery's Constitution from Revolution to Ratification* (New York: Hill & Wang, 2009); Paul Finkelman, *Slavery and the Founders: Race and Liberty in the Age of Jefferson* (Armonk, N.Y.: M.E. Sharpe, 1996); Garry Wills, *"Negro President": Jefferson and the Slave Power* (Boston: Houghton Mifflin Co., 2003); Davis Brion Davis, *The Slave Power Conspiracy and the Paranoid Style* (Baton Rouge: Louisiana State University Press, 1969); Leonard L. Richards, *The Slave Power: The Free North and Southern Domination, 1780-1860* (Baton Rouge: Louisiana State University Press, 2000). Don E. Fehrenbacher and Ward M. McAfee, *The Slaveholding Republic: An Account of the United States Government's Relations to Slavery* (New York: Oxford University Press, 2001), ix, see this as an unintended result over time, rather than a "conspiracy" intentionally installed at the beginning of the nation.

No Northerner was elected to the presidency more than once, regardless of his stance on slavery. The northern-born, pro-slave presidents of the 1850s (Millard Fillmore of New York, Franklin Pierce of New Hampshire, and James Buchanan of Pennsylvania) continued this pro-slavery trend to the Civil War.

"Additionally, the Speaker of the House generally was a slaveholder and the longest serving speakers were all Southerners, Henry Clay (Kentucky), Andrew Stevenson (Virginia), and Nathaniel Macon (North Carolina). The chairmen of the powerful House Ways and Means Committee (which determined what legislation reached the floor) were slaveholders most of the time, too. Over half of the Supreme Court justices from the same period were from the Old South, as were the two more important chief justices, John Marshall (Virginia) and Roger B. Taney (Maryland).

"There is more involved in this political ascendancy than the three-fifths compromise in the Constitution, which guaranteed the Old South twenty-two extra congressmen in the 1850s, based on the enumeration of slaves in the U.S. census. This Southern dominance was made possible by the support that non-slave holding, Northern congressmen, Democrats after the rise of Jackson, rendered to Southern positions on slavery. These men actually came to the fore during the debates on the Missouri Compromise. It was their votes that made the adjustment of sectional argument over the admission of Missouri as a slave state possible. They were condemned as 'unblushing advocates of domestic slavery' by their opponents in the North.

"But it took the invective of a Southerner, who distrusted them as much as their Northern critics, to give them the sobriquet by which they would be forever known all the way to the

Civil War. John Randolph of Roanoke, Virginia, called them 'doughfaces,' Northerners of Southern principle, and he despised them for being bought off by political patronage and deemed them unreliable for the future.[92]

"Martin Van Buren organized these doughfaces, and others of like philosophy, into a paramount part of his New York political machine, the Albany Regency. Known as Buck Tails, from their identifying hat adornments and, buttressed by New Englanders, Pennsylvanians, and North Westerners of similar political leanings, they became an important segment of Van Buren's new national Democratic Party that made Andrew Jackson and his successors president."[93]

"I did not know that Van Buren was so important. He was a failed President because of the, how do you say it? The Panic of 1837, right? I remember my father talking about that."

"But he was a great political organizer. Unfortunately, Randolph proved correct in his prediction of their final fecklessness, but it would take the bitter anti-slavery quarrels of the 1850s and the rise of the Republican Party to cause the doughfaces to break their bond with the Old South. Those who had stayed loyal to the Southern wing of the Democratic Party, the old Jacksonians from New York and elsewhere, men who had traditionally delivered 15-25 votes in Congress to protect Southern rights in slaves and territorial expansion, ultimately either became strong anti-slavery men or lost election to Republicans or Free Soil independents. The concept of the Slave Power Conspiracy was impossible to beat."

---

92  On Randolph, see Russell Kirk, *John Randolph of Roanoke: A Study in American Politics* (Indianapolis: Liberty Press, 1978).
93  On Van Buren, see Robert V. Remini, *Martin Van Buren and the Making of the Democratic Party* (New York: Norton, 1970 ed.) and Richard P. McCormick, *The Second American Party System: Party Formation in the Jacksonian Era* (Chapel Hill: University of North Carolina Press, 1966).

"I reckon!" Sarah interjected.

"Almost everyone, who was anyone, North or South, believed in it. Yankees like U.S. Senator William H. Seward (New York, Republican presidential candidate and later Lincoln's secretary of state), one-time U.S Representative Abraham Lincoln (Illinois, president of the United States-to-be), and U.S. Senator Thomas Morris (Ohio, who coined and popularized the term "Slave Power Conspiracy" during the Jackson administration), backed the notion of a Slave Power Conspiracy.

"So did Southerners like U.S. Senator James H. Hammond (South Carolina secessionist), and James L. Petigru (who called South Carolina "too small for a Republic and too large for an insane asylum"), and U.S. Representative Alexander H. Stephens (Georgia, close congressional friend of Lincoln, later vice president of the Confederacy, who called slavery the "cornerstone" of Southern civilization).

"That is amazing!"

"To sum up, the ability of the Old South to control much of antebellum national politics, through the use of the clause in the Constitution that based representation in Congress on the white population plus three-fifths of the Old South's slaves, led to the notion that there was a conspiracy to deny the more populous North its fair share of national power, which came to be labeled the Slave Power Conspiracy. But the real key to the Old South's ability to control the government came from its Northern allies, the doughfaces, men who had disappeared by the time of the congressional by-election of 1858 and presidential election of 1860 in favor of Republicans. With them went an important political influence that led to Republican victory and boosted the Old South's interest in secession. By 1860, the Old South could still block legislation, but it could no longer advance its program defending the extraterritoriality of slavery it the territories because of the loss of its Northern allies."

"So the protection of slavery outside the South, like in the Western Territories had been compromised." Sarah said. She thought a moment and went on, "and so had expansion into area of the Caribbean, like the Knights of the Golden Circle wanted!"

"Correct! Despite its constitutional victory in the Dred Scott Case, the South felt the loss of its political power in Congress as early as 1859, when the Whig Representative from Baltimore's Fourth Congressional District, in my home state of Maryland, Henry Winter Davis, switched sides to vote Republican William Pennington in as speaker of the house, and was promptly censured by the State Legislature. But the damage was done. In control of one house of Congress, the Republicans were on the march to a presidential electoral victory in 1860, with only 39% of the popular vote.[94]

"Their cordon against slavery had finally become a possibility," Sarah mused

"Yes, and in spite of all this, I was still a cooperationist and against secession in 1861."

"I am flat worn out, Mr. Booth. Can we call it a day?"

---

94 William W. Freehling, *The Road to Disunion II: Secesionists Triumphant* (New York: Oxford University Press, 2007), 323. See also, in general, Brenda Weinapple, *Ecstatic Nation: Confidence, Crisis, and Compromise, 1848-1877* (New York: Harper, 2013).

# 6

## THE DISSATISFIED WHIG

"The major charges I will advance against Lincoln here," Booth began, "are sufficient to impeach the most famous and respected of public men, as the Republican Party claims he is. More would only overdo."⁹⁵

"Gracious!" Sarah exclaimed.

"Lincoln was a complicated man whose public life went through several periods," Booth said. "The first was when he was a Whig, which stretched from his becoming an adult until the passage of the Kansas-Nebraska Act in 1854. This Lincoln was the economic man or 'High Whig' influenced by Henry Clay's American System. Here he believed that law was law and scripture was scripture. But he evidenced two disturbing qualities that marked him as a dangerous man. These were his faith in necessity and a feeling that he alone knew its disposition for the future, both revealed in his 1838 'Springfield Young Men's Lyceum Speech.'"

"What was that?" Sarah asked.

---

95   M. E. Bradford, "The Lincoln Legacy: A Long View," in his *Remembering Who We Are: Reflections of a Southern Conservative* (Athens: University of Georgia Press, 1985), 144. Many of Bradford's arguments were presaged in brief in Frank Meyer, "Lincoln Without Rhetoric," *National Review*, 17 (August 24, 1965), 725 and his "Lincoln Again," *ibid.*, 18 (January 25, 1966), 71, 85. See also, Thomas J. Pressly, "'Emancipating Slaves, Enslaving Free Men': Modern Libertarians Interpret the United States Civil War," *Civil War History*, 46 (No. 3, 2000), 254-65; Wilson (ed.), *A Defender of Southern Conservatism*, 19. For a critique of Bradford, see John McKee Barr, *Loathing Lincoln: An American Tradition from the Civil War to the Present* (Baton Rouge: Louisiana State University Press, 2014), 11-12, 231-41, 304, 336.

"A speech that Lincoln gave as a young man, in which he saw himself as essentially the man on a white horse, an elected dictator, who would free the salves and enslave the white men. You see, on all levels, Lincoln was not a man of the people. He believed in republican government of the best citizens, not democracy of the masses. Lincoln married into the Todd-Stuart-Edwards clique of Illinois politics, and he lusted after office like most men lust after women and money."[96]

Sarah snickered. She knew much, perhaps too much, about lusting after women and money. After all, she was lusted after often—indeed, she really would have had it no other way.

As Booth saw it, "Lincoln's economic policy was full of contradictions. Far from being the little man's president as reputed, Lincoln supported and was supported by great wealth. From his first days in 1832 at New Salem, Illinois, to the end of his life, Lincoln supported the party of privilege and monopoly in the Antebellum Era, the Whigs. It is something requiring explanation," Booth contended, "that Lincoln, who is held up as an apostle of liberty, who himself along the way said so much of the Declaration of Independence and Jefferson, turned in his youth to the rhetorician and Whig Party leader Henry Clay and clung to him into maturity, and followed his lead essentially to the end."[97]

"Clay was the champion of that political system which doles out favors to the strong in order to keep their adherence to the government," Booth said. "Lincoln was ashamed of the poverty of his youth and moved as an adult to be one of, and associate with, the rich. While there are many tales of Lincoln defending the poor in court, his real income came from being a corporate

---

96 Edgar Lee Masters, *Lincoln, the Man* (New York: Dodd, Meade, 1931), 68-73, 202, 215-18. For a critique of Masters, see Barr, *Loathing Lincoln*, 187-93, 331-32, 335-36, and *passim.*
97 *Ibid.*, 3, 4, 26.

lawyer, the representative of the Illinois Central Railroad which drove squatters and settlers, like the Lincoln family of his youth, from their desired rights of way."

"He must have been a busy man," Sarah opined.

"Actually," Booth went on, "Lincoln as essentially a lazy attorney who relied on his partner, Billy Herndon, to do all the legwork on a case.[98] Lincoln's laziness made him not an original thinker. For this he relied economically on Henry Clay's American System. This was a program, originally developed by economist Matthew Carey (Clay was an indolent thinker, too), which promoted a national banking system, internal improvements, and the liberation of American slaves and their return to Africa. Clay originally hoped to finance this with a high tariff designed to exclude foreign imports and the sale of land in the western territories at $1.25 an acre. But by the 1850s, the notion of land sales had evaporated in favor of homesteading the land for free, causing the rest of the program to rely on the tariff alone for its financing—a tariff paid predominantly by the South, which imported European goods in exchange for its cotton."[99]

"No wonder the South seceded," Sarah mused.

"It was for this reason that Lincoln refused to join the initially antislavery Republican Party," Booth contended. "Until it adopted the American System, which had been continually rejected by the American voter from Thomas Jefferson to James Buchanan, the Republicans had little to offer Whigs like Lincoln. But once this was achieved by 1856," Booth explained, "Lincoln and the Republican Party were chiefly concerned with

---

98  Ibid., 11, 13, 84, 116, 118, 122, 141. See also, Martha L Benner and Cullom Davis (eds.), *The Law Practice of Abraham Lincoln: Complete Documentary Edition* (3 DVDs, Champaign: University of Illinois Press, 2000). See also, Gerald J. Prokopowicz, "'A Superior Opportunity of Being a Good Man," at http://www.papersofabrahamlincoln.org/DEReview.htm.
99  Masters, *Lincoln, the Man*, 122, 297. For the American System, see Glyndon G. Van Deusen, *The Jacksonian Era, 1828-1848* (New York: Harper & Row, Publishers, 1959), 51.

letting in a new set of thieves to the public treasury, but they came in through the election of 1860 under the guise of piety and humanitarianism, the Cordon of Freedom. The Republicans then proceeded to loot the nation during the hostilities and the Reconstruction that followed under the cover of a war to liberate the slaves and preserve the Union.

"The corruptions of the Republican Era began under Lincoln's direction or sponsorship", Booth said, "under the guise of military necessity.[100] Basically," Booth explained, "creditors got the upper hand over debtors of the first time since Andrew Jackson destroyed the Second Bank of the United States. The government became the sponsor of a great transfer of wealth using the protective tariff on foreign imports (which rose from 18.84% in 1861 to 47.56% in 1865), the massive funding of internal improvements (especially the Pacific Railroad), a national banking system (that sponsored the creation of $480 million in fiat paper money to enhance credit for big business at the expense of small businesses and farms), and the Homestead Act (in which less than 19% of the lands have gone to actual farmers, the rest to big businesses). The Northern policy of importing immigrants with the promise of this land, only to force them into the ranks of General Grant's meat grinder or into near slavery in the cities of the East," Booth said, "requires little comment."

"From the beginning of the Republican Party Lincoln warned his associates not to talk about their views on these subjects," Booth asserted. "Lincoln blithely encouraged the rotten army

---

100 See, *e.g.*, Samuel Langhorne Clemens [Mark Twain] and Charles Dudley Warner, *The Gilded Age* (Hartford: American Publishing Co., 1873); Mark W. Summers, *Era of Good Stealings* (New York: Oxford University Press, 1993). See also Summers other pieces, "'A Band of Brigands': Albany Lawmakers and Republican National Politics, 1860," *Civil War History*, 30 (1984), 101-19; *The Plundering Generation: Corruption and the Crisis of the Union* (New York: Oxford University Press, 1987); and *Railroads, Reconstruction, and the Gospel of Prosperity: Aid Under the Radical Republicans* (Princeton: Princeton University Press, 1984).

contracts system, massive thefts of Southern property, allowing special cronies and favorites of his friends to trade in Southern cotton, and a calculated use of the patronage and the pork barrel that resulted in almost $10 million being pumped into local Republican organizations. All of this was accomplished on Lincoln's watch," Booth concluded.[101]

"Then Lincoln was crooked?" Sarah asked.

"Well, Lincoln himself seemed monetarily honest," Booth said, "but he turned a blind eye to what was happening. But he did see to it Congress enacted the American System, the basis of the corruption, which he signed. And he kept the war going, refusing all attempts at compromise. The reason was that Lincoln and the master minds of the Republican Party, the offshoots of Henry Clay, had for further purposes, seeing the industrial advantages that now revealed themselves," Booth said. "They cared nothing for the Union compared to what they cared for money and power."[102]

"Money and power? What about slavery and emancipation?" Sarah questioned.

"Well, above all, Lincoln was a political chameleon of many colors. In northern Illinois (above the National Road,[103] settled by Yankees), according to his arch opponent, Stephen A. Douglas, Lincoln was a 'black abolitionist,' in Egypt, that is Southern Illinois (below the National Road, settled by Southerners), he was a 'white supremacist,' and in middle Illinois, Lincoln was something in between, as the audience called for. He was against slavery in the abstract alone. In reality he was for leaving the institution be in the South, but he was for keeping it

---

101 Bradford, "Lincoln Legacy," 146-49. See also the exchange between Bradford and Gabor S. Boritt, in Boritt (ed.), *The Historian's Lincoln: Pseudohistory, Psychohistory, and History* , 87-123.
102 Masters, *Lincoln, the Man*, 214-32, 444-45, 446, 483, 487.
103 Old U.S. Highway 40, roughly Interstate 70 today.

out of the territories, especially above the Missouri Compromise line. Beyond that, between 1858 and 1860 Lincoln stated he was against equal rights for blacks at least twenty-one times, and for white supremacy eight times.[104]

"Really?" Sarah interjected with amazement.

"Oh, yeah. The key to understanding Lincoln," Booth maintained, "is that, like his political mentor, Henry Clay, he was against slavery in the abstract. He rarely concerned himself with real slavery or real blacks. Lincoln was from Illinois, the state with the worst Black Code of any free state and many slave states, which Illinois toughened six times between statehood and the Civil War. None of that bothered Lincoln. He supported Illinois' Black Code and the Federal Fugitive Slave Act of 1850 without protest. He also introduced five emancipation decrees, all of which called for gradual, compensated abolition, with a long apprenticeship program and compulsory colonization abroad in Africa (Lincoln believed that all American slaves originally came from Liberia), Haiti (Isle la Vache) or Central America (where the colony was named Lincolnia by a cynical press), or locally in Florida or Texas for all those freed.[105]

"To justify the Republican war," Booth asserted, "Lincoln had to get the South to fire the first shot to distract Northern opponents from the Republican economic program through a war-inspired patriotism for Union. This maneuvering and duplicity surrounding Ft. Sumter and Lincoln Administration relief efforts dovetailed with a Confederate objective—to get the rest of the slave South to secede and join the seven states already compromising the Confederacy. Here, both sides were half successful with four of the eight slave states left in the Union leaving

---

104  Bennett, *Forced into Glory*, 74, 219-27, 229-30, 305-34.
105  *Ibid.*, 183-86, 188, 192-96, 197, 227, 233, 237-38, 241, 242, 244-45, 261, 267, 271-85, 286-97, 381-87, 452-65, 527, 539, 546-47, 553-54.

over Lincoln's call for volunteers from all the states to quell what he and his cohorts called the War of the Rebellion. Lincoln also claimed secession to be illegal, following a dubious constitutional theory advanced (1832) and later repudiated (1850) by Daniel Webster, that the Union preceded the states in origin."

Booth again called this, "Lincoln's Spectacular Lie'. There is no clause creating perpetual Union in the Constitution. The states had declared independence and signed the Treaty of Paris in 1783 as separate entities, and that three states (Virginia, New York, and Rhode Island) had ratified the Constitution, reserving secession as a right that might be exercised later."[106]

The second period of Lincoln's political life Booth called "the artificial Puritan years, from 1854 to Lincoln's accession to the presidency. Here Lincoln began to place more faith in necessity and spoke out on the slavery issue wholly for effect, opposing the Kansas-Nebraska Act, especially demanding no extension of slavery into the western territories. He showed a sense of his own destiny as the Caesar he had spoken of in his Lyceum Address, who would gain absolute power by 'emancipating slaves or enslaving free men.' Lincoln had begun to mix law with scripture.

"Finally, there was the Cromwellian phase of the public Lincoln during the war itself," which Booth called "the worst. The real is defined in terms of what is to come and only Lincoln understood what it was. He emancipated the slaves and enslaved the free, because God told him so. Lincoln's law was now scripture.[107]

---

[106] DiLorenzo, *The Real Lincoln.*, 5, 85-129.
[107] Bradford, "The Lincoln Legacy: A Long View," 143; and M. E. Bradford, "Dividing the House: The Gnosticism of Lincoln's Political Rhetoric," *Modern Age*, 23 (Winter 1979), 10-21, especially 20-21. The second stage of Lincoln's political development is detailed in Bradford, "Lincoln and the Language of hate and Fear: A Southern View," in his *Against the Barbarians and Other Reflections on Familiar Themes* (Columbia: University of Missouri Press, 1992), 229-45.

"God told him, huh? Is that not a form of blasphemy?" Sarah was dismayed.

"Yes, but Lincoln's willingness to be associated with 'higher law' doctrine allowed him to ally his trampling of the Constitution and law with the purpose of God," Booth grumped.[108] "Lincoln, I hear, was immersed in Hebraic-Christianity from his earliest years which is something deeper than belonging to a church or professing a creed. He was a Jehovah [Old Testament] man all his life; and he early realized the advantage of using the Bible for his appeals to the people. Indeed," Booth claimed, "Lincoln was the first president to invest the government, his government, with Christianity and to put its poisonous inoculation deep down in the flesh of the Republic."

Booth went on, "in Lincoln's case the subjugation of the South had to be smeared over with religion, with the whole rank and file of Calvinism, with the nauseating piety and sadistic righteousness of America as a Christian nation. The War Between the States was for God," Booth said, "and Lincoln made it so. But there was nothing in Lincoln's religious philosophy, which forbade riches and privileges; it was rather the contrary. Hence he laid the foundation for missions of irreverence and plunder." Booth adjudged that "Lincoln was truly America's patron saint of despotism, big business, and hypocrisy. "[I]t is not for lack of facts that the myths have grown up and are growing up about Lincoln," Booth concluded. "The facts have been disregarded in order that the portrait of him might be drawn that the Republicans wanted."[109]

"So the Lincoln we know is a false image!" Sarah said.

"Exactly! Booth trumpeted. Booth assailed more of Lin-

---

108 Masters, *Lincoln, the Man.*, 81-82.
109 Masters, *Lincoln, the Man*, 21, 34, 124, 149, 150, 151, 154-56, 480, 490, 491, 493-94.

coln's record as Cromwellian president. "Lincoln's dishonesty and obfuscation with respect to the African Americans, slave and free, was a key ingredient to Lincoln's political success," Booth pointed out. "Lincoln was able to appear 'anti-Southern or anti-slavery' without at the same time appearing to disparage the beginnings of the Republic, which was pro-Southern and pro-slavery. He moreover mastered this position without appearing pro-Negro. He was the first Northern politician of any rank to successfully combine these attitudes," according to Booth.

"Lincoln's political skill and duplicitous rhetoric on the freed slaves' place in American society allowed him to combine and unite elements in the North that might ordinarily have been hostile," Booth went on. "It enabled him to compromise the Northern Democratic party by culling out its antislavery members and thus destroying the traditional national Democratic majority that had dominated American politics since the days of Thomas Jefferson. Lincoln insisted the black race was included in the Declaration of Independence ('all men are created equal'), but hinted that this need not apply to blacks in the North—or even in the South, after it had been morally purged of the 'peculiar institution,' as Southerners like to refer to slavery.

"Well, I do declare!" Sarah muttered, almost whispered, as she wrote furiously.

"Under Lincoln," Booth maintained, "once the nation was freed from the blight of slavery, African Americans would experience nothing more than a technical freedom comprised of empty words.[110] Lincoln left the nation with a durable heritage of pious

---

110 William C. Harris, "The Hampton Roads Peace Conference: A Final Test of Lincoln's Presidential Leadership," *Journal of the Abraham Lincoln Association* (Winter 2000), 31-61. There is some dispute if Lincoln's phrase to what would happen in the South after the war, "root hog, or die," applied to whites, blacks, or both. See arguments in Lincoln Discussion Symposium, Books, Mr. Lee, posts 8, 18, 20, 22, 23. But the Vice President of the Confederacy,

self-congratulation. Victorious Yankee America now evidences a habit of concealing its larger objectives behind a façade of racial generosity, of using the Negro as a reason for policies and laws which make only minimal alterations in his condition, and of seeming a great deal more than it is truly willing to give."[111]

"Another thing Lincoln did upon being elected president," Booth continued, "was to promise the South that his administration would not interfere with slavery where it existed, and backed a proposed constitutional amendment to that effect. He had his cabinet pledge to support the Fugitive Slave Act of 1850. Lincoln would not, however, compromise on Republican opposition to slavery in the territories, which Congress would end in June 1862. Even with the firing on Ft. Sumter, Lincoln stuck to his position that a rapid return of the South would preserve slavery as an institution. When individual army tried to free the slaves in their command areas, Lincoln reprimanded, sacked, or demoted them.[112]

"Well, Miss Nettie," Booth said. "You are undoubtedly tired of writing and I am tired of talking. How about you tale a look at my leg and we continue this tomorrow?"

---

Alexander Stephens, claimed it referred to the freed slaves alone, *New York Times*, Article on Hampton Roads Conference, June 26, 1865. Stephens made the same reference to the slaves in his memoirs, *A Constitutional View of the Late War between the States* . . . (2 vols., Philadelphia: National Publishing Company, 1870), II, 615.

111 Bradford, "Lincoln Legacy," 144-46. See also, Bradford, "Dividing the House," 10-21, *passim*; and Bradford, "Commentary on 'Lincoln and the Economics of the American Dream'," in Gabor S. Boritt (ed.), *The Historian's Lincoln: Pseudohistory, Psychohistory, and History* (Urbana: University of Illinois Press, 1988), 107-123, and Dilorenzo, *The Real Lincoln*, 3-4, 10-32.

112 Bennett, *Forced into Glory*, 5, 13-14, 30-31, 246-54, 336, 337, 339, 340, 346-48, 358.

# 7

# Unconstitutional Presidential Dictator

"Lincoln's corruption was not only economic," Booth complained the next time he and Sarah met. He seemed anxious to start lambasting the Lincoln administration right off. "Much of the corruption was governmental, resulting in Lincoln's expansion of the powers of the presidency and his alteration of the basis for the Federal Union. Indeed, Lincoln defined himself through his use of the presidential war powers. There were no logical limits to Lincoln's use of the war powers so long as he could use them in a holy cause. Others have maintained that Lincoln acted much as the Committee of Public Safety during the French Revolution, except there were no executions on a massive scale. Since Lincoln's War of the Rebellion was an internal contest (among the states), it became an engine not only for defeating the Confederacy and preserving the Union. It also became an instrument for transforming the Union's very nature," Booth posited.

"Well, this war seems to have done that!" Sarah commented.

"There is reason to believe that there had to be a war to end slavery in the United States was to guarantee the institution of Henry Clay's American System," Booth said, "of which Lincoln was the prime proponent in 1860. Under the cover of saving the Union, Lincoln, by executive fiat, and the new Republican majority in both houses of Congress, could pass their economic system, so long blocked by Democrats, particularly from the South. Indeed, Lincoln seethed in frustration at the lack of constitutional and popular support for the American system. Lincoln's plan was an old Eighteenth Century mercantile ideology, a system that used faulty economic theory to build empires and subsidize individuals or groups or industries favored by the state. It was financed by a protective tariff, which prevented free trade competition and raised local prices to consumers. It was a fancy cover for corporate welfare for select Yankee industries.[113]

"Because Southern Democrats had been so long the central group around which opponents to the American System had coalesced," Booth said, "it was imperative to keep the South out of the Union long enough to allow the Republican majority to enact its programs as war measures. By late 1862 or early 1863, Congress had enacted the American System in full with the new National Banking System and its paper money to inflate credit, the Pacific Railroad Act, and the Protective Tariff. Indeed, the tariff with its new rate of 80% was so central to Republican economic aspirations that secession was merely an extension of the old Nullification argument over the Tariff of Abominations of Andrew Jackson's day. And like in 1832, Lincoln expected that the South would come crawling back to the Union, in time."[114]

"Well, the South certainly has lost this war on the battlefield," Sarah said glumly.

Sarah's comment brought Booth to what he called "Lincoln's unconstitutional and illegal centralization of political authority in the Federal government, embodied in one word— despotism. From the time of Jefferson, for over fifty years, republican (not Republican) principles of state sovereignty and government of

---

113 DiLorenzo, *The Real Lincoln*, 3, 4-5, 54-84, 234.
114 *Ibid.*, 118-19, 121, 126, 128-29.

the people had held sway over the American government. But all the while," Booth asserted conspiratorially, "a patient, secret, self-conscious influence was gathering power—appropriating it from the people and the states and storing it in a central government for the purposes of business and money, and under the guise of law and order, of religion, and even of liberty. From the very first Lincoln was a centralist, a privilegist, an adherent of the non-principled Whig Party, which had laid the foundation of the Republican Party," Booth said.[115]

"Lincoln's Illinois opponent for the U.S. senate seat in 1858, Stephen A. Douglas, tried to warn the voters what Lincoln was about during the Lincoln-Douglas debate at Chicago," Booth maintained. "Douglas believed that the American system would have to impose a uniformity upon the states from Washington, D.C. to function. Deep in its haughty plans, Douglas said, was a hidden agenda to abolish the state legislatures, blot out state sovereignty, merge the rights and sovereignty of the (then) thirty-two states into one consolidated empire, and vest the Federal government with state police power and the right to make all domestic law.

"This was in violation of the cardinal instruction of American government," Booth stated, "where the state legislatures are constituent assemblies that can pass any law not expressly prohibited by state and Federal Constitutions, while Congress is not a constituent assembly and can pass only those laws warranted by an actual grant of power from the states in the Federal Constitution. There would be a uniformity of despotism throughout the land," Booth claimed, "exactly what the plutocratic interests of the time wished, and they were deploying the abolitionists, who

---

115 *Ibid.*, 497.

knew nothing about the nature of the Union and cared less, to bring this consideration about."[116]

"This sounds most frightful," Sarah shuddered as chills ran up her back.

"Upon entering office, Lincoln effected many unconstitutional acts—the invasion of the South, the declaration of martial law, the creation of a naval blockade of Southern ports, the suspension of the writ of habeas corpus, the imprisonment of dissenters without trial, the shut down of critical newspapers, the censorship of telegraphic transmissions, the nationalizing of private railroads, the creation new states without the consent of the citizens of the states from which they came, the interference in local elections by Federal troops, the deportation a member of Congress, the confiscation of private property and firearms, and the gutting of the Ninth and Tenth Amendments."

"Do not Northern people see this?" Sarah inquired.

"It is most dismaying that while the Northern public recognized Lincoln as dictator," Booth asserted, "they have usually tempered their notice by calling him a good or great one. The basic theme is that Lincoln's violation of the Constitution actually preserved it and those who disagree are dismissed as extremists. The wartime Republicans were not so smug. Congress passed an indemnity act to declare all presidential, cabinet, and military actions valid in 1863. The measure passed the House of Representatives but not the Senate. The presiding officer of the Senate was up to the task—he simply declared it passed. [117]

"The result", according to Booth, "was a bevy of unconstitutional Lincolnian acts in response to the secession of the South that are glossed over with the remark that what he did before

---
116 Ibid., 302, 345.
117 Ibid., 5-6, 130-69. For a different view, see John Avery Emison, *Lincoln Ueber Alles: Dictatorship Comes to America* (Gretna, Louisiana: Pelican Press, 2009).

Congress met on July 4, 1861, was validated by that Congress and made lawful for his great purpose of saving the Union. But Lincoln acted during that time and others intentionally, when Congress was out of session, as a satrap with full despotic power and his rightful masters, the people, had had no word to say about it. He ruled exactly as did the British King Charles I or Oliver Cromwell—without Parliament. [118]

"How so?" Sarah asked.

"Lincoln increased the size of the regular army," Booth said," circumvented Congress by calling up the militia and volunteers with the connivance of Republican state governors, spent funds appropriated for one governmental agency in another, suspended the writ of habeas corpus, replaced civil courts with military commissions, imposed an illegal blockade against the South, declared privateers with letters of marque to be pirates (the Declaration of Paris in 1865 had outlawed privateers, but the U.S. had failed to sign on), arrested suspect members of the Maryland state legislature to guarantee a Union majority, ignored a decision of the Chief Justice of the United States Supreme court while riding circuit, created a national police force to enforce loyalty, and invaded a foreign land, the Confederacy, or as dismissive Yankees liked to refer to it, 'Jeff Davis' Wheel Barrow Concern.' It was a coup d'etat in every essential feature," Booth complained, "a government made a nation from a confederacy of states by the glorious acts of an army headed by Lincoln." In Booth's most damning statement, "You know, the Constitution was shot to pieces, literally shot to death at Gettysburg.[119]

"Thus Lincoln became our first dictatorial president as he summoned the militia, spent unauthorized millions, sanctioned

---

118 DiLorenzo, *The Real Lincoln*, 113, 373, 399-400.
119 *Ibid.*, 4, 398-414, 422.

recruiting, decreed a blockade, defied the Supreme Court, and pledged the nation's credit. He also established new units of government, appointed military officers to rule over the conquered sections of the South, seized property, arrested as many as 20,000 and put them in a Yankee 'Bastille,'[120] closed over 300 newspapers, imported at least 500,000 foreign mercenaries (immigrants), and interfered in local elections in 1864 that garnered him a second term (when 38,000 votes might have changed the result). He also made a new state out of an old one using creative constitutional theories, dismissing it all as 'expedient.'"[121]

"Why that is awful!" Sarah remonstrated.

"Oh! There is more. As the action of Congress demonstrated," Booth maintained, "Lincoln abandoned the accepted international rules of war, which had just been codified in Geneva in 1863, and micro-managed the war effort himself. Lincoln initiated his own code of war, the so-called Lieber Code, which had an important exemption clause at the end that permitted military commanders to ignore it if necessary. Federal armies practiced rampant vandalism without any Lincoln rebuke," Booth said. "Lincoln had the South punished for its intransigence by burning out towns and sacking plantations."[122]

"How positively awful," Sarah said emphatically.

"Even more 'expedient' and more damning," in Booth's eyes, which were blazing as black as burning coals, "was Lincoln's role as military leader, as commander and selector of Northern generals,

---

120 See, *e.g.*, John A Marshall, *American Bastille: A History of the Illegal Arrests and Imprisonment of American Citizens in the Northern and Border States on Account of their Political Opinions During the Late Civil War* (2 vols., Philadelphia: Thomas W. Hartley & Co., 1883).
121 Bradford, "Lincoln Legacy," 149-50.
122 Dilorenzo, *The Real Lincoln,* 6-7, 171-99. Whether Yankee occupation practices in the conquered South were measured and more-or-less controlled or vicious and running rampant is argued by Mark Grimsley, *The Hard Hand of War: Union Military Policy Toward Southern Civilians, 1861-1865* (New York: Cambridge University Press, 1995); and Walter Brian Cisco, *War Crimes Against Southern Civilians* (Gretna, La.: Pelican Publishing Company, 2007).

chief commissary of Federal forces, and head of government in dealing with the leaders of an opposing power. In this role the image of Lincoln grows to very dark—indeed," Booth whispered, "almost sinister." Basically, Booth maintained that Lincoln did his best to keep the war going at all cost until he had achieved his domestic political purposes. He appointed known corruptionists, at lower levels and winked at their activities, even after he had to fire Secretary of War Simon Cameron as a sacrificial lamb, in favor of Edwin McM. Stanton in January 1862.

"But all such mendacity was nothing in comparison to the price in blood paid for Lincoln's attempts to give the nation a genuine Republican [military] hero," Booth argued. "Until Generals U. S. Grant, W. T. Sherman, and P. H. Sheridan emerged late in the war, Yankee generals seemed to disapprove of Lincoln's policies or character. Lincoln threw many of the professionals (G. B. McClellan, FitzJohn Porter, W. B. Franklin, and D. C. Buell) to the Radical Republican wolves on the congressional Joint Committee on the Conduct of the War, which included as its only Democrat our present Chief Executive, Andrew Johnson. Then he assigned 'Republican' generals, champions of the 'new freedom,'" in Booth's words (taken from "The 'Gettysburg Address"), "in their places (N. P. "Commissary" Banks [who supplied Confederate troops through his constant losses on the battlefields], B. F. "Beast" Butler [who looted Louisiana and the Gulf coast, while declaring New Orleans women who opposed him to be common prostitutes], J. C. Frémont [first Republican presidential candidate in 1865], John Pope [son of an old family friend], Franz Sigel [prominent German political leader], Lew Wallace [later author of Ben Hur], "Fightin' Joe" Hooker [who immodestly offered to become America's first military dictator], A. E. Burnside [who admitted to his inadequacies before he took command], and J. A. McClernand [a loyal Democrat convert from Illinois]). Unfortunately, all of them stunk militarily."

"That is truly outrageous!" Sarah cried.

"All Lincoln asked of the ordinary Billy Yank," Booth said, " was that he be prepared to give himself up to no real purpose—at least until Father Abraham found a general with proper moral and political credentials to lead him to Richmond. The heroes he found to lead his armies were the most vicious practitioners of war to date, laying the South to waste. In 1864, as in 1861, Lincoln rejected out of hand all peace feelers from the Confederate side, regardless of terms.[123] He wanted total victory," Booth asserted. "He needed a still-resisting, impenitent Confederacy to justify his 1864 re-election." Booth airily blamed "the deaths of over 100,000 Americans on Lincoln's refusing an 'inexpedient' peace."[124]

"Indeed," Booth believed, "Lincoln was a cold man in general, referring to his acquaintances solely by their family names. He was much like the icy French revolutionary leader Maximilien Robespierre, but at least Lincoln possessed a marvelous sense of humor. This, combined with his intellectual and critical faculties, coupled with a sort of sluggishness and indifference, created a man ordinarily full of black despondency, who gloried in cruel, insensible tales of the destruction of the South, dismissing the hundred of thousands of casualties as God's will, though the whole land be made one tomb. But Lincoln's psyche was tempered with a strange duality," Booth admitted. "He also had a bright side, as seen in his assertion of 'with malice toward none.'"[125]

---

123 Frank H. Severance, *The Peace Conference at Niagara Falls in 1864* (Ithaca: Cornell University Library, 1914).
124 Masters, *Lincoln, the Man.*, 150-53.
125 Bennett, *Forced into Glory,* 139, 140, 142, 143, 145, 244, 427, 429, 431.

"That is his bright side? After he had welshed on so many promises already?" Sarah said, amazed.

Booth chuckled at Sarah's anger. "Next," Booth said, "I charge Lincoln with causing the war in the first place, the most serious of Lincoln's violations of the presidential responsibility. Lincoln well knew that his accession to office would produce a crisis of Union. But once secession took place, Lincoln expected to defeat it swiftly with a combination of persuasion, force, and Southern loyalty to the Union. The last of these," Booth stated, "Lincoln completely overestimated. Lincoln never expected a full-scale Southern revolution, a revolution of all classes of white men against the way he and some of his supporters thought."[126]

"Lincoln hoped for some small insurrection," Booth surmised, "something that he could use to unite the nation and stop secession cold. He needed a crisis, and to keep the United States Congress out of session, so that he could institute his new political order through executive fiat as war measures. Lincoln also refused to publicize the South's offer to pay for Federal installations like Sumter, and to keep the Mississippi River open to commerce. It might have led to business as usual, compromise as in the past.[127]

"Lincoln directed the nation away from the usual instinct to agree with the Constitution," Booth said, "to see law as a means to limit government and the authority of temporary majorities, and of revisions in the law as the product of the ordinary push and pull within a pluralistic society, not as a response to the

---

[126] The notion that Lincoln never was much of a Southerner despite his Southern birth, is in William J. Cooper, "The Critical Signpost on the Journey toward Secession," *Journal of Southern History*, 77 (No. 1, February 2011), 16. A contrary view of Lincoln as perpetual and sympathetic Southerner, is in James G. Randall, *Lincoln and the South* (Baton Rouge: Louisiana State University Press, 1946).

[127] Roy P. Basler (ed.), *The Collected Works of Abraham Lincoln* (8 vols. and index, New Brunswick: Rutgers University Press, 1953), VIII, 29-30, 41-42, 379-85, 402, 403. The First Inaugural Speech is in Basler (ed.), *Collected Works*, IV, 262-71.

extralegal authority of some admirable abstraction like equality. Lincoln's cult of equality is a secular religion, and most misery is caused by the pursuit of abstract happiness, which can never be achieved.[128]

"Lincoln has opened the way for the development of an omnipresent president who as a spokesman for the people might consider himself entitled to do whatever he felt was good for the nation, irrespective of the interests and rights of the states, Congress, the judiciary, and the individual."[129]

"What a self-centered peacock! The man had become a virtual religion in his own right." Sarah said, as she reached for a new pencil in her reticule.

"When Lincoln announced the preliminary Emancipation Proclamation in late 1862," Booth said, "he was hoping to hold the Republican majority in Congress. His implementation of the Proclamation in January 1863 was not a seizure of property, but the urging of domestic slave rebellion. As president," Booth maintained, "Lincoln took no oath to preserve the Union or end slavery. He took an oath to protect the Constitution. In the end, Lincoln showed that he too had some reservations about declaring emancipation as part of a military policy through an executive proclamation. His hope was that Congress would enact compensated emancipation instead.[130] It was nothing more than Military Emancipation by force and presidential edict.

"On New Year's Day 1863, Lincoln freed any slave in any

---

128 M. E. Bradford, "On Remembering Who We Are," in his *Remembering Who We Are*, 11, 13; and *id.*, "Not So Democratic: The Caution of the Framers," in *Ibid.*, 36. On the ideological unity of white, secessionist Southerners against Lincoln, see also, *id.*, "All To Do Over: The Secession of 1861," in *A Better Guide than Reason: Federalists and Anti-Federalists* (New Brunswick: Transaction Publishers, 1994), 153-167; and *id.*, "The Heresy of Equality: Bradford Replies to Jaffa," *Modern Age*, 20 (Winter 1976), 62-77.
129 Bradford, "Lincoln Legacy," 153-55. The final statement is a quote from Gottfried Dietz, *America's Political Dilemma: From Lincoln to Unlimited Democracy* (Baltimore: The Johns Hopkins University Press, 1968), 58.
130 *Ibid.*, 317, 435, 437, 439, 453-54.

jurisdiction he did not have control of, namely, in the seceded Confederate states," Booth chuckled. "That is to say he freed no one, but those few who had been confiscated or fled slavery since the start of the war. On the other hand, the Emancipation Proclamation guaranteed the extended enslavement of nearly one million blacks, who lived in the loyal Border States or occupied areas of the Confederacy exempt under the edict. Moreover, as a presidential decree of wartime necessity, "Booth pointed out, "the Emancipation Proclamation was of doubtful legality.[131]

"Much nation-wide anti-Negro feeling came out in the aftermath of the Emancipation Proclamation," according to Booth. "200,000 Northern white soldiers deserted in its aftermath; 120,000 more evaded conscription at home; and 90,000 fled to Canada to avoid any possibility of military service in Lincoln's Union. All this, despite that fact that the Emancipation Proclamation freed no slaves but those the Union forces could not touch," Booth claimed. "And all the time, the real purposes behind the Emancipation Proclamation was to keep European monarchies our of the war and to incite a slave rebellion to assist the floundering Union invasion of the South."[132]

"I never hear of any of that!" Sarah said.

"Very few have, it is not something that would promote Northern support of the war effort." Finally, Booth found highly objectionable "Lincoln's changing American political language

---

[131] *Ibid.*, 6-8, 13, 17-20, 25-26, 434-35, 468, 497, 505-508, 537, 540-41. This figure is 10 times more than the one given in William C. Harris, "After the Emancipation Proclamation: Lincoln's Role in the Ending of Slavery," *North and South*, 42-53, although Seward's figure is from 1865 and Harris' is from 1863.

[132] DiLorenzo, *The Real Lincoln*, 4, 33-52, especially 45. See also, Bennett, *Forced into Glory*, 8, 21, 58, 518-19, 534. A more conservative approach both praiseworthy and critical of Lincoln is William K. Klingaman, *Abraham Lincoln and the Road to Emancipation, 1861-1865* (New York: Viking, 2001. For a contrary interpretation favoring Lincoln's role in freeing the slaves, see Allen C. Guelzo, *Lincoln's Emancipation Proclamation: The End of Slavery in America* (New York: Simon & Schuster, 2004). On the Thirteenth Amendment, See Michael Vorenberg, *Final Freedom: The Civil War, the Abolition of Slavery, and the Thirteenth Amendment* (Cambridge ; New York : Cambridge University Press, 2001).

to prevent future generations from reversing the ill effects of the trends he set in motion with his executive proclamations. Lincoln is our first Puritan president. He had the habit of wrapping up his policy in the idiom of Holy Scripture, concealing within the Trojan horse of his gasconade and moral superiority an agenda that would never have been approved if presented in any other form.

"Americans would be wise to recognize that under this political system, some 'truths' are more important than Lincoln's Truth. Even the Truth that we have a political tradition that is conservative and contrary to Lincoln. It is truly an irony of history," Booth concluded, to "make an Illinois White supremacist the signer of the Emancipation Proclamation, ... [and to] make a Virginia slaveholder the author of the Declaration of Independence, and with the same results."[133]

---

133 Bradford, "Lincoln Legacy,"155-56. See also, *id.*, "The Heresy of Equality: Bradford Replies to Jaffa," in *id., A Better Guide than Reason*, 29-53, quote on 52. The tracing of Puritan influence from the English Civil War to the American Revolution to the American Civil War, without Master's or Bradford's censuring of Lincoln, is the theme of Kevin Phillips, *The Cousin's Wars: Religion, Politics, & the Triumph of Anglo-America* (New York: Basic Books, 1999).

# 8

## Military Emancipation

Booth was on a tear this day. "No one was fooled by Lincoln's first inaugural speech. No interference with slavery in the states, indeed!"

"Is that not what Lincoln did? Or did not do?" Sarah inquired.

"The Democrats in the North accused the Republicans of trying to get around the constitutional guarantees on slavery by acting indirectly against what the South called the 'peculiar institution' by nibbling at the edges of the slave system, attacking the domestic and international slave trade, and refusing to enforce the fugitive laws."

"But what bout the South?" Sarah asked.

"Southern Democrats said much the same, calling the Cordon of Freedom an 'inflammatory circle of fire.' The spearhead would be more domestic insurrections inspired by would-be John Browns."

"Southern cooperationists, those who opposed immediate secession, had no quarrel with the Northern Democrats, did they?" Sarah pondered aloud.

"No. But Southern cooperationists and Northern Democrats pointed out that for the South to leave the Union would lessen the Democrats' political power in Congress and negate Republicans' obligation to obey the Constitution or any laws protecting slavery. Secession would lead to direct invasion and the imposition of immediate Military Emancipation, the second part of the Republican policy against slavery.

"So the Republicans wanted the South to secede so they could start the war and use that so-called Military Emancipation?" Sarah quizzed Booth once more.

"Indeed," Booth said. "Many Republicans actually favored Southern secession through which to attack the slave institution at once. So Lincoln and the Republicans intentionally refused to compromise the one issue that could have postponed the war; namely, the spread of slavery in the territories that Chief Justice Taney ruled as constitutional in the Dred Scott case. Lincoln and the Republicans decided to forget the Cordon or Freedom and proceed directly to Military Emancipation."

"But the war has been so long and bloody," Sarah said. "Why would anyone or any group want that?"

Booth came back quickly, "What if Lincoln and the Republicans misjudged how long a Civil War might last and how fiercely the South would fight to maintain its social, cultural and economic institutions? What if the Republicans began to attack slavery even before Lincoln was inaugurated and, with the new President's connivance, never relented?"[134]

"How would we ever know?" Sarah wondered.

"The place to look for this plot to effect immediate Military Emancipation is not at the machinations leading up to the firing on Ft. Sumter," Booth mused, "but rather during the 'Winter of Secession' prior to Lincoln's inauguration in the U.S. Senate's Committee of Thirteen, chaired by John J. Crittenden of Kentucky."

"What did the Senator do?"

---

134 Oaks, "Was the Civil War Actually about Slavery?" [3].

"What Crittenden and his committee proposed was a modification of the Missouri Compromise—even though Justice Taney and the Supreme Court had ruled the original unconstitutional in Dred Scott. The new plan was to extend the 36° 30' line to the eastern border of the free state of California. Slavery was to be protected in the West in all territory possessed by the United States at that time and also 'hereafter acquired' below the Missouri Compromise line. Crittenden thought that reasonable".

"So do I!" said Sarah, emphatically.

"But there was a critical procedural rule in the committee," Booth cautioned. "The proposal would have to be endorsed by a majority of Democrats in the committee, and a majority of Republicans, too. Key Southerners on the committee thought Crittenden's plan acceptable. But the five Republicans on the committee would have none of this. Crittenden's plan would break the Cordon of Freedom around the South. Especially objectionable was the phrase, territory 'hereafter acquired.' This smacked of encouragement of Southern pseudo-military filibustering expeditions throughout the Caribbean to acquire more slave territory below the Missouri Compromise line."

"But Lincoln was not in Congress or on that committee, was he?"

"Lincoln did not have to be there," Booth explained. "Led by William H. Seward, the Republicans on the Crittenden Committee voted en masse not to accept the Compromise. The secessionist fire-eaters in and out of Congress were more than happy with the result. They brooked no compromise, either."[135]

---

135 How the slightly differing viewpoints merged is explained in Robert J. Cook, William L. Barney, and Elizabeth R. Varon, *Secession Winter: When the Union Fell Apart* (Baltimore: The Johns Hopkins University Press, 2013), 1-9, 86-90; Charles B. Dew, *Apostles of Disunion: Southern Secession Commissioners and the Causes of the Civil War* (Charlottesville: University Press of Virginia, 2001.

"So Lincoln views did not count?" Sarah seemed astonished that a President-elect did not have more influence.

"I think that there is more to it than that," Booth went on. "Lincoln, like most Northerners, had heard all this secession braggadocio in 1798, 1832, 1850, and incessantly for the past few years. They all believed that it was nothing but drivel spouted by a few loudmouths soon to be put down by sensible Union men all over the South, as it had been in 1850.

"It seems more likely that Lincoln had internalized the common Northern antislavery image of the South. It was a society of rudely domineering, rich planters, and cowering non-slaveholding yeoman farmers. The average Southerner, believed Lincoln, was like Lincoln himself, a conservative unionist with little attachment to slavery, whose family had fled the South of slavery when he was but a boy. This is what Lincoln and the Republicans saw, so the South had little to fear from their Cordon of Freedom or even Military Emancipation. Pro-slave secession would fold in a minute before the might of such Southern freeholders.[136]

"If the Southern slaveholders could not understand this, well then, they could simply leave the Union, and accept invasion and eventual subjugation and seizure of their slave property. They would no longer have the protection they had once enjoyed from the Constitution, the rulings of the U.S. Supreme Court, or the laws of Congress, made possible by an unjust Slave Power Conspiracy."[137]

"So," Sarah opined, "the South took up Lincoln's suggestion in December 1860 and seven states seceded by February 1861."

"All Lincoln needed then," Booth asserted, "was to conceal

---

[136] William J. Cooper, "The Critical Signpost on the Journey toward Secession," *Journal of Southern History*, 77 (No. 1, February 2011), 16.
[137] James Oaks, "Was the Civil War Actually about Slavery?" *Salon*, August 29, 2012, [4].

the real reason for an armed conflict by goading the South into firing the first shot and calling the nation together to avenge this insult to the American flag. It took place at Ft. Sumter, South Carolina. Three-quarters of a million dead Americans later, including the Yankee Tyrant himself, Lincoln's suppositions proved completely wrong. The South had fought at last, slaveholders and freeholders united, with tremendous fury.[138]

"But Lincoln got his Military Emancipation. It started just like he and his Republican Party pledged, immediately. By August 1861, Congress had passed the First Confiscation Act, confirming that slaves fleeing "disloyal" masters could be forfeit to the United States. Congress passed a Second Confiscation Act in July 1862, which freed all slaves in Rebel areas of the South—if they could but get to Union lines. But to put the freedom section of the Second Confiscation Act into effect, Congress had instructed the President to issue a proclamation saying so.[139]

"Lincoln delayed his presidential order until the Yankees had won a battle at Antietam, Maryland, turning back a Confederate invasion of the North. Then he issued a preliminary Emancipation Proclamation to put the freedom sections into effect. The preliminary Emancipation Proclamation gave the Confederates 100 days to come back into the Union or else Lincoln would free all slaves in the Confederacy.[140]

"To sweeten the pot, on December 1, 1862, Lincoln once

---

138 See, James M. McPherson, "What Caused the Civil War?" *North & South*, 4 (November 2000), 12-22; Jeffrey R. Hummel, "Why Did Lincoln Choose War?" *ibid.*, 4 (September 2001), 38-44; Webb Garrison, *Lincoln's Little War* (Nashville: Rutledge Hill Press, 1997); Thomas J. DiLorenzo, *The Real Lincoln*, 89-125.

139 *An Act to Suppress Insurrection, to Punish Treason and Rebellion, to Seize and Confiscate the Property of Rebels, and for Other Purposes (July 17, 1862)*, Public Acts of the 37th Cong., 2nd sess., ch. cxcv, sect. 5. See also, John Syrett, *The Civil War Confiscation Acts: Failing to Reconstruct the South* (New York: Fordham University press, 2005).

140 Oaks, *Freedom National, passim*. The characterization of the 100-day grace period is from Lerone Bennett, *Forced into Glory*, 505-508. See also, Don Thomas, *The Reason Lincoln Had to Die* (Chesterfield, Va.: Pumphouse Publishers, 2013), 9.

more tried to win over the loyal Border State slaveholders exempted from the Emancipation Proclamation by offering a new plan which would grant compensation for all those loyal slaveholders who voluntarily freed their slaves by January 1, 1900. This was essentially the Cordon of Freedom under another guise.[141]

"The outraged Republican Congress, now imbued with the notion of Military Emancipation, refused to consider Lincoln's new program of gradual, compensated emancipation. It smacked too much of allowing Southerners the right to own, exploit, beat, and rape slaves and their descendants for at least another half-century.[142] Likewise, the Confederacy and the loyal Border South refused to budge and accept Lincoln's newly offered Cordon of Freedom. So on January 1, 1863, the Northern President issued the permanent Emancipation Proclamation, the Republican Congress' Military Emancipation writ large, freeing all slaves in the Confederacy (but not in the whole Union). Recently, I hear that Congress has passed a Thirteenth Amendment that will free all slaves everywhere. The states are considering that one now.

"I see why you shot him. He got his wish of no slavery, but at such cost!"

"He freed the black slaves but enslaved the white freemen. Damned right, I shot him."[143]

---

141 Bennett, *Forced into Glory*, 513-18. The Lincoln plan is in Basler (Ed.), *The Collected Works of Abraham Lincoln*, V, 529-37. Lincoln never got over the notion that American ex-slaves should be colonized abroad, given their innate inferiority to whites. See Peterson, *Lincoln in American Memory*, 394, quoting Richard Current, *The Lincoln Nobody Knows* (New York: Hill and Wang, 1958), 230.

142 This definition of slavery in a different context is from Barr, *Loathing Lincoln*, 253.

143 Pressly, "'Emancipating Slaves, Enslaving Free Men'," 254-65.

# 9

## GUILTY AT LAST

John Wilkes Booth smirked inwardly, silently, maintaining a calm exterior, as the courtroom exploded around him. He leaned on his crutches. He had beaten every charge against him but one—the military execution (as Booth saw it) of the President. Counselor O'Connor just stood there and gaped at the scene. He had never seen anything like this in a court, any court, before. Would Booth actually go free?

O'Connor did not think so, but if he did, surely the crowd would attack and overcome the guards and hang everyone else to the nearest tree. Or would the public relations campaign bring out the latent Southern sympathies of the population of the nation's capital and save the day? No, that could not happen. These were veteran military men, combat generals, realists who knew the political demands of the occasion.

The Clerk cleared his throat. He licked his lips. The crowd suddenly went silent. It was appropriately quiet as a tomb. As ordered by General Barry, he began to read"

CHARGE IV. Murdering a member of the Government of the United States, in violation of the laws and customs of war.

Of the charge and the specification [the clerk

paused, a lady in the crown sucked in air noisily, with a barely audible screech], GUILTY!

The audience went wild with uncontrolled cheering, applause, and whistling. It took nearly five minutes before General Barry could quiet the unruliness. Finally, he pointed his Colt's Dragoon revolver at the ceiling, fired a booming shot, and screamed in a basso profundo voice, "ORDER! Order in the court. I will have order! ORDER!"

"John Wilkes Booth, you have been found guilty of the murder of the President of the United States and commander-in-Chief of the Armies and Navy, by a unanimous vote of this Military Commission. I hereby sentence you to hang by the neck until dead oat 10 A.M., July 4, 1865. May God have mercy on your soul."

General Barry nodded to the Clerk, who shouted hoarsely from his raw throat, "COURT DISMISSED!"

Motioned to by the Sergeant of the Guard, Booth and O'Connor slipped out a door behind the court members. The military judges followed closely behind. The audience pushed and shoved, newspaper reporters running down the stairs and heading for their houses of publication. Everyone was yelling, "Guilty, by God! He will hang, thank God!"

Later, O'Connor met Booth in his jail cell.

"I am sorry, Mr. Booth," he said.

"As my father would have said, 'the good do not always win.'"

O'Connor looked miserable.

"Do you want to tell me what happened in there? I expected a 'guilty' vote of all charges and specifications."

O'Connor reached into his frock coat and pulled out a newspaper. The masthead was of the National Intelligencer, a noted

Washington sheet since 1800. The paper had lived on government patronage until the political parties split in the 1820s over the rise of Andrew Jackson, Martin Van Buren and his Democrats. Then the National Intelligencer went with the opposition Whigs and stayed there until the Civil War, when it refused to support Lincoln and the Republicans.[144]

In 1865, John F. Coyle and a consortium of investors bought the National Intelligencer. Because of his opposition to many of Lincoln's wartime policies, it was to Coyle that Booth sent his missive on why he killed Lincoln. Coyle maintained that he had never received the letter, supposedly mailed by Booth's theater actor friend, John Matthews. So Booth's letter disappeared, allegedly burned by Coyle or Matthews, both afraid of government repercussions after Lincoln's death.[145]

Booth opened the folded newspaper and looked at the headline. It was a quote from the French philosophe, Francois-Marie Arouet Voltaire: "Killing A Man Is Murder Unless You Do It To The Sound of Trumpets." It was a four-page synopsis of his many interviews with Sarah Slater, "Miss Nettie."

"This came out a few days ago. The whole city has been atwitter with it since. You were heard without the Court. That is what happened and why you beat most of the charges. Well, not all. The real problem was that the only ones who really knew about your conspiracy were your co-conspirators. And they could not testify under the rules of what is admissible evidence. I waited until now to bring this to you, because I was afraid that

---
144 Frederic Husdon, *Journalism in the United States from 1690 to 1872* (New York: Harper & Bros., 1873), 258-59.
145 See various essays in David Dillon (ed.), *The Lincoln Assassination: From the Pages of the Surratt Courier* (Clinton, Md.: The Surratt Society, 2000), Part I, 25-50. See also Coyle's testimony in Pitman (comp.), *The Assassination of President Lincoln and the Trial of the Conspirators*, 83.

the guards would seize it. Now, after your conviction, no one cares."

"I thought Coyle had betrayed me. I looked in vain for this while Davy Herold and I were hiding in the swamps. This is much better than my letter," Booth said scanning the newspaper.

"Would you like to hear the whole story of how this came about?"

"Certainly! Has Coyle been arrested?"

"No, but it was close-run thing. Here is what I know from various sources, which will remain unnamed, for obvious reasons."

Booth listened as O'Connor related this story: Secretary of War Edwin McM. Stanton was not in a good mood when he reached his office in the War Department building. It was colloquially called the "lunatic asylum" for obvious reason, most of which originated from Stanton's work ethic, which was intense to say the least.[146]

The Secretary had a newspaper folded under his arm. He was "hopping mad" in the vernacular of the day. "Get me Baker!" he stormed to the Acting Assistant Adjutant General, a lieutenant who was sort of a clerk and go-fer all wrapped into one.

Baker was Brigadier General Lafayette C. Baker, the head of the National Detective Police. His outfit was just the sort of organization any good bureaucrat needed—slightly irregular when necessary. And Baker was just the sort of man any good bureaucrat needed—slightly shady in his practices when neces-

---

[146] A good brief characterization of Stanton is in Roy Z. Chamlee, Jr., *Lincoln's Assassins: A Complete Account of their Capture, Trail, and Punishment* (Jefferson N.C.: McFarland & Company Inc., Publishers, 1990), 35-44, 159. Stanton's gruff manner in daily matters, is from George Alfred Townsend, *Washington: Outside and Inside*. (Hartford: James Betts & Co., 1873), 359-60. The Secretary's course in the wake of Lincoln's assassination is examined in Beverly Bone, "Edwin Stanton in the Wake of the Lincoln Assassination," *Lincoln Herald*, 82 (Winter 1980), 508-21. See also, Hamilton Gay Howard, *Civil War Echoes: Character Sketches and Secrets* (Washington: Howard Publishing Co., 1907), 226-36; and Otto Eisenschiml, "Stanton's Reign of Terror," in his *In the Shadow of Lincoln's Death* (New York: Wilfred Funk, 1940), 191-213.

sary. He and his men were known for brutal methods, operating just barely on the right side of the law ordinarily, and on the wrong side when necessary.[147]

Baker's bailiwick was located across the street from Willard's Hotel, a location whose bar and saloon was guaranteed to bring close at hand all sorts of spies, crooks, and assorted malefactors. He arrived with a rush up the central stair to Stanton's second floor office.

"You called, sir?"

"You know John F. Coyle of the National Intelligencer? Go get him. Arrest him and bring him here. Do it in person. I want you back here with him."

About an hour after Baker left, Judge Advocate General Joseph Holt rushed into the office, out of breath. "Stanton, have you seen this?" He waved a copy of the National Intelligencer with Booth's four-page missive in it.

Stanton waved his copy back.

"Well," Holt asked, "what are we going to do about this?"

"Here is your answer now," Stanton said, pointing to Baker, who had just arrived and roughly shoved Coyle through Stanton's office door.

"Dammit, Coyle, what the hell is this drivel doing on the streets of the nation's capital? I have been pretty easy going on your challenging every policy we Republicans have put forward to win the was with the so-called Confederacy." One never referred to the Confederate States of America anyway else around Edwin Stanton. I have half a mind to throw you in the Old Capitol Prison for the duration of the conflict, short as that may be."

"You do that Mr. Secretary, and you will be doing nothing

---

[147] See Lafayette C. Baker, *History of the United States Secret Service* (Philadelphia: L. C. Baker, 1867; Jacob Mogelever, *Death to Traitors: The Story of General Lafayette C. Baker, Lincoln's Forgotten Secret Service Chief* (New York: Doubleday & Company, 1960).

but proving Booth's major points in that 'drivel,' as you call it. Every newspaper in the city will condemn you in their next issue. You forget that the war has essentially been won and this unconstitutional disparagement of the First Amendment will not wash any longer."

"This outrageous crap will be in every newspaper in every major city in the North, not to mention the so-called Confederacy, what is left of it, by tomorrow, certainly. How did you get this? I want that reporter's name immediately!"

"You cannot touch her, and you know it. She is your favorite nemesis, the French Woman."

"Who? Sarah Antoinette Slater? Again? How did she get this? I was told Booth had visits from a nurse, good-looking female nurse. She was the one? God damn it, she has a French passport. I had to let her go last time I had her arrested for messing up Booth's diary. She gutted the whole thing and made it useless. We could have arrested and hanged half of the leading Rebels in the so-called Confederacy with those missing pages."

"Hell, we ought to hang everyone from brigadier general on up, including members of their Congress and Senate, anyway" Holt grumbled. "And hanging a few like Miss Slater would not hurt our cause either. Too many Southern women acted as spies in this war."[148]

Stanton fumed as he ran the options over in his head. "Alright, Coyle, get out of here. And remember we have our eyes on you. Try to keep your nose clean. The war is not over yet."

"Why did you do that?" Baker asked after Coyle thundered down the wooden stairwell. He obviously did not want to be around in case Stanton changed his mind.

---

148 On Holt and the assassination agenda, see, *Lincoln's Forgotten Ally*, 200-15, and *id.*, *Lincoln's Avengers: Justice, Revenge, and Reunion after the Civil War* (New York: Norton 2004), 67-137, *passim*.

"He is right," Stanton said. "The war is over and it is more important that the right story of Lincoln get around. I, and you, Holt, will go around to our Republican friends and see to that. Booth will be hanged on July 4$^{th}$ and he will soon be forgotten as a traitor to his country and a murderer of the greatest President we have ever had. We will have people voting Republican for generations in the memory of 'Martyred, Honest Abe,' 'the Rail-splitter.'"[149]

"So there you have it, Booth, your statement against Lincoln get printed and given ou to the public, Coyle gets off, and you do not."

"Why was I convicted of merely one charge?"

"That was so because Major Rathbone was the single independent witness to your shooting President Lincoln. All the others were tainted as actual or possible co-conspirators. Especially in the 'To Whom It May Concern' letter,[150] where you signed the names of all of your co-conspirators. I told you that you were smart on day one of our association."

---
149 Alonso Taft to Benjamin Wade, September 8, 1864, David Rankin Barbee Papers, Box 3, Archives, Georgetown University.
150 See Rhodehammel and Taper (eds.), *The Writings of John Wilkes Booth*, 153.

# 10

## WHAT PROFIT HATH A MAN FROM ALL HIS LABOR?[151]

Lawyer O'Connor came in on July 4, a hot, humid, typical Washington summer day. It was an hour before the traditional hanging time in English-speaking countries, 10 A.M.

"You might be interested that there were so many volunteers to spring the trap that they had to draw lots."

"I hope they are sober enough to do the job correctly,' Booth said dryly.

"Yeah, there were a lot of bars open all night. The walls of the arsenal are already full. Some have climbed into the trees for a better view."

"If you want, we can have a minister come in and pray," O'Connor suggested.

"No, right or wrong, God will judge me, preacher or no preacher."[152]

Booth looked at O'Connor intently. Then he smiled.

"Well, looks like you lost another one, huh, Counselor?"

"Please, Mr. Booth. This is no time to joke."

"I disagree. This is a fine time to joke. All else is pretty grim. You know, I attended the hanging of Old Osawatomie John Brown back in '59 as a member of the Richmond Grays, the First Militia. While I abhor his stand on getting rid of slavery,

---
151 Eccl. 1:2-3, RSV.
152 Rhodehammel and Taper (eds.), *The Writings of John Wilkes Booth*, 124.

I admire him for his cool manner in approaching the noose. He was stronger that most of the militiamen sent to guard him from an abolitionist attempt to free him before the hanging. I only hope I face death with such equanimity."[153]

"Do you think you can make it up those thirteen steps with only one leg and a crutch without help? I can have a couple of soldiers help you."

"No. I want to try it on my own."

"I figured you for that. I have had a second crutch brought over to make it easier. Or better yet, use the hand rail."

"We shall see."

"How was your last meal? Satisfactory?"

"Prison food is prison food, no matter the choice on the menu."

O'Connor and his client sat in the cell for a few minutes. There was a stirring in the hall. A sergeant stepped up to the door and turned the lock with his key.

"Time to go, gents."

O'Connor shook Booth's hand. "God bless you and give you the strength to meet Him like a man."

"Thank you, Mr. O'Connor, for all you have done for me. It cannot have been easy to represent the greatest criminal of the century. I hope that your reputation has not been unduly damaged."

"It has not." O'Connor patted Booth on the shoulder as he stepped into the aisle out side the cell. The sergeant left the cell door open and stepped around Booth. The four guards shouldered their bayonetted rifles and stood one pair ahead of Booth the other pair behind him.

---

[153] Glenn Tucker, "John Wilkes Booth at theaHanging," *Lincoln Herald*, 78 (Spring 1976), 3-11.

"Harch!" The group moved forward, O'Connor trailing behind.

The bright sunlight made every one flinch a bit. But Booth stood as tall as his use of the crutches would let him. He looked to one side. There were a couple of dozen civilians there to witness the execution. Booth nodded to them and smiled. A few smiled back but most scowled at what they saw as his insolence.

The scaffold had been built for the bigger hanging of his fellow conspirators that would follow in a few days. A captain moved over to him—the Yankee hangman.

"Looks like I will be the man who tests the whole shebang, huh, Captain?"

"Yes, I guess you could say that, Mr. Booth. I am Captain Christian Rath, by the way."

"Do a good job, sir, if you please." Booth reached out to shake his hand.

Startled, Captain Rath at first withdrew a step. But he saw that Booth was sincere and he advanced to grasp his hand. There was something in it. It was a twenty dollar gold piece. Booth was tipping the executioner as in medieval times, like in the days if Richard III. He was the consummate actor to the end.

Booth and his escort marched around the scaffold to the rear. There they were, the thirteen steps to perdition or glory. The guards stood aside, a pair in each side of the stairs. Captain Rath led the way up. Booth advanced to the steps. He paused. Which way to do this? He stepped up on the first tread, but swung weakly to one side. He dropped one crutch and grabbed the railing.

"Guards!" Rath snapped, "Assist him to climb!"

Before Booth could protest, two of the guards began to help him ascend the stairs. On top, Booth was given the crutch he had lost by another guard who had followed him up. Rath guided Booth forward where the rope dangled menacingly before them.

"Mr. Booth, the traditional manner is to place the noose behind the right ear, but because of your leg I will place it over your left, so as to easier break your neck in the drop. Place the crutches close under your arms, as we will have to tie your hands behind you."

"Whatever you say, Captain. I have never been hanged before, " Booth chuckled. Booth felt the cloth strips bond his hands and his legs above the knee."

"If you have any last words, now is the time."

"Deo vindice!" Booth shouted in his best stage voice that carried through the prison yard, over the wall and out into the street. It was the motto of the Confederacy, "God will vindicate." Rath put a cloth sack over his face and adjusted the rope so it fell over Booth's left shoulder, as promised. The floor creaked and shook a bit as the Captain moved back to safety.

"Deo vindice!" Booth shouted again. Even though the bag over his head muffled the sound, his voice still carried mightily to the observers on the ground and the wall and the trees. He stood tall and defiantly. Suddenly, the trap fell open with a sound midway between a rumble and a crash.

# PART IV

## "I Care Not to Outlive My Country"

We should accord Booth the "respectability of rational political motivation." Booth "deserves a measure of respect we so generously and indiscriminately pay to men on both sides of the war who fought, killed, and died for what they believed. When we are able to make this concession to Booth, we will truly understand how terrible the Civil War was."

—William Hanchett, John Wilkes Booth and the Terrible Truth about the Civil War (Racine: Lincoln Fellowship of Wisconsin, Historical Bulletin No. 49), 34-35.

# 1

## BETWEEN HEAVEN AND HELL

Booth awoke with a start. He was not in heaven. He was in his own sort of personal hell—surrounded by Yankee soldiers and the Garrett family. Nothing had changed. Lucinda Holloway moistened his lips with a rag that tasted of cheap wine. Damn! He was still in Virginia.[154]

"Kill me," he muttered, half-heartedly.

"Oh, no, Booth. We do not want you to die," Baker said. "You were shot against orders."

"We don't want to kill you. We want you to get well," Conger affirmed, an evil smirk spreading across his face as he looked through the dairy once more. "My God," he said quietly to

---

[154] In general for the contents of this chapter, see Dodels, "The Last Days of John Wilkes Booth," 22-28; Mogelever, *Death to Traitors*, 357-60; Reuter, *The King Can Do No Wrong*, 46-51; Chamlee, *Lincoln's Assassins*, 155-57; Roscoe, *Web of Conspiracy*, 387-98; Oldroyd, *Assassination of Abraham Lincoln*, 70-78; Laughlin, *Death of Lincoln*, 147-53; Townsend, *Life, Crime, and Death of John Wilkes Booth*, 32-39; Kauffman, "Booth's Escape Route: Lincoln's Assassin on the Run," 49-50; Barbee, "Lincoln and Booth," 959-84, *passim*, DRB papers, GU.

See also, Conger's and Baker's testimony, R. Sutton, *et al. (comps.), The Reporter: Containing. . . Trial of John H. Surratt, on an Indictment for Murder of President Lincoln* (Washington: Sutton, 1867), III, 260-73; Doherty's "Official Report on the Capture of John Wilkes Booth," *Surratt Courier*, 25 (May 2000), 3-7; Baker, "An Eyewitness Account of the Death and Burial of J. Wilkes Booth," 425-46; Statement of Miss Halloway, in Wilson, *John Wilkes Booth*, 208-22; Otto Eisenschiml, "Death Visits Garrett's Farm," *Why Was Lincoln Murdered?*, 153-61.

See also, Wilson, *ibid.*, 171-93; Miller (ed.), "A Trooper's Account of the Death of Booth,"5-9; Fleet (ed.), "A Chapter of Unwritten History: Richard Baynham Garrett's Account," 388-407, more easily accessed in Richard Baynham Garrett, "End of a Manhunt," *American Heritage*, 17 (June 1966), 40-43, 105. Richard Garrett returned the lock of hair to Edwin Booth, some years later.

himself. "We have them all! Everyone! It is all in Booth's own hand!"

"I ... care not ... to ... outlive my ... country," Booth choked, as if he were some Civil War version of Nathan Hale.

"I daresay that neither your country nor its traitorous leaders will out-live you, sir." Conger was still simpering with the irony of it all, when he stepped from the veranda and collared Sergeant Andrew Wendell. "Who shot this man, Sergeant?"

"Sergeant Corbett claims he did it sir. But the men do not believe him. He is kind of a queer sort, full of Hell-fire and damnation, don'tcha know? Glory seeker—and I don't mean the glory of God, like he always claims, either."

"Go get him. Bring him up here, now!"

By this time the trooper sent to Port Royal returned with Dr. Charles Urquhart, Jr. He examined the wound. "He is mortally wounded, gentlemen," he said to the three Union officers.

"I cannot ... stand it! I ... want ... to die!" Booth screamed, summoning all the strength he had for the occasion.

"You will, sir," Dr. Urquhart said gently, placing his hand on Booth's shoulder reassuringly. "But in God's good time."

There was a rustle of men approaching through the grass and trees.

Sergeant Wendell called out to Conger, "Here is Sergeant Corbett, sir."

Corbett stood at attention; shoulders squared, back straight, eyes front, hands along his legs, his thumbs pointing down the yellow stripes on his trousers.

"Corbett, what in Hell did you shoot for?"

The sergeant never blinked. "Providence directed me, sir."

"Let me see your pistol, Sergeant."

Corbett handed over his Remington .44 caliber Army model

sidearm. Conger sniffed the barrel. Nothing. He pulled back the hammer and examined the cylinders. All of them were loaded. The weapon had not been fired.

Conger stood looking at the man before him for some time. "Well," he said finally, shaking his head in disbelief, "I guess He did or you could not have hit Booth through that crack in the barn." He handed the pistol back to the religionistic Sergeant. "You may go, Corbett."[155]

Corbett saluted smartly, and Conger returned it half-heartedly. The men know Corbett very well, he mused to himself. Very well indeed.

"How long will he live, Doctor?" Conger inquired aloud as he returned to the porch.

"As little as a half hour ... maybe an hour or more. But he does not have long. He will not see noon," Urquhart said as he watched Booth twitch and sigh in lengthening intervals. In the east, the first light of dawn painted the sky an eerie red that highlighted the yellow flames and billowing smoke rising from the still-burning barn.

Conger motioned to Baker. They went through Booth's pockets and removed everything they could find. Conger placed the small items, including the diary, in his coat pockets. He wrapped the two holstered revolvers and the sheathed Bowie knife in Booth's belt, and tied the bundle to his McClellan cavalry saddle. Then he picked up Booth's carbine.

"I am going on ahead to report," he said to Baker. "You await Booth's death and follow along. We want our story to get to your

---

[155] On Boston Corbett, see Richard F. Snow, "Boston Corbett," *American Heritage*, 30 (June-July 1980), 48-49; and Laurie Verge, "The Killer of John Wilkes Booth," Kauffman (ed.), *In Pursuit of . . .* , 111-12. Corbett's own intriguing tale is in Steven G. Miller (ed.), "Boston Corbett's Long-Forgotten Story of Wilkes Booth's Death," *Surratt Courier*, 26 (May 2001), 5-7; *ibid.*, 26 (June 2001), 4-6

cousin and Stanton before Doherty, or anyone else, can poison the well, so to speak. We must secure the fame and the reward due us."

"How long should we wait for Booth to, die? What if he lives?" Baker wanted to know.

"Wait an hour," Conger decided, after pondering a bit. "If he is still alive, send over to Belle Plain for a military surgeon from one of the gun ships. If he dies, get the best conveyance available and bring him on to the City."

Baker returned to the corpse—for, in truth, Booth was little more than a still-talking, dead man. "Miss," Baker said to Lucinda Holloway, who was still kneeling beside Booth and regularly moistening his lips, "could you rub his forehead and temples with your fingers, ever so gently? It might relieve some of his agony."

Miss Holloway nodded her head, yes. She crawled over, took Booths head in her lap, and tenderly began caressing his head.

"Lift . . . my . . . hands," Booth rasped.

Baker looked at him quizzically, "Hands?"

Lucinda Holloway repeated, "Yes, his hands."

Baker lifted them so Booth could see the palms of the appendages that had snuffed out the life of the leader of the Union twelve days earlier. Momentarily, halo-like, Lucy Hale's ring twinkled in the pale light of the dying fire. Booth seemed transfixed by the sight.

"Useless," he mumbled. "Useless."

At least that is what Baker heard. Some of the troopers, standing farther away, thought that he said, "Lucy, Lucy." But as one of them said dismissively later, "Who the Hell is Lucy?"[156]

---

156 Booth's standard last words, "useless, useless," may be a figment of Byron Baker's imagination. At least that is what Northerners *wanted* Booth to say, to make some sort of apology. J. Denis Robinson, "The 'New' Dying Words of John Wilkes Booth," *As I Please*, 2 (No. 5; April

With that, the death rattle drifted up his throat, and he heard from afar the gypsy's curse from his childhood one last time, "You are born under an unlucky star. You have got in your hand a thundering crowd of enemies—not one friend—you will make a bad end. . . . You cannot escape it. All that we see or seem, is but a dream within a dream."

The voice drifted into silence. A peaceful fog came over mind. His neck and head stiffened and relaxed. Dr. Urquhart checked his pulse, looked up at Baker, and shook his head slowly, side to side. With a scalpel, he deftly snipped a curl from Booth's head and unobtrusively pressed it into Miss Holloway's hand. His fingers passed over the staring, hazel eyes, hiding them forever behind those pallid lids rimmed with perfect, black lashes. Then the good doctor closed Booth's jaw for the last time. The voice that had mesmerized America with its love of Shakespeare, and hatred of the cause of forced Union, would be heard nevermore.

Lucinda Holloway silently shed a tear as she slowly lowered his head to the porch and got up, still carrying her lock of Booth's hair, to join the Garrett family, watching from near the front door.

Doherty and Conger questioned the family to confirm that the man lying dead on the porch was the same one who had stayed with them the last day and half. They all said it was, but

---

20, 1998) at seacoastnh.com, believes that Booth was looking at the ring Lucy Hale had given him, when Lt. Baker raised his hands. He uttered "Lucy, Lucy," but his tongue was nearly paralyzed so the words came out as Baker thought it ought. He suggests one hold the tip of one's tongue and try it. Maybe Robinson and we are guilty of what we accused Baker of--hearing what *we* want. It should have happened that way, even if it did not. Booth's trouble in making himself understood is directly related to his difficulty in breathing, which led eventually to his asphyxiation. No matter what his last words were, Dr. Blaine V. Houmes, "The Last Words of John Wilkes Booth . . . Or Were They?" *Surratt Courier*, 32 (June 2007), 3-7, believes that Booth could talk in some fashion after being shot as his vocal cords were undamaged.

*William L. Richter*

denied knowing him by any other name than John W. Boyd, until Richard had told them differently just moments before.[157] Out in the yard, Old Man Garrett was allowed to climb down from the improvised gibbet, at last. His health would never be the same again. The dank, chill air of this night just passed, like the cold hand of death that now held John Wilkes Booth in its grasp, had penetrated to his very soul and would hold tightly to him. It was April 26, destined to be remembered in much of the South thereafter as Confederate Memorial Day.[158]

---

157 The notion that Booth survived the barn holocaust became popular over the years following the assassination. It received a real boost with the publication of Finis L. Bates, *Escape and Suicide of John Wilkes Booth, Assassin of President Lincoln* (Memphis: Pilcher Printing Co., 1907), and is instrumental to those who claim to be direct descendents of Booth, Forrester, *This One Mad Act*, and Nottingham *The Curse of Cain*. They are all torn apart, Bates specifically, in a 1907 letter written by Reverend Richard B. Garrett, see "A Garrett Speaks Out," Dillon (ed.), *The Lincoln Assassination: From the Pages of the* Surratt Courier, XI, 13-14; and an article by William G. Shepherd, "Shattering the Myth of John Wilkes Booth's Escape: An Adventure in Journalism," *Harper's Magazine*, 68 (Nov. 1924), 702-19. See also, "The Booth 'Mummy'," Dillon (ed.), *The Lincoln Assassination: From the Pages of the* Surratt Courier, XII, 1-17; Mark L. Siegel, "The Flight of John Wilkes Booth and the Corpse Brought from Garrett's Farm," *Lincoln Herald*, 84 (Winter 1982), 210-17.

But the argument continues. Otto Eisenschiml, "Was Booth Killed at Garrett's Farm?" in his *Why Was Lincoln Murdered?*," 147-55, believes that the lack of tattoo marks on the 1903 corpse rules out Bate's story. It was Booth who died in 1865. Nate Orlowek (see Timothy Crouse, "A Conspiracy Theory to End All Conspiracy Theories: Did John Wilkes Booth Act Alone?" *Rolling Stone*, 216 [July 1, 1976], 42-42-44, 47, 91--92, 94) has spent a lifetime believing that Booth got away. A complete discussion of where things stand currently is in the Surratt House Museum publication, Verge (ed.), *The Body in the Barn*. The most recent study is C. Wyatt Evans, *The Legend of John Wilkes Booth: Myth, Memory, and a Mummy* (Lawrence: University Press of Kansas, 2004). See also, Erich L. Ewald, (ed.), "'The Butcher's Tale': The Primary Documentation of Chris Ritter's' Confrontation with Louis Weichmann," Dillon (ed.), *The Lincoln Assassination: From the Pages of the* Surratt Courier, XI, 5-10, and two statements by Richard B. Garrett that Booth was dead and he saw him die, *ibid.*, XI, 11-14.

The official government position is still that Booth died in the barn. See Dillon (comp.), *John Wilkes Booth: The FBI Files*, passim. But just recently, Booth's distant relatives have asserted that they believe the actor was not in the Garrett barn and hope that modern DNA research will prove their argument to be beyond reproach. See Edward Collmore, "On the Trail of the Assassin," *Philadelphia Inquirer*, April 26, 2008, A1-A11.

158 Confederate Memorial Day is celebrated on April 26 in Mississippi, Alabama, Florida, and Georgia. But it is celebrated in May 10 in the Carolinas, and in Virginia on May 30, while in the rest of the South it is celebrated on June 3, the birthday of Jefferson Davis.

# 2

## LINCOLN SHALL BE KING

John Wilkes Booth's assassination of President Abraham Lincoln still haunts our political history today, even as it has been consigned to a brief, often barely mentioned, almost esoteric interlude between the grand eras of Civil War and Reconstruction.[159] It is mentioned in passing in most history classes; studied by a few dedicated buffs and historians whom many dismiss unfairly as mere antiquarians. But it was not always so. Lincoln's administration of the U.S. Government and his death continued to affect American government for years after his assassination.[160]

Who was this "Assassinator" everyone either ignored or professed interest in? Until recently, few historical studies have focused at any length on Booth. Suddenly, here in the twenty-first century, he has become ubiquitous. As the new titles demonstrate (for example, H. Donald Winkler's, Lincoln and Booth), Booth is mostly appended to studies on Lincoln, receiving a second billing that must hurt Booth's all-encompassing ego, even from beyond the grave.

Less hesitant than the historians to tackle the topic, novelists have had a field day with the actor-turned-assassin, churning out volumes featuring Booth as the star performer. In large part they have muddled, rather than clarified, what we know about

---
159 James M. McPherson, *Battle Cry of Freedom: The Civil War Era* (New York: Oxford University Press, 1988), 852; Eric Foner, *Reconstruction, 1863-1877: America's Unfinished Revolution* (New York: Harper & Row, 1988), 75.
160 This is a central theme in Thomas DiLorenzo, *The Real Lincoln*.

Booth. His fictional personalities and activities run from the mundane to the fantastic.[161]

The common denominator in all these theories was the not-too-subtle notion that John Wilkes Booth was not wholly sane. This was the favorite assumption of the time,[162] and has never been supplanted in the mind of the American people, who seem to like their assassins to be a brick short of a full load. Crazy killers do not threaten the inherent nobility of the American system of government. Booth's alleged insanity covered up a lot of sin—be it of omission or commission—personal, familial, or governmental.

The Booth family was instrumental in affirming Johnny's unbalanced mind. This absolved them of any complicity in their brother's evil act. Edwin Booth spoke for all when he asserted that, unlike the rest of them, Johnny "was a rattle-pated fellow, filled with Quixotic notions ..., [a] wild-brained boy ... insane [about secession] ..." Lincoln's 1864 reelection, Edwin maintained, "drove [poor ole Johnny] beyond the limits of reason."[163] Lamentably, this ignored certain pronounced eccentricities of father Junius Brutus, mother Mary Ann, older brother June, older sisters Rosalie and Asia, younger brother Joseph, and Edwin, himself, or as Booth crony and fellow actor Edwin Forrest once intemperately snorted, "All those goddam Booths were crazy."[164]

---

161 Constance Head, "John Wilkes Booth in American Fiction," *Lincoln Herald*, 82( (Winter 1980), 455-62; Steven G. Miller, "John Wilkes Booth and The Lincoln Assassination in Recent Fiction," *Surratt Courier* (June 2004), 4-9. For a recent non-fiction biography of Booth, see Terry Alford, *Fortune's Fool: The Life of John Wilkes Booth* (New York: Oxford University Press, 2015).

162 See, e.g., the statement of Joseph Bradley, Sr., in defense of accused conspirator John Surratt, Jr., quoted in Wilson, *John Wilkes Booth*, vii.

163 Edwin Booth to Nahum Capen, July 28th, 1881, in Stern, *Man Who Killed Lincoln*, 396-97. For Joseph A. Booth, see Junius Brutus Booth to Edwin Booth, October 20, 1863, in Rhodehamel and Taper (eds.), *The Writings of John Wilkes Booth*, 79n.5.

164 Quoted in Stanley Kimmel, *The Mad Booths of Maryland*, 272. For a discussion of all of this in detail see, Richter, Sic Semper Tyrannis, 84-89; *id.*, *Last Confederate Heroes: The Final*

Yet Booth was not insane at all. He understood what the war was all about. It all revolved around who would reconstruct and govern the restored Union, the power-grasping President or constitutionally endowed Congress. As those opposed to Republican military and civil policies said it; they wanted "the Union as it was, the Constitution as it is." Booth put the problem more succinctly in his favorite refrain of an anti-Lincoln folk tune of the period; it was all about "in 1865, when Lincoln shall be king."[165]

In our modern age, the notion that a President ought to rule and badger Congress through presidential decree and position papers is not as controversial as it was in Booth's nineteenth century. The nineteenth century was still too close to the rule of the colonies by the prerogatives of the King of England (the colonies broke from this with the Declaration of Independence), so our first national constitution was the Articles of Confederation, where our President was a non-entity elected by Congress from its own membership, in effect, the executive committee chairman. All power rested with the unicameral Congress, each state having one vote. The individual states were even more assertive of legislative power in their own constitutions.[166]

The result was government on all levels that operated inefficiently, if at all.[167] It was no accident that the Federalists, mostly former Continental Army officers (centralists like George Wash-

---

*Struggle for Southern Independence & the Assassination of Abraham Lincoln* (2nd ed., Laurel, Md.: Burgundy Press, 2007), xviii-xix.
165 Terry Alford (ed.), John Wilkes Booth: A Sister's Memoir by Asia Booth Clarke (Oxford: University Press of Mississippi, 1996), 88.
166 John Fiske, *The Critical Period of American History* (Boston: Houghton Mifflin, 1897), challenges the abilities of the government under the Articles; Jackson Turner Main, *The Sovereign States, 1775-1783* (New York: New Viewpoints, 1973), looks at state government.
167 Merrill Jensen, *The New Nation: A History of the United States during the Confederation, 1781-1789* (New York: Vintage, 1950), questions the inadequacies of government under the Articles.

ington and Alexander Hamilton) who sought to amend the Articles of Confederation, turned out to be counterrevolutionaries who wrote an entirely new document. This Constitution of 1789 increased federal power through a more powerful president and split up the legislative body into a bicameral Congress to weaken the power of the states.[168]

The new Constitution, which Booth would rely on in making his arguments as a Constitutional Unionist before he became a belated Secessionist,[169] was sold to the American people through the Federalist Papers (propaganda written by Hamilton, John Jay and James Madison), which falsely promised that the new document was as respectful of states rights as the Articles. Opponents of the new Constitution (like Thomas Jefferson, John Hancock, and Patrick Henry) were condemned as Anti-Federalists, backward-looking men in favor of a weak country susceptible to un-American English and French influences.[170]

The rift continued after the ratification of the Constitution, made possible by the first ten amendments and the Federalists carefully buying the votes of still reluctant states with cold cash and political sops (Hancock was falsely promised the presidency to win over Massachusetts), and threatening laggard Rhode Island with blockade and war.[171] Political parties formed around the scope of the new federal power—the Federalists (Washington, Hamilton, and John Adams) in favor, the Democratic-

---

168 Forrest McDonald, *Novus Ordo Seclorum: The Intellectual Origins of the Constitution* (Lawrence: The University Press of Kansas, 1985); M. E. Bradford, *Original Intentions on the making and Ratification of the United States Constitution* (Athens: University of Georgia Press, 1993).
169 Rhodehammel and Taper (eds.), *Writings of John Wilkes Booth*, 55-64 (Constitutional Unionist), 124-27 (Secessionist).
170 Jackson Turner Main, *The Anti-Federalists: Critics of the Constitution, 1781-1788* (Chicago: Quadrangle Books, 1961).
171 Forrest MacDonald, *E Pluribus Unum: The Formation of the American Republic, 1776-1790* (Boston: Houghton Mifflin, 1965), for a different than usual view on the deals made to get the Constitution ratified.

Republicans (no relation to later anti-slavery Republicans) for the old-time states rights. Disappointed in the rise of political parties (which the Founding Fathers condemned as pernicious "factions"), Madison changed from being for the centralized Constitution he helped write and joined Jefferson and his New York ally, Aaron Burr, against its expanded powers. But when the Jeffersonians gained power in 1800, each side reversed its position, seeking to deny full national political power to the other.[172]

As newer states, western and southern, joined the Union, the Federalists found themselves a minority political party confined to New York and New England. Almost everyone became a Democratic-Republican in response to the War of 1812 (even John Quincy Adams), and, in its aftermath, the Democratic-Republicans came to adopt the concept of massive Federal governmental powers, the exact opposite of their stance in 1800.[173]

In 1820 and 1824, so few Federalists were left that the Democratic-Republicans ran unopposed (the so-called Era of Good Feelings). But not all younger Democratic-Republicans believed that the new philosophy of no parties was for the best. They were led by Martin Van Buren, whose front man was Andrew Jackson, and who envisioned a new party based on de-centralized government that he would call the American Democracy.

But the winning presidential candidate in 1824 was John Quincy Adams, as close to an old-time Federalist as one could

---

[172] Stanley Elkins and Eric McKitrick, *The Age of Federalism: The Early American Republic, 1788-1800* (New York: Oxford University Press, 1993) for the politics of this era. See also, an interesting analysis of the changing Constitution in Jill Lepore, "The Commandments: The Constitution and Its Worshippers," *The New Yorker*, 86 (January 17, 2011), 70-76.

[173] The first American political system is discussed in Joseph Charles, *The Origins of the American Party System* (New York: Harper & Row, 1961); William Nisbet Chambers, *Political Parties in a New Nation: The American Experience, 1776-1809* (New York: Oxford University Press, 1963. For the dirty tactics endemic to American Politics, see Jill Lepore, "Party Time: Smear Tactics, Skullduggery, and the Debut of American Democracy," *The New Yorker*, 82 (September 17, 2007), 94-98.

be, minus the name. He joined with Speaker of the House of Representatives Henry Clay of Kentucky, who also had Federalist economic leanings (he called his policy the American System, which would be the centerpiece of Republican political platforms in the latter part of the nineteenth century), in the "corrupt bargain" to deny the real anti-federalist, Andrew Jackson, the first presidential election to be decided in the House.[174]

A friend of Booth's father, who once wrote him a threatening letter while drunk,[175] Jackson was hopping mad over the Corrupt Bargain, as only he could be. He and his followers joined in a four-year campaign to unseat Adams, which they did in 1828. His opponents, angry that the Jacksonians had grabbed the name the American Democracy for themselves, and that Jackson tended to rule by fiat, called themselves Whigs. This indicated that they were against "King Andrew of Veto Memory" as much as the original Whigs (Patriots) of the American Revolution were opposed to the king-like powers of old George III.[176]

Because they had a hard time in electing Presidents (William Henry Harrison died after a month in office, John Tyler switched to the Democrats and annexed Texas, Zachary Taylor died after two years in office, and Millard Fillmore or Henry Clay just plainly could not win a national presidential election), the Whigs developed the notion of Congressional Supremacy. This meant

---

174 On the second American party system, whose prime architect was little-known President Martin Van Buren, see Robert V. Remini, *Martin Van Buren and the Making of the Democratic Party* (New York: Norton, 1970); Richard P. McCormick, *The Second American Party System: Party Formation in the Jacksonian Era* (Chapel Hill: University of North Carolina Press, 1966); and for the downfall of the preceding political system, Norman K. Risjord, *The Old Republicans: Southern Conservatism in the Age of Jefferson* New York: Columbia University Press, 1965.

175 Stanley Kimmel, *Mad Booths of Maryland* (2 ed., rev. and enlarged, New York: Dover Publications, 1969), 13-92.

176 For the Whigs, see E. Malcolm Carroll, *Origins of the Whig Party* (Durham: Duke University Press, 1925); George Rawlins Poage, *Henry Clay and the Whig Party* (Chapel Hill: University of North Carolina Press, 1936); Arthur Charles Cole, *The Whig Party in the South* (Gloucester, Mass.: Peter Smith, 1962).

that the President ought to be subordinate to the wishes of Congress, where all the real Whig leaders of importance resided. Ideally, U.S. senators and representatives could be instructed, in turn, on how to vote by the members of their state legislatures or residents of their congressional districts back home.[177]

In the mid-1850s, in response to the failure of the Wilmot Proviso (no slavery in the territory obtained from Mexico in the recent war) and the passage of the Kansas-Nebraska Act (which repealed the Missouri Compromise of 1820 and opened the entire West to slavery through popular sovereignty),[178] the Northern Whigs and Northern anti-slavery Democrats combined to create the Republican party that would put Abraham Lincoln in office in 1861. Since the Republicans had so many old-line Whigs in their ranks, and the Democrats controlled the presidency during the 1850s through Franklin Pierce and James Buchanan, Congressional Supremacy became an immediate Republican Party staple.

At the same time, the Southern Whigs (located predominately in Booth's home state of Maryland and Louisiana) went over to the pro-slavery Democrats, with the exception of Booth's own congressman, Henry Winter Davis, who became a Radical Republican.[179] The party lines were now drawn for the miniature pre-Civil War of Bleeding Kansas (1854-1861) won by the anti-slavery forces; the John Brown Raids (1856 Kansas and 1859 Virginia); Lincoln's loss to Stephen A. Douglas in the debates

---

[177] For Congressional Supremacy, see William L. Richter, *The ABC-Clio Companion to the American Reconstruction, 1862-1877* (Santa Barbara, Ca.: ABC-Clio, 1996), 100-101.

[178] Rhodehammel and Taper (eds.), *Writings of John Wilkes Booth*, 64, 65; Bestor, "State Sovereignty and Slavery," *passim.*

[179] The realignment of the two political parties can be followed in Roy Franklin Nichols, *The Disruption of the American Democracy* (New York: Macmillan, 1948); Kinley J. Brauer, *Cotton Versus Conscience: Massachusetts Whig Politics and Southwestern Expansion 1843-1848* (Lexington: University of Kentucky Press, 1967).

for the senatorial election (1858), the election of Lincoln as President (1860); secession of the lower (Gulf) South (1860-1861), and the Civil War (1861-1865). But Republicans could be smug because they had won the presidency and control of Congress with the secession of the South.[180]

Unfortunately, the party had reckoned without considering the political timber of their new leader, Abraham Lincoln. The just-elected President refused to call the Congress into session as the war began. He declared the South to be in Rebellion and called up called up the militia (causing the Upper South to secede), accepted ninety-day volunteers from the several states, expanded the size of the Regular Army and Navy, established new American rules for war through General Orders No. 100, Adjutant General's Office, created an illegal blockade of the South (under international law), denied the writ of habeas corpus (allowed under Congress' powers in the Constitution), threatened to execute Southern privateers as pirates, eman-

---

180 William L. Richter, *Historical Dictionary of the Old South* (Lanham, Md.: Scarecrow Press, 2006), 61-63,155, 175-76, 200-207, 215-17, 234-35, 253-56, 263-64, 271-72, 277, 287-95, 365-66, 373-74. See especially the introduction, 1-29, which explains the Southern political mind before during secession and during the War of Northern Aggression. For a comprehensive study of the North-South struggle, see William W Freehling, *The Road to Disunion* (2 vols., New York, Oxford University Press, 1990-2007).

Shorter, more specific studies include Richard H. Brown, "The Missouri Crisis, Slavery, and the Politics of Jacksonianism," *The South Atlantic Quarterly*, 65 (Winter, 1966): 55-72; Robert Pierce Forbes, *The Missouri Compromise and Its Aftermath: Slavery and the Meaning of America* (Chapel Hill: University of North Carolina Press, 2007); Freehling, *Prelude to Civil War: The Nullification Controversy in South Carolina, 1816-1836* (New York: Harper & Row, 1965); Chaplain W Morrison, *Democratic Politics and Sectionalism: The Wilmot Proviso Controversy* (Chapel Hill: University of North Carolina Press, 1967); Holman Hamilton, *Prologue to Conflict: The Crisis and Compromise of 1850* (New York: Norton, 1964) who points out that Stephen A. Douglas was probably more responsible for the Compromise than Henry Clay as a recent biography admits, Robert V. Remini, *Henry Clay and the Compromise that Saved the Union* (New York: Basic Books, 2010); The Kansas Missouri Border Wars are detailed in James A Rowley, *Race and Politics: "Bleeding Kansas" and the Coming of the Civil War* (Philadelphia: Lippincott, 1969).

But nothing beats Arthur Bestor's lengthy study of the South's political philosophy that led to Northern defeat during the 1850s in the Kansas-Nebraska Act and the Dred Scott case in the U.S. Supreme Court than the classic "State Sovereignty and Slavery, 117-80.

cipated slaves within the Confederacy, and transferred funds between the several executive branches of government without proper appropriation to pay for it all.[181]

Congress saw no way around it—when it finally came into session it would have to pass a law endorsing every action Lincoln took. The U.S. Supreme Court would follow suit, approving Lincoln's executive decisions, until after the war. But the political battle between the executive and legislative branches of the Federal government had just begun. It would be the primary issue during the war and the reconstruction that followed, and Booth saw himself as a political slave beset by Yankee tyranny on all sides.[182]

---

181 Richter, *Historical Dictionary of the Civil War and Reconstruction* (Lanham, Md.: Scarecrow Press, 2004, soon to be reissued in a second revised edition), 227-31. For congressional approval of Lincoln's executive actions, see David Herbert Donald, *Lincoln* (New York: Simon & Schuster, 1995), 305, arguably the best one-volume study of the sixteenth President to date.
182 Rhodehammel and Taper (eds.), *Writings of John Wilkes Booth*, 130.
Alford (ed.), *John Wilkes Booth*, 88, 107.

# 3

# A New Birth of Freedom

While the Republican-controlled Congress was more than willing to endorse President Lincoln's use of the executive proclamation to advance the Union war effort, it angered Republican legislative leaders that their roles had been reduced to being rubber stamps for the executive. Booth felt the same. It was executive tyranny writ large.[183] Lincoln was willing to acquiesce in their passage of the 1860 party platform, essentially Henry Clay's economic program, the American System, and Lincoln, as Clay's outspoken Whig acolyte for years, was more than willing to grace measures like the National Banking System, high protective tariffs, land grant colleges, and the Union Pacific railroad with his presidential signature. Congress saw this as Congressional Supremacy in action.

But party leaders wanted more. They wanted to set the policy for the reconstruction of the reunified nation—bringing the wayward South back into the Union with a new Constitution purged of all of the evils that prewar Southern society represented. These included slavery, white planter supremacy in state governments, the alleged degradation of non-slaveholding white farmers (called "plain folk" by modern historians or condemned as "po' white buckra" by enslaved blacks who took on the airs of their wealthy owners), the lack of a productive factory-based

---

183 Richter, *Historical Dictionary of the Civil War and Reconstruction*, 240-43.

economy in favor of staple agriculture, and most of all, the Slave Power Conspiracy, the Southern domination of the Federal Government by control of the presidency (Lincoln would be the only Northerner to be elected to two terms in the first eighty-seven years of the nation's history, and only the third elected president opposed to slavery after the Adamses, John and John Quincy), Congress (through committee assignments and the counting of 3/5 of the slaves for representation even though they could not vote), and the Supreme Court (two of the five chief justices were Yankees, meaning slave owners John Marshall of Virginia and Roger B. Taney of Maryland dominated the bench for 64 years, right on through the Civil War).

Hence the North had wanted to reconstruct the South and the Union long before the powder smoke and report of the first shot fired on Ft. Sumter had dissipated, which naturally irritated Booth and all "right-thinking" Southerners. Republicans, and certain "War" Democrats in Congress, saw secession and the battlefield conflict as their golden opportunity and Congressional Supremacy as their weapon of choice to expand the theory and practice of American democracy.[184]

Oddly congressional Democrats made the first attempts to reconstruct the nation during the secession crisis. In separate plans, before the war started, senators R.M.T Hunter of Virginia and Stephen Douglas of Illinois suggested that some sort of economic alliance be drawn up that provided for common

---

184  Eric Foner, *Free Soil, Free Labor, Free Men: The Ideology of the Republican Party before Reconstruction* (New York: Oxford University Press, 1970); Frederick J. Blue, *The Free Soilers: Third Party Politics, 1848-1854* (Urbana: University of Illinois Press, 1973). Some notion as to dates of Reconstruction and how they have changed from the traditional (Kenneth M. Stampp, *The Era Of Reconstruction, 1865-1877* [New York: Vintage, 1967]; William A. Dunning, *Reconstruction: Political ands Economic, 1865-1877* [New York: Harper Bros., 1907]) to the more modern (W. E. Burghardt DuBois, *Black Reconstruction, . . . 1860-1880* [New York, Harcourt Brace, 1935]; Harold M. Hyman [ed.], *The Radical Republicans and Reconstruction, 1861-1870* [Indianapolis: Bobbs-Merrill, 1967]; Eric Foner, *Reconstruction: America's Unfinished Revolution, 1863-1877* [New York: Harper & Row, 1988]).

foreign policy, tariffs, trade regulations, patents, and copyright laws. All domestic institutions like slavery were to be state functions except that slavery was to be guaranteed in the territories until statehood whereupon any state could prohibit it (popular sovereignty), basically Chief Justice Taney's Dred Scott decision. But these plans all recognized secession and Congress rejected them, much to Booth's vocal disappointment.[185]

The minute the North refused to give up Southern forts, it occupied Confederate territory and could reconstruct it, come what may, which is what Booth and all Constitutional Unionists feared. The result was a second secession of the Upper South.[186] Beginning in 1861, various Northern agencies ranging from the Army to the Treasury Department to private reconstruction organizations to various religious denominations flooded the occupied South to purify it. Starting around Fortress Monroe in the Virginia Peninsula, then New Orleans, the southeastern third of Louisiana and the Mississippi Valley north through Mississippi and Arkansas to Memphis, Tennessee, the process went forward in a disjointed fashion, freeing slaves (declared contraband of war), seizing cotton (to pay for the war) and abandoned plantations, putting freed slaves to work under U.S. Army supervision, and saving souls.[187]

---

185 Robert W. Johannsen, *Stephen A. Douglas* (New York: Oxford University Press, 1973), 832-34; Jeffrey J. Crow, "R.M.T. Hunter and the Secession Crisis, 1860-1861: A Southern Plan for Reconstruction." *West Virginia History* 34 (April 1973), 273-90. On Booth's attitude, see Rhodehammel and Taper (eds.), *Writings of John Wilkes Booth*, 64.
186 Richter, *Historical Dictionary of the Civil War and Reconstruction*, 585-86.
187 Foner, *Reconstruction*, 35-76. It is commonplace in the Surratt Society to roundly condemn Leonard F. Gutteridge and Ray A. Neff, *Dark Union: The Secret Web of Profiteers, Politicians, and Booth Conspirators that Led to Lincoln's Death* (New York: John Wiley & Sons, Inc., 2003) in the harshest words (Edward Steers, Jr., and Joan Chaconas, "Dark Union: Bad History," *North & South*, 7 [No. 1, January 2004], 12-30). This may hold for the assassination theories put forth in the book (pp. 69-210), but the corrupt machinations of the various military, religious, benevolent organizations and government officials (pp. 1-68) during early wartime Reconstruction are remarkably accurate. For similar stories of Reconstruction shenanigans, see, *e.g.*, Willie Lee Rose, *Rehearsal for Reconstruction: The Port Royal Experiment* (New York: Vintage, 1967); Louis S. Gerteis, *From Contraband to Freedman: Federal Policy toward Southern Blacks,*

But this was all icing on the cake. The real reconstruction was to be political. It was here President Lincoln and his Republican Party came to blows over Congressional Supremacy. This was particularly true of Lincoln and his successor, Andrew Johnson, and one branch of the Republican Party, those called the "ultras" or the Radicals, as Booth and all American quickly found out. The Radical Republicans believed in several non-negotiable principles. They thought the newly freed slaves possessed certain civil rights. First of these was the right to vote. Blacks were the only obviously loyal, potentially Republican group in the South. Ironically, the end of the Civil War brought about increased representation to the Southern states because blacks would be counted not as 3/5 of a person but as one person.

The Radicals found other civil rights were important, too, like national citizenship previously denied all blacks, slave or free, by the Dred Scott case; the right to own property even though confiscation of Rebel property (the legendary "forty acres and a mule") proved too much for Civil War era congressmen; trial by a jury of their peers; equal protection under the law; and education (to cast an intelligent vote and protect other rights).

Although they bestowed citizenship upon the black population, with the rights and privileges that went with it, the Radicals believed that full benefits and rights ought to be denied white Rebels until, guided by Congress, they did penance for their secession and the war. And, most of all, Congress was to be the controlling institution of Reconstruction. The President had a role to perform, but it was definitely subordinate to Congress. Congressional Supremacy was the word of the day.

---

*1861-1865* (Westport, Conn.: Greenwood Press, 1973); Ludwell H. Johnson, III, *Red River Campaign: Politicians and Cotton in the Civil War* (Baltimore: Johns Hopkins University Press, 1958); and Martha M. Bigelow, Freedmen of the Mississippi Valley, 1862-1865," *Civil War History*, 8 (1962), 38-47.

Most confusing to Booth and others was that one might be a Radical Republican on some issues and a moderate or Conservative on others.[188] The balance within the party changed constantly. But all Republicans believed that conditions ought to be placed against automatic readmission of the Southern states back into the Union. What motivated these Radicals? Revenge (it had been a hard war), political advantage (the South had to have a viable Republican base, the black voter), guarantee of the wartime Republican accomplishments (tariffs, taxes, freedom of slaves), the Pacific railroad out of Chicago, and the National Banking System, all played a part. There was a fear of a lost peace otherwise.

Finally, idealism moved the Radicals; a desire to help freed slaves gain their rights as a freed people, to amend the old Constitution and to make it a "New Birth of Freedom," in Lincoln's words, which Booth continually scoffed at. The Radicals were men of unusual principle not normal in American politicians. In ordinary times they might not have even been elected. As it was, those Republicans from the safest seats in Congress generally were the most radical. As their seats were threatened by Democrat opponents, Radicals became Moderates (for some Reconstruction), or if seriously endangered, they became Conservatives (for little Reconstruction). But all Republicans agreed with the Radicals to some degree at one time or another.[189]

---

188 Donald, *The Politics of Reconstruction, passim.*
189 T. Harry Williams, *Lincoln and the Radicals* (Madison: University of *Reconstruction*, xvii-lxviii; Hans L. Trefousse, *The Radical Republicans. Lincoln's Vanguard for Radical Justice* (New York: Knopf, 1969); David H. Donald, *The Politics of Reconstruction, 1863-1867* (Baton Rouge: Louisiana State University Press, 1965), and his "The Radicals and Lincoln," in Donald (ed.), *Lincoln Reconsidered* (New York: Vintage, 1956), 103-27. The standard historical debate on how important the fight between Lincoln and the Radical Republicans was is Donald, "Devils Facing Zionwards," who says it was of little import and Williams, "Lincoln and the Radicals," who argues it was a key inter-party fight. See Grady McWhiney (ed.), *Grant, Lee, Lincoln and the Radicals* (Evanston, Il.: Northwestern University Press, 1964), 72-91, 92-117, respectively

# 4

# CONGRESS EMERGES SUPREME

Although Booth would not live to see it all, Political Reconstruction went through three distinct phases: Conservative (Presidential), Moderate (Congress seeking accommodation with the President), and Radical (Congressional Supremacy as put forth by the Radical Republican leadership with increasing support from their more moderate and conservative colleagues). Gradually the cautious Radical beginnings became a torrent of demands endorsed by the Northern voters in the congressional election of 1866 for obedience from the executive and judicial branches of the recalcitrant Yankee government and the defeated but defiant Confederate South to guarantee the results of the Union victory through a more thorough peace process.

Prior to Lincoln's Emancipation Proclamation and employment of black soldiers, the Radicals complained that Lincoln was moving too slowly to defeat the Confederacy through necessary policies, which was fine with Booth. They organized the Committee on the Conduct of the War to speed things up through Congressional Supremacy over domestic policy and removing ineffective generalship from the battlefield.[190]

But after the Emancipation, the Radicals objected to Lincoln

---

190 Bruce Tap, *Over Lincoln's Shoulder: The Committee on the Conduct of the War* (Lawrence, Kan.: University Press of Kansas, 1998); E. B. Long, "The Committee on the Conduct of the War," *Civil War Times Illustrated*, 20, (August 1981), 20-27. A good listing of sources on Lincoln and Reconstruction is in David A. Lincove (ed.), *Reconstruction in the United States: An Annotated Bibliography* (Westport, Conn.: Greenwood Press, 2000), 77-81.

moving too quickly to readmit the wayward South back into the Union. This was irritated Booth, too. It was time for a strong application of Congressional Supremacy to slow the Reconstruction process. The clash came after Lincoln introduced his suggested plan of Reconstruction, commonly known as the First Presidential or Ten Percent Plan.

Part of his annual message to Congress, December 8, 1863, the President proposed that whenever ten percent of the population of a seceded state signed an oath of future loyalty to the Union and recognition of the acts of Congress passed since secession, they could elect a constitutional convention to draw up a new state constitution, elect a loyal state government, and send representatives and senators to the U.S. Congress. No mention was made of slavery, as Lincoln feared that the Emancipation Proclamation was unconstitutional. Higher officials in the state and Confederate governments were not allowed to participate until later. Finally, the state had to be occupied by Federal troops.

The Radical Republicans went wild. How dare Lincoln act alone without consulting them? Reconstruction was a congressional prerogative under the dictates of Congressional Supremacy. Ten percent? This was an infinitesimal number in any democracy. Where were the demands that the South free their slaves? What was this war for anyhow?

Lincoln called these objections "pernicious abstractions." He, of course, was thinking that he would be lucky to get ten percent of the Confederate white population to cooperate with him during the war. And he was not going to allow slavery to prolong the conflict. He saw emancipation as a gradual process, lasting to 1900 and beyond. Like Henry Clay before him, Lincoln saw the colonization of American slaves to a place in Latin America or back to Africa as the ideal means for resolving the "Negro

Question." Failing this, Lincoln believed that blacks would be doomed to second-class citizenship in the states, North or South, something Booth would have agreed to.[191]

Congress hit back at Lincoln's conservative approach to Reconstruction immediately that summer. Under the leadership of senate Radicals Benjamin Wade of Ohio and Henry Winter Davis of Maryland (Booth's old congressman from the 1850s, now a Radical Republican, par excellence), Congress passed the Wade-Davis Bill. This called for more severe conditions for readmission of the seceded states. It assumed that if the states were not out of the Union they were so far gone Congress could set special conditions.[192]

When fifty percent had taken an oath of future loyalty (the idea was more than democratic—this would postpone Reconstruction until after the war when Republicans were better prepared to look at it), the offending state could call a new state constitutional convention. This body had to abolish slavery, disfranchise higher Confederate and state officials, and repudiate the Confederate war debt (the debt made the Confederacy a nation, to repudiate it denied that). Then the new state could elect a state government and present representatives and senators to Congress, which might accept them and readmit the state back into the Union. Many Republicans abstained from voting, but it was passed July 2, 1864. Congress then adjourned.[193]

---

191 William B. Hesseltine, *Lincoln's Plan of Reconstruction* (Chicago: University of Chicago Press, 1967); Peyton McCrary, *Abraham Lincoln and Reconstruction* (Princeton, NJ: Princeton University Press, 1978). Lerone Bennett, *Forced into Glory*, an expansion of his "Was Lincoln a White Supremacist?" *Ebony*, 23 (1968), 35-38, 40, 42, is harshly critical of Lincoln's notions of white supremacy. For a much more complimentary approach, see Harold M. Hyman, "Lincoln and Equal Rights for Negroes," *Civil War History*, 12 (1966), 258-66.

192 Herman Belz, "Henry Winter Davis and the Origins of Congressional Reconstruction," *Maryland Historical Magazine*, 67 (1972), 129-43; Gerald Hentig, *Henry Winter Davis: Antebellum and Civil War Congressman from Maryland* (New York: Twayne Publishers, 1973), *passim*.

193 Herman Belz, *A New Birth of Freedom: The Republican Party and Freedmen's Rights*

The end of the congressional session meant that President Lincoln could pocket veto the Wade-Davis Bill without comment. But Lincoln spoke out against it anyway. He said he feared that his emancipation provisions were unconstitutional and an amendment was needed to end slavery. But, the President further stated that he preferred not to be limited to any one approach. Should any ex-Confederate state, however, prefer to use the provisions of the harsher Wade-Davis Bill, he would honor their choice.[194]

How typically Lincoln! Clever, slippery, indirect, and to the Radicals, insulting. The Radicals responded with the Wade-Davis Manifesto. It unfairly and inaccurately accused the President of interfering with Congressional Supremacy to forward his own suspicious, milder Reconstruction goals in the South for personal political gain. Indeed, Lincoln spoke out on April 11, 1865, delivering a speech, which some historians believe pushed assassin John Wilkes Booth to the breaking point, saying that it was better to accept his ten percent governments in Louisiana, Arkansas, Tennessee, and Virginia rather than start anew. But he was willing to reconstruct the rest of the South by a congressional plan. He only suggested that the more intelligent blacks and Negro soldiers who fought for the North receive the right to vote, the notion that alienated Booth so thoroughly that he, in a typical wartime response, violently ended Lincoln's life—as Brutus did Caesar's do long ago.[195]

After the death of Booth and Lincoln, the sparring over which branch of the government was the strongest led to the first

---
(Westport, Conn.: Greenwood, 1976), 57-62.
194 Foner, *Reconstruction*, 61-62.
195 Michael W. Kauffman, *American Brutus: John Wilkes Booth and the Lincoln Conspiracies* (New York: Random House, 2004), 209-10. For an interesting paranormal study of Booth's acting as Brutus, see Diana L. Rubino, *A Necessary End* (N.p.: Solstice Publishing (2014).

congressional impeachment of a president in American history, Andrew Johnson. Although Johnson was not found guilty, the Radicals won anyway. His successor was the war hero, Lt. Gen. U.S. Grant, a believer in Congressional Supremacy.[196] For the rest of the nineteenth century, a slew of ineffective presidents served (can you name them?), allowing Congressional Supremacy to reign supreme. Not until Theodore Roosevelt came to power because of William McKinley's assassination did the pattern change. Aptly, McKinley, a major in the 23d Ohio Volunteer Infantry, was the last of the Civil War veterans to serve as president. The sad heritage of Abraham Lincoln's assassination had passed. Roosevelt and Woodrow Wilson introduced a new legacy for the century that followed—one dominated by strong presidents not Congress, and through that legacy, Abraham Lincoln would be remembered as a strong president, one of the greatest power artists as executive the nation had known.

Booth suspected this future all too presciently. As he told his captors before passing away in the arms of Lucinda Holloway on her sister's front porch at Locust Hill Farm, "I care not to outlive my country." Providentially, he did not.

---

196 David L. Wilson, "Ulysses S. Grant and Reconstruction," *Magazine of History*, 4 (Winter 1989), 47-50.

CPSIA information can be obtained at www.ICGtesting.com
Printed in the USA
BVOW02s0050290615

406554BV00001B/95/P

9 781627 872706